MOVE, glass, please . . .! Perhaps if I really concentrated I might shift it by sheer force of will. I closed my eyes tightly, until there was nothing but the glass, shimmering like the Holy Grail, in the dark space of my mind.

Like I said, it was just a game to begin with. I mean, I never *really* expected it to move. When Lauren snuffled that 'Someone must be pushing it,' I actually gasped.

Marina stuck up her hand for silence. 'Shush a minute. It's trying to tell us something.'

Typical of Marina, of course, to be so totally cool, hardly raising an eyebrow as the glass jerked uncertainly about the perimeter of cut-out letters, as if testing its boundaries.

The glass, or whatever it was inside the glass, teased us at first. It skittered, first this way, then that, skating towards the word YES, then NO. Whooshing back and forth, it skimmed the table surface with an uncanny squeaking sound.

Marina commanded, 'If there is a spirit present, then please tell us who you are!'

www.kidsatrandomhouse.co.uk

Also available by Susan Davis

the sequel to THE HENRY GAME:
DELILAH AND THE DARK STUFF

THE HENRY GAME

THE HENRY GAME
A CORGI BOOK: 0552 54793X

Published in Great Britain by Corgi Books,
an imprint of Random House Children's Books

This edition published 2002

5 7 9 10 8 6 4

Papers used by Random House Children's Books are natural,
recyclable products made from wood grown in sustainable
forests. The manufacturing processes conform to the
environmental regulations of the country of origin.

Set in 12/14½ pt Bembo

Corgi Books are published by Random House Children's Books,
61–63 Uxbridge Road, London W5 5SA,
a division of The Random House Group Ltd,
in Australia by Random House Australia (Pty) Ltd,
20 Alfred Street, Milsons Point, Sydney, NSW 2061, Australia,
in New Zealand by Random House New Zealand Ltd,
18 Poland Road, Glenfield, Auckland 10, New Zealand
and in South Africa by Random House (Pty) Ltd,
Endulini, 5a Jubilee Road, Parktown 2193, South Africa

THE RANDOM HOUSE GROUP Limited Reg. No. 954009

A CIP catalogue record for this book is available from the British Library.

Printed and bound in Great Britain by
Cox & Wyman Ltd, Reading, Berkshire

The Henry Game

SUSAN DAVIS

CORGI BOOKS

For my mum, Kath, who read the very first stories but did not make it to see this one. RIP.

For Terry, who kept the faith, and me with it. Also Mia, Joby and Josh.

Acknowledgements
Thanks to my agent and fairy godmother, Mary Pachnos, whose energy, wit and professional insights have made all things possible.

To the team at Random House Children's Books: Annie Eaton, Harriet Wilson and especially Charlie Sheppard for her warm enthusiasm and expertise.

And not forgetting Nicola and Mel.

Finally thanks to Henry VIII for being there when I needed him.

Chapter One

I suppose there *was* a time *before* Henry, although it's hard to imagine it now. It's almost like talking about the time before the Ice Age, or the Big Bang. Like the time before you were born, a time that maybe never was, that you can't possibly imagine in a million years. A time when we were just normal girls, fifteen going on sixteen, and doing the stuff that normal teenagers do.

BH. Before Henry. A time before that sultry July afternoon in Marina's kitchen, blind drawn against the sun, the filtered light striping our fingers greeny-gold on the glass. This was how it began.

'A seance,' I said to the others. 'We'll call up the spirits. A pity we haven't got a real Ouija board. Still, all we need is a few letters and a glass. Then we just stick our fingers on it and concentrate. Couldn't be easier.'

You see it was all my fault. I take the blame. We might have done anything that afternoon. Anything *normal* girls do, that is, with their exams behind them and the summer stretching ahead. We might have toasted ourselves on Marina's lawn, rattled the double glazing with her new sound system, or read our horoscopes aloud from *Crush*. We might even have come over all swotty and discussed our project on the Tudors, which Henry Purviss, our history teacher, had set for all of us intending to take A-Level history next year.

But there I was busily scribbling letters and cutting them into squares. 'Well, come on, you lot. Not chicken, are you? It'll be a laugh. Unless you've got any better ideas?'

They shook their heads. They hadn't got any better ideas. So that was how we came to be sitting five minutes later, Marina, Lauren and me, fingers glued to the glass, waiting for the spirits to come.

You couldn't blame the spirits really, for being a bit reluctant. I mean the location wasn't exactly ideal. Marina's space-age kitchen with its whizzy appliances, and the black slab worktops that reminded me of head-stones. And then there was the low churning rumble of the tumble-dryer.

'Can't you turn it off?' I whispered to Marina after another five minutes had ticked by. 'It might be putting them off.'

Marina snapped that no she could not. 'I've got two more loads to do.'

Then Lauren's stomach was making gurgly noises, like one of those cheap squeaky toys that kittens play with.

'Do you have to?' I glared at her.

Lauren reminded me crossly that she needed to eat every three hours, something to do with her low-protein, allergen-free diet. 'I can't help my bodily functions, can I?'

I prayed silently: *Please, God, spare us from Lauren's 'bodily functions'*.

Lauren was what you might call a serious hypo-chondriac. She could have been quite pretty with her hazel eyes and shiny brown hair, if not for that agonized expression of hers, as if someone had just told her the world was about to end in, like, five minutes.

Now she scratched her knee, and the table shifted slightly. 'Oh look. It's levitating.'

I took a deep breath. 'Lauren, this is serious. Can you, like, stop fidgeting?'

This was asking for trouble of course. I had no idea, Lauren said, what an eczema-sufferer like her had to go through. 'It's like insects, millions of creepy-crawlies all scritching and scratching and burrowing under your skin. And anyway, how much longer is this going to take?'

'Well how do I know? It's not like waiting for a bus or anything, is it?'

At that time, I didn't know much about spirits. But it stood to reason they couldn't be rushed. They had to be lured, surely? Tempted into the land of the living with spooky panpipes, and flickering candles. Yet here we were, the place we always gathered after school for some reason, Marina's kitchen with its electrical hum and cooker buzzers. Enough to frighten the living, never mind the dead.

'You have absolutely no concept of what it's like,' Lauren was groaning.

'I think we have. You look like you're possessed already. Or is that shoulder-wiggling thing you're doing some kind of work-out for your pecs?'

'Hah, very funny. I'm dying for a really good scratch.'

'Die then.' Marina gave her that look of hers, a kind of disdainful snarl that she'd honed to perfection and was much admired for.

'Yeah,' I said, backing her up, 'you're always *dying* for something.'

It was all Lauren's fault, I was sure, for scaring the spirits off. Still, what else could you expect from someone with those chewed, ridged fingernails?

Cheiro's Book of the Hand was my Bible in those days. And the fingers pressed to the glass that afternoon told me all I needed to know about their owners.

Take Lauren for instance. Her flabby white palms were a sign of poor health (Cheiro was spot on there), what with her allergies to pollen, cat fur, the house-dust mite, and practically everything else under the sun. Apart from the skin rashes, she also suffered from blocked sinuses. Sometimes in class, she'd snort. I mean a really disgusting farmyard, piggy kind of snort. I willed her not to do that today. One snort from Lauren and the spirits would go wafting back to the other side, to their immaculate green garden, which I once read about in *Spiritualist Monthly*.

But Marina was taking charge. 'Take deep breaths . . . empty your minds . . .' She sounded all wise and mystical, like one of those voices on a Learn-to-Meditate tape. She closed her eyes, and Lauren and I followed suit. Marina had that effect on people; a natural authority. If anyone could tempt the spirits from their flowery paradise then Marina could. With her psychic fingers, I just knew she had the power to make my seance work. The Psychic Hand, it's one of the highest types.

Actually it was that hand which had brought Marina and me together in the first place. I'd taken Cheiro's book to school with me one breaktime, and found it worked like a magnet. Girls who barely gave me a second glance normally were thrusting their hands at me. 'Do mine . . . please do mine next!'

Really it was only *Marina's* palm I was interested in.

12

She seemed so exotic compared to the other girls in our class. While they prattled on about celebs and pop stars, Marina's talk was all of gods and goddesses. Aphrodite, the goddess of Love and Beauty for instance; the way Marina talked about her, you'd think she was a real person, a distant cousin or something.

'Wow! You have got an unbelievable Mount of Venus.' Holding her small hand in my own, I had flattered her shamelessly.

'Really?' Marina had tried hard not to sound impressed. Still she couldn't resist asking, 'Is that good then?'

'It's quite unusual actually. I've never seen one like it before.'

This was enough for Marina, to be special, different from everyone else. After that, well, I knew I had her hooked.

Now I opened my eyes a fraction and saw her forefinger pressed to the glass, her dark head tilted dramatically towards the ceiling. Lauren looked as if she was trying to stop a sneeze coming. Another minute, and it would all fall apart. My brilliant idea of communing with the spirits declared a joke, a complete and utter failure.

MOVE, glass, please . . . ! Perhaps if I really concentrated I might shift it by sheer force of will. I closed my eyes tightly, until there was nothing but the glass, shimmering like the Holy Grail, in the dark space of my mind.

Like I said, it was just a game to begin with. I mean, I never *really* expected it to move. When Lauren snuffled that 'Someone must be pushing it,' I actually gasped.

Marina stuck up her hand for silence. 'Shush a minute. It's trying to tell us something.'

Typical of Marina, of course, to be so totally cool, hardly raising an eyebrow as the glass jerked uncertainly about the perimeter of cut-out letters, as if testing its boundaries.

The glass, or whatever it was inside the glass, teased us at first. It skittered, first this way, then that, skating towards the word YES, then NO. Whooshing back and forth, it skimmed the table surface with an uncanny squeaking sound.

Marina commanded, 'If there is a spirit present, then please tell us who you are!'

The glass hesitated, as if it was thinking about it.

'Spirit. We wish to communicate with you. Please tell us your name.' Marina's sweep of dark hair nudged a few of the letters out of place, and I quickly poked them back in line.

The glass responded to Marina's command. It swung decisively to the circle edge. It began to spell a word, the three of us repeating the letters aloud. 'H . . . E . . . N . . . R . . . Y . . . Henry.' We all spoke the name together.

It was kind of a disappointment, I suppose. Somehow, we hadn't been expecting a Henry.

'Not Henry Purviss, is it?' Lauren wondered.

I glared at her. 'How can it be? He's not even dead. Well, *half*-dead maybe.' I was thinking about that mind-numbing stuff Purviss had given us on the Tudors a few weeks back.

'Shhh!' Marina hissed. 'It's moving again.'

The glass jerked, faster this time, and again we repeated the letters aloud . . .

'Hal?' We looked blankly at each other.

'Well, hey, Hal, how you doing?' I said finally. 'Do you, like, have a surname or anything?'

The glass swept at once to the letters K . . . I . . . N . . . G.

'Hal King,' I shrugged. 'Hal King mean anything to you lot?'

Perhaps, seeing our dumb looks, the thing in the glass offered another clue: OF HAMPTON COURT.

'Hal King of Hampton Court,' Lauren repeated slowly. She was frowning like a contestant on a quiz show, as if getting the wrong answer would lose her thousands of pounds.

'Hampton Court!' I was almost bouncing up and down in my chair by now. 'Oh wake up, Lauren, you prune. Hampton Court! There *is* only *one* Hampton Court, isn't there?'

'But didn't King Henry the Eighth live at Hampton Court?' Lauren said.

'Yes! She finally got it. Go to the top of the class,' I sighed with impatience. 'Look, forget Hal King. Hal was kind of a Tudor nickname for Henry. *King Henry*, get it? Hampton Court was, like, Henry's Des Res. Well, Marina's been reading about him for her project. I'm right, aren't I, Marina?'

But Marina was already way ahead of us. She was gazing at the glass as if she was about to get down on her knees any minute. 'It was the King's favourite. It was his favourite palace.' Marina spoke in a kind of churchy whisper, as if she was actually being received in the golden splendour of the famous Long Gallery.

15

'But, Henry of Hampton Court . . .' Lauren doggedly persisted. 'I mean, what are you two trying to tell me? I mean, it can't be . . . it can't really be . . .'

'King Henry the Eighth? In the glass?' Marina's eyes were bright. Huge. 'Why not? We called up a spirit, didn't we? It could have been anyone. Why not someone important? Famous. Why not the most notorious English king ever? Give me one good reason.'

'It's a bit of a coincidence though, isn't it, Marina?' Lauren suggested. 'I mean, you said you were choosing Henry the Eighth for your project next term, and now he just turns up.'

'Well, why shouldn't he?' I snapped in Marina's defence. 'Better if it had been one of the six wives though, like Anne Boleyn for instance.'

I'd decided on Anne for *my* project. What with all those lovers and her snappy dressing, Anne had real style I reckoned.

'But,' Lauren squinted in disbelief, 'I mean, he's been dead for at least . . . at least . . .'

'He came to the throne in 1509,' Marina stated coolly. 'He died in . . .' She hesitated for a moment. 'He died in 1547.'

'So he comes back nearly five centuries later, just to say "hi" to us lot? I don't want to spoil the fun or anything, but you've got to be joking.'

But this time, the glass spelled out the words without hesitation. A whole, gob-smacking sentence. SWEET LADY I DO NOT JEST.

I do not jest, it said. *He* said rather. Henry VIII. The same Henry who had burned heretics and beheaded wives, and snogged anything in a farthingale like there was no

16

tomorrow, had just given Lauren a telling off for her cheek.

I suppose that was the, like, *defining moment*. The moment when we could have just dumped the letters into the bin, and sauntered off to the park to check out the talent. But, this is the whole trouble with *defining moments*, you never recognize them until years after, when it's too late. How could we have known then, that one of the worst male chauvinist pigs known to history was about to disrupt our entire lives? And anyway it was too late. Already our world had shrunk to that upturned brandy glass, to its squeak and slither and glide. As that afternoon ticked on into evening, all our energy seemed concentrated in the very tips of our fingers. Henry was taking us for a ride.

We didn't need to ask questions. Henry's messages came without prompting. There was hardly even time to interpret.

MY LADY IS A GOGGLE-EYED WHORE, Henry said. Then, THAT MADAM IS A POISONED LILY.

It didn't take too many brain-cells to figure out who he was on about. Anne Boleyn. Anne who flirted with half the hunks at court and lost her head for it. Of course, the fact that she couldn't give Henry a son and heir didn't help much either. Still, as if she hadn't paid enough for her misdeeds, Henry had to gripe about her. He had to give us three girls the old 'my wife didn't understand me' line.

THAT MADAM IS A WITCH, Henry said.

'Poor Anne Boleyn,' I whispered. 'He hasn't forgiven her. After all this time. He must have fancied her once though.'

17

At once the glass whirled out a reply: FANCY . . . ALL SWEET LADIES TAKE MY FANCY . . .

' "Sweet ladies".' I couldn't resist a snigger. 'Dirty old devil's getting it on with us. Oh God. Sorry. That just . . . that just about cracks me up.'

Maybe it was the tension of the past hour or so, I don't know. But sometimes, when you start laughing you just can't stop. Especially when someone's glaring at you, all disapproving, like Marina was. It felt like a kind of sacrilege almost. Like getting the giggles in church, or at someone's funeral.

'Sweet ladies . . .' My hysterical giggles turned into hiccups. 'That's US, you realize. Eugh! Pass me the sick bag . . . puh . . . lease!'

Well it wasn't *all* my fault. I mean, it could have been Lauren's explosion of sneezing that scattered the letters. But the glass, suddenly disorientated, spelled out a string of gibberish with the remaining letters. Something like MWEGLTOFCOT. Then nothing. The glass was motionless, just an old upturned brandy glass again. Henry, if it was Henry, had abandoned us in a fit of royal pique. I could even see him, strutting back to the other side with a dismissive swirl of his ermine-lined cape, and a roar of disgust. Like Anne before us, we were in the black books.

'Did you have to? Just when it was getting interesting?' Marina said. If looks could kill, Lauren and I would shortly be headed for the spirit realm ourselves.

Lauren mumbled an apology: 'I think it's that perfume Abbie's wearing.'

'*Oh, Frenzy*, you mean.' Just to annoy her, I took a slurping sniff of my own armpit. 'Fancy a squirt?'

'It's not funny, Abbie. You could have shown more respect, you of all people.' Marina released the blinds, and the kitchen was flooded with rosy light. 'We've just been talking to a *king*. Not just any common old everyday spirit, but *royalty*. Doesn't that mean anything to you two?'

She glanced up at the clock and I saw the look of alarm flash across her face. It was six already. At once she began setting up the ironing board, ready to slip into her little housewife role.

The Pauloses kept a small grocery store in Commerce Road, dark and pungent with yeast and spices, exotic fruits, and hessian sacks spilling odd beans and seeds. Marina's parents never returned home from their shop much before nine, but she had a list of chores to do before then, pinned to the cork notice board above the fridge.

Anxious to make amends, Lauren bent to clear up the letters while I replaced the brandy glass in the drinks cabinet. It was funny to think of Marina's father coming home and filling it with the other kind of spirits. And where was Henry now? Somehow I couldn't visualize him floating among the herbaceous borders described in *Spiritualist Monthly*. A Tudor knot-garden maybe, with herbs and secret arbours and fountains. Or was he banished to some outer darkness until we took out the letters again? Or maybe he was still hovering in the kitchen, watching greedily as Marina prepared the evening meal, old hungers and memories stirring.

Marina's lounge had a stuffy smell. You could smell the carpet, which was new, and the velour suite, all padded and plumped and tasselled. The lampshades were tasselled

19

too, and the curtains swagged in loops and scallops across the French windows, like old-fashioned ball-gowns. The mock chandelier hanging from the ceiling reminded me of a giant jelly-fish. Every surface was cluttered with family photos; different versions of Marina's own dark eyes following my every movement, as if to say, 'Hey, English girl, what are you doing here?'

'I'm her friend,' I felt like saying to all those aunts and cousins and grandfathers. 'Best friend actually.' The mysterious eyes dismissed me. What did friends matter? Family was what counted, family.

I slid the glass door of the cabinet softly back. As I straightened, I noticed one of the plumes of dried pampas grass that sat either side of the electric log-fire. It seemed to be waving ever so slightly . . . if you looked at it, half squinting . . . surely? The windows were closed. They always were for security reasons, no matter how hot it got, Marina said. There wasn't a breath of air in the place.

Back in the kitchen, Marina left off ironing her father's shirt to take lamb chops from the fridge.

'I think I might do Elizabeth I for my project actually. The Virgin Queen.' Lauren was brushing her hair with her pure bristle brush. 'Eugh! You're not eating red meat, are you?'

Marina sighed. 'That was the plan. Lauren, would you mind *not* brushing your hair over the cooker?'

'Sorry. I'm just telling you what I've read, like it takes your body two whole days to rid itself of the toxins in red meat. Chicken's even worse. Boys are actually growing boobs from eating too much chicken, because of the hormones and everything.'

Marina caught my eye. We both smiled secretly, to show how sick we were of Lauren's health lectures, we who had higher concerns in the spirit realm.

'Wooh,' I said, in my mock-impressed voice. 'That explains some of the dorks in our class. That Andrew Warrender really should wear a trainer-bra, don't you think?'

'Hormones aren't funny, Abbie,' Lauren reprimanded me. 'Anyway, I should go. I want to call in at the library before it closes, so I can make a start on my project. You coming?'

'No. No, not just yet. See you tomorrow, yeah?'

The chops were sizzling in the pan by now. It was quite a relief as Lauren trundled off, vanquished by the smell of charred flesh. Marina tossed me the potato peeler. 'Catch! If you're staying, you can make yourself useful.'

This was the time I liked best, when I had Marina all to myself. It seemed only fair. Hadn't I got to her first? I was admiring Marina's Mount of Venus, calculating her birth number, long before Lauren came snivelling round.

'I'm sorry,' I said. 'For what happened earlier, laughing, I mean. I think it was nerves actually.'

'You did go a bit white when the glass began moving,' Marina conceded. She was very nifty with that iron, angling it just right for the collar. This was the bit about her I didn't get. How domesticated she was. Almost mumsy. 'You're not scared, are you, Abbie?'

We began talking about tomorrow, how we would create a more fitting atmosphere for Henry, with music and incense, the works.

'Not exactly *scared*. Why should I be? It was my idea. I mean, if he suddenly materialized right there on the table, then I'd be scared. As long as he stays in the glass, we're all right.'

I pretended to concentrate on the potatoes, removing the peel in thin unbroken curls. As long as he stayed in the glass. Would he though? I couldn't imagine old Henry staying anywhere he didn't want to. Confined by a silly circle of letters.

'Why? Are *you* scared?'

Stupid question. Marina was never afraid of anything. She didn't even bother to reply, just smiled her mysterious smile, padding barefoot between cooker and ironing board. Marina was small and curvy, yet she moved with such grace, she might have been gliding through citrus groves, a basket of Cyprus oranges balanced on her head. I watched her shake out a pillowcase. Imagine if Henry could see her too, as I did. What would he think? I reckoned Henry would have been really gone on Marina, he'd have fallen for her, just like he did for the unlucky Anne, his 'goggle-eyed whore'.

'Anyway, we might get someone else next time. Henry might have been a sort of one-off.' I took up another potato, the peaty skin making me cough.

'A one-night stand you mean?' Marina said. She was shaking her head. Henry would be back, she was certain of it. She felt it in her bones, deep in her gut, underneath her skin. She just *knew* it. 'As long as Lauren doesn't back off.' She stared at me, her dark eyes wide. 'Lauren can be a pain, but we need her to make up the numbers. As long as you don't get cold feet. As long as you and me are here, then Henry will come.'

'I'll be there. I'm not that much of a wimp.' I felt myself flush with pride. It thrilled me to be bonded in this way with Marina. Me and Marina, a potent psychic combination, irresistible to the unseen forces.

'We must keep it between the three of us though.' Now that the mound of potatoes was done, she padded behind me to the front door. 'Whatever you do, Abbie, don't talk about it to anyone. People are so dumb. They'd think we were making it up, that we were freaks or something.'

Marina had a kind of shimmer about her as she stood framed in the doorway. She looked all misty-eyed. She looked the way people look when they're in love. 'Henry,' she said. 'I'm sure he's come to teach us something. You know, like a spirit guide.'

It was still hot outside. Thick privet hedges wafted their tangy scent, and nearly every front garden in Arcadia Avenue had one of those sugar-pink lavatera things trumpeting into the sky. I broke into a jog. After the quiet cool of Marina's house, the buzz of traffic on the main road was somehow a shock.

Joining the queue at the bus stop, I thought of Henry. I imagined him, left behind in that kitchen. The King as he had been in life, sucking meat from the chop bones, shaking snowstorms of salt with his pudgy jewelled fingers. His ermine-trimmed cap would perch on the kitchen stool; the gold-sheathed dagger would mist in the steam from the pans. He would suck the bones clean, then chuck them over one shoulder. Then he would gaze at Marina, and lick his mean red little lips. Slowly.

Chapter Two

One thing was for sure, no way would the ghost of Henry VIII want to materialize in *my* house. I lived about five bus stops away from Marina, just round the corner from the tube station. There were no lavateras in our front gardens. Actually, there *were* no front gardens, only strips of concrete wide enough for a dustbin. Smedhurst Road. Number sixty-two. Not even a house, but a maisonette, which is kind of like two flats together, one up, one down, both sharing a porch. We shared the porch with Mrs Croop from downstairs.

That night I burst in, clumping up the stairs two at a time as usual. Then stopped. The living-room door was open. Through it, I had a telescopic view of our elderly neighbour, enthroned in one of the fireside chairs. And there was my mother, crouched at her feet, as if she was paying her some sort of homage. In fact, she was most likely doing something unmentionable to our neighbour's toenails.

Mrs Croop's eyes lit up when she spotted me. 'Here's your Abbie, bless her. Hallo, my ducks! Your mum's just been giving me a quick seeing to. My old feet have been giving me gip, I don't mind telling you.'

This was the trouble with Mrs Croop. She didn't mind telling you *anything*.

'Oh,' I said, very sniffy, making it plain how utterly

disgusted I was. I mean having a chiropodist for a mother was bad enough, without having to witness the grisly procedures under your own roof.

'Well, I'll be off then.' Mrs Croop levered herself from the chair. 'I don't want to hold up your tea, ducks.'

'Why does she have to call me "ducks"?' I said when she'd gone.

My mother decided to ignore my 'sick' noises. 'I'll just hoover these toenails up, dear, and then I'll get your tea.'

I thought of Henry suddenly. Henry would probably have had crones like Mrs Croop flung in the Tower dungeons. Somehow that thought made me feel better, as I spread out my project work on the table.

No, no self-respecting spirit would be seen dead in this house. It was bad enough inviting my friends round, what with Mum's collection of teapots on the gingham-frilled dresser, and Dad's favourite picture of *The Crying Boy* who looked, my dad said, as if he was crying 'real' tears.

'I hope you washed your hands, Mother,' I remarked.

Having disposed of Mrs Croop's remains, my mother was laying the table for tea: salad with jars of gherkins and pickled onions and all that stuff that gives you dog's breath, and ensures that no man will ever want to kiss you in a million years.

Not that I had a man – a boyfriend rather. This much the three of us girls had in common at least. Lauren because her constant snuffling was a bit of a turn-off, Marina because her dad never let her out of the house, and me . . . well I was working on it. One day, I would go to bed looking like Quasimodo and wake up like Kate Winslet, and the phone would never stop ringing.

'Of course I did. Is that history you're doing, dear?' My mother was trying to lay the table around me.

'Anne Boleyn,' I told her. 'She's my character for my project.'

'Is she, dear? Wasn't that the poor woman who got her head chopped off, just for having a lovely little baby girl? Disgraceful.'

'I don't think that was the only reason, Mother,' I said. 'There was a bit more to it than that. Actually she had six fingers on one hand, and that, as you may not know, was the classic sign of a witch.'

'A witch! What superstitious nonsense. A simple operation would have put that right. I had a patient once, and she had an extra little toe on her . . .'

'Mother please! Spare me the details.'

'Sorry, dear.' She began that tuneless humming, a sort of medley of hymns and TV theme tunes, which nearly drove me insane, and I knew that she was wondering about Anne Boleyn's feet and the state of her toenails.

My mother didn't believe in witches of course, or spirits, or anything that didn't walk on two feet. I longed to lift her from the lowly heights of cutting old folks' toenails, from their bunions and corns and hard skin, lift her into another spiritual dimension, onto another plane. Maybe I would tell her about Henry. On second thoughts, what was the point? I knew exactly what she would say: 'That's nice dear,' humouring me as if I was six again, and chatting to my imaginary friend.

Glancing up at *The Crying Boy*, I tried to reassure myself. Beyond our poky flat was a world of art and culture, of poets and media people, and musicians.

'Is that an original?' Lauren had sniggered, when first

she saw *The Crying Boy*. I had to agree with her, of course, that it was entirely lamentable. In fact it made me want to cry myself. 'My dad thinks they look like real tears,' I said. Then felt ashamed for making fun of my dad's taste. I felt angry with Lauren too. It was all right for her. Her parents, like the parents of most kids in our class, were divorced. She lived with her mother, Izzie, who wore big earrings and boogied to Van Morrison while she fired her pots in the basement. Izzie even had a boyfriend. Whereas my mother was always fussing about in her crochet tank top and stretch pants, making plates of sandwiches cut in silly triangles and calling my friends 'luvvy'. Most embarrassing of all though, she'd been forty-seven, practically geriatric, when she found she was pregnant with me.

'I'd given up all hope of falling,' she was fond of boasting, 'and then Abigail came along!'

She made it sound like a miraculous birth, as if she'd had a visit from God or something. In my opinion, sex should be banned for the over-forties. It made me feel sick to think about it.

'What are you making that face for? I thought you liked salad?' Mum peered closely at me. She was always doing that. I think she'd read in some magazine to check your teenaged children for dilated pupils or something, a known sign of drug-taking.

'I'm fine, it's just that . . .'

'Yes?'

'Oh, nothing.' I packed Anne Boleyn away, until later. It had been on the tip of my tongue to tell her about Henry after all, but then I remembered Marina saying we should keep it to ourselves.

'People are so dumb,' Marina said. She was right of course. It seemed a pity though.

Meeting up at Marina's house next day, it struck me that we should have dressed up a bit.

'I mean, denim and crop tops aren't really the thing for a seance, are they? Especially when we're like half-expecting a Royal Visit.'

'Speak for yourself,' Lauren scoffed. 'Personally I thought I *was* dressed up.'

Maharishi trousers, she meant; her shoulders were square and bony in a strappy T-shirt. A pity we couldn't replace Lauren with some genuine Romany mystic, but we were stuck with her. Just like we were stuck with blue sky and sunshine, when thunder and lightning would be so much, well, spookier.

The temperature must have been in the high twenties again. On the other side of that blind, summer was humming, wafting its scents of camomile and privet and melting tar and sweat. We must have been mad to shut ourselves in that green-gold gloom with Henry, when out there it was all happening. Or waiting to happen. Yet we did.

This time, drawn blinds and a rumbling tumble-dryer weren't enough. We had to create the right mood, Marina decided. She draped her purple silk shawl over the blind for extra black-out, then we lit the patchouli incense and enough candles to light up the dark side of the moon.

The lounge would have been a better setting of course, with its velvet and tassels, its creepy unused feeling, but Marina said no. The lounge was very much her parents' domain. And anyway, there was that gilt-framed picture of the Virgin Mary over the electric log-fire, which would be a complete turn off for Henry, what with him quarrelling with the Pope and everything.

'I brought *The Dance of the Blessed Spirits*.' Lauren produced a CD from her vast library of classics. She added in a despairing kind of voice, 'Marina's heard it before. I don't imagine you have though, Abbie.'

'*The Blessed Spirits*? Yeah, I play it every night, don't I, before I go to bed.'

'Listen, we've got to do this properly.' Marina pushed her hair back from her face, watching me as I sorted the letters into their circle. 'There's really no point in summoning a king, or any spirit come to that, if we act like it's all a joke. What are we going to ask him for a start? Has anyone thought of a good question?'

'We could ask if he had regrets,' I suggested.

Marina stared coolly at me. 'Regrets?'

'Like wasn't he a bit harsh on poor Anne for example? Couldn't he have just sent her to France for a long holiday?'

'No, I think we should stay off the subject of Anne Boleyn,' Marina decided. 'This isn't, like, *Hello Magazine* you know, Abbie.'

'Yeah,' Lauren drawled. '*Exclusive interview with Royal, Henry tells it like it is*. Honestly, Abbie . . .'

'*Henry dishes the dirt on Annie*,' I joined in. '*Warts 'n' all profile of a royal marriage*. No, actually I'm serious. Don't forget I'm doing Anne for my project. It might be helpful to get, like, the inside story.'

Lauren sighed. 'Marina's right though. We don't want him to think he's talking to a bunch of bimbos. Why don't we ask him about the Reformation, and the dissolution of the monasteries?'

'Eugh . . . excuse me!' I gave a great exaggerated jaw-cracking yawn as the first tremulous notes of *Blessed Spirits* fluted through to us from the lounge. 'Haven't we had enough of that stuff from Purviss?' Two whole double history periods in fact, about how Henry got more powerful than the Catholic Pope and went around pensioning off the monks and wrecking the monasteries. 'Anyway, I'll get the glass, while you're thinking about it.'

In Marina's lounge, the door of the cabinet slid smoothly back. Strange, but the minute my fingers closed on the brandy glass, a sort of tingle buzzed through them. It was one of those sultry July days, when you stick to everything you touch, and yet, as I took the glass, a cold-ness shivered through me. Would Henry come at all this time? I almost hoped he wouldn't.

'What *are* you *doing* in there, Abbie?' Marina called out. 'For God's sake, let's get on with it.'

Marina had been right. Henry *did* come. He came at once. We didn't even get the chance for Marina to demand in her velvety tones, *Is there anybody there?* It was as if he'd been waiting for us, impatient for his chance to live again beneath our fingers. The glass scooted back and forth to the letters, so fast we could hardly keep up.

GREETINGS SWEET MAIDS FROM YOUR SOVEREIGN LORD HENRY.

'See,' Marina said, smugly assured, 'I told you he would come back.'

We looked at each other, flustered. What should we say back? Now that we had Henry's attention, what to do with it? Mad as it was, I almost felt we should curtsy, as if we three had been summoned to court, to recite poetry, to dance quadrilles for the King's entertainment.

GREEN GROW THE HOLLY O, the glass spelled out, as if picking up my thoughts.

'Is that one of your favourite songs?' I asked.

The glass responded. YESNOYESNOYESNO ... HEY NONNY HEY NO HOLLY O.

It seemed we'd hit on the right subject. The glass practically danced round the circle, spelling out snatches of poetry, and ballads, none of which we recognized. There were lots of 'nonnies' and 'lullies' and something about a 'maid with paps like silken pillows'.

'He means "boobs",' I hissed to Marina.

'I think we can all guess what "paps" are.' Marina cleared her throat. 'Perhaps, Sire, we might ask you a few questions?'

'Sire?' Sire seemed to be going a bit far. Marina sounded like a chat-show hostess, sucking up to some dumb celebrity. 'Please, Sire, please tell us this, what is it *actually like*, where you are now?'

Ah! This could be interesting. I grinned at Marina, to show my approval. Henry, though, seemed a bit confused. The glass crept half-heartedly, a few inches to the right, then back, then gave up altogether.

'Maybe he doesn't know,' I whispered. 'He's an earth-bound spirit. He doesn't know what it's like. He doesn't even know he's dead. Imagine!'

Lauren cleared her throat. 'It must seem a bit dull, where you are now. Do you miss the royal court?'

This time, alarmingly, the glass answered. WHAT SAY'ST THOU MAID PRITHEE, TAUNT ME NOT WITH RIDDLES.

'What about your wives?' I decided to come straight

31

to the point. 'Which one did you love the best?'

This was more like it. Swiftly the glass spelled out what I already knew from the history books, that timid (and let's face it, *boring*) Jane Seymour had been the favourite.

SWEET JANEJANEJANEJANE . . .

'Why Jane though? I mean, OK, she bore you a son, but I mean, was that all? Was there something about her you particularly fancied? Something you go for in women? What about us lot? Which one of us girls d'you fancy the most?'

Even while Lauren and Marina were groaning, Henry answered chivalrously, just like the day before, that ALL SWEET LADIES TAKE MY FANCY.

'You must have a favourite though. Tell us. We can take it.'

For a minute or two, the glass skittered this way and that, confused.

Funny, even though the others agreed that this line of questioning was completely dumb, and totally out of order, this didn't stop them from adjusting their poses, Marina tossing back her lustrous hair as if the very weight of it was a burden to her, Lauren stuffing her tissue up her sleeve and attempting to suck in her cheeks. There wasn't much I could do, except to fluff up my copper-blonde crop a bit. I made sure not to smile though. Thanks to a slight gap in my front teeth, I'd probably have to wear a brace for the rest of my natural life; it seemed unlikely that the Tudors would go for a fetching glint of metal among the pearly whites.

Luckily we didn't have to wait too long for Henry's decision. Before we knew it, the glass was on the move again, sweeping our fingers towards the letter M so that we sighed and gazed at Marina, even before it finished spelling her name.

M . . . A . . . R . . . I . . . N . . . A.

I nudged her gently. 'Wow, Marina, you've scored!'

. Well who else could it possibly have been, but lovely dusky Marina, with that expression on her face, as if she was purring contentedly, deep deep inside herself? Only when Henry began to elaborate, suggesting that Marina was indeed FINER THAN THE NIGHT CROW, did she blink and flush a little.

'The Night Crow!' I leaned forward, rocking the table slightly. 'That was another name for Anne Boleyn. Some evil old cardinal called Wolsey hated Anne, and spread all these rumours about her being a witch and everything. If you're "finer than the Night Crow", Henry must think you're even more of a looker than Anne was. Hey, that's some compliment, Marina! Anne was like the Catherine Zeta Jones of her day. She could make a bloke's tongue hang out at the mere flick of an eyelash.'

'Shhh!' Marina flashed. She was intent on the glass, as well she might be. Henry was giving her the works, pulling out all the Tudor chat-up lines in one go. Marina was his DARK EYED DOVE. Marina was his TRUE MAIDEN. Marina was of such FLESHLY VERTUE THAT MIGHT RARE BE FOUND.

Well. Henry was going over the top a bit, I felt. Yet here was Marina, coolly lapping up compliments as a cat laps cream.

'What does he mean "True Maiden"?' Lauren was gazing at Marina with a devotion that made me want to throw up.

'I've heard the "Dark Eyed Dove" bit before,' I said. 'That was what he called Anne before he dumped her. Maybe he's mixing Anne up with you, Marina.'

Lauren simpered that it wasn't hard to see why. 'It's true, Marina, really, you've got this natural nobility about you, hasn't she, Abbie?'

This time Marina couldn't resist a smirk of pleasure. 'It's probably just that we've got the same colouring.' She gave a dismissive shrug.

The glass had been motionless for at least five minutes.

'You know all that stuff about Jane being the favourite is crap,' I said. 'If you ask me, Jane was like the good little stay-at-home wifey, but when it came to looks, forget it. No contest. Anne could twist old Henry round her little finger. I got this out of the library today . . . *The Pleasure of Kings*. You wouldn't believe some of the stuff that's in it.'

At once the glass joined in. POISONING WHORE, said the glass. Then, oddly, adding, NO HEAD IS TOO FAIR.

'Too fair for chopping off, he must mean,' I said, as the glass resorted now to the gobbledygook of the day before, stuttering out a string of 's's and 'G's. Without any warning, Marina reached out and snatched it up. 'I forgot to say, my parents could be home early tonight.'

It seemed a bit rude, as if we'd just dumped old Henry without so much as a 'so long, your highness, see you around maybe'. What happened to Marina's bowing and scraping? Her, 'oh if you please, Sire, this and please, Sire, that'? Was it the thought of her parents, or a sudden fear of what Henry might say next, that made her ditch him so suddenly?

'It's Wednesday. They often close early on a Wednesday,' Marina said. Behind us, the blinds rattled up. Dust spirals danced in the shafts of light.

'Wow, what about that then?' I couldn't help teasing her a bit. 'With a Hey Nonny No . . . and a Green Grow the Holly O . . . Marina is fairer than the old Night Crow . . .'

'Marina is the "True Maiden".' Lauren blew her nose so hard, she made it sound like 'glue maiden'.

'True Maiden. Virgin, he must mean,' I said. 'Marina is my true virgin.'

'Look, I don't want to rush you or anything.' Marina was slapping the lid on the tin of letters. 'But I'd rather my father didn't find you two here, OK?' She turned her back on us, twisting her hair into a smooth coil, filling a pan with water.

I thought I understood why she was so touchy. It was that word 'Maiden'. Technically, of course, we were all still virgins, but we had, like, *messed about* a bit. Even Lauren, who had had a few dates a while back with some Simon bloke she met at the allergy-testing clinic. Only Marina would have qualified as 'pure'; innocent of gropes and fumbles and sloppy kisses, for what chance did she have to mix with boys? The boys at Bromfield High hardly counted. They were all computer nerds with Neanderthal stoops from playing with their joy-sticks every moment they got. Marina's parents did sometimes drum up male cousins to accompany her to the cinema at weekends, but even then, they were chaperoned by an aunt, or a married female cousin.

Poor Marina. Whenever a conversation turned to sex, which it did quite often, she would fall silent, her enigmatic look suggesting she'd romped her way through the entire *Kama Sutra*. Lauren and I knew different of course. Yet no one ever challenged her. We understood that Marina, of all people, had to keep face.

'Aren't you scared to be alone, Marina?' Lauren took a scoop of Kalm-Wax and slicked her bunches into what looked like spaniels' ears. 'I know I would be. I mean, imagine if he's watching you when you go to the loo, or you're having a bath and everything?'

'Come on.' I was prodding Lauren down the passage towards the door. 'Why would he want to watch her on the loo anyway? Honestly. He's not a pervert.'

'How do *you* know?'

'Because as far as I know, the Tudors had a romantic view of women. They weren't just after ripping their knickers off.' At the front door, I turned to Marina. 'You'll be OK?'

'I'm fine.' She frowned as if to say, why would she not be? 'I'm going to write it all down tonight, as a matter of fact. Record what Henry says. Otherwise we might just forget. And then we can analyse it later.'

'The Night Crow,' Lauren said, as we strolled down Arcadia Avenue. 'You know that's really creepy. In fact the whole thing is creepy. Henry picking Marina out, as if he could actually *see* her. I mean surely, spirits (not that I'm sure I believe in spirits), but if they do exist, then how can they physically see the living? I mean, they can't. Can they?'

She turned to me, as if I had all the answers to life, death and the universe. Everything.

'Well don't look at me. Brilliant I may be, but I don't

have, like, a hotline to the other side or anything. I imagine they just kind of tune in to our energy-waves and auras and stuff.'

'So, maybe Marina has beautiful energy-waves?' Lauren sounded doubtful.

'Maybe she has. We won't know, will we, until we're dead ourselves.'

'I suppose not,' Lauren said miserably, as if that day were not too far off.

'Anyway, don't look so worried,' I called after her, as she waited to cross the main road for the Highgate bus. 'Who knows what turns a ghost on? Just be thankful old Henry hasn't taken a fancy to you.'

Lauren laughed. At least I thought she did. It was hard to tell the way she was sneezing and spluttering into the stream of traffic. Traffic fumes. Another thing she was allergic to.

When my own bus lurched into sight, five minutes later, I jumped on it, glad to be alone. To think about the seance. To try to make sense of it all. Leaning my head against the dirt-streaked window, I wondered about auras and energy-waves. Was there really something special about Marina's? Could she really seduce the dead from their eternal sleep with her totally spiritual drop-dead gorgeousness? And what would she be doing now, at this minute? I imagined her once we'd left, rushing to sit before the mirror, smoothing her hair, gazing deep into her own dark eyes. Henry was the first male admirer she'd ever had to my knowledge. I supposed it was bound to go to any girl's head. And Anne Boleyn had lost her head twice over Henry. I just hoped that Marina wasn't about to do the same.

Chapter Three

Hardly a day passed, when we didn't gather at Marina's house to play the Game.

Now, whenever I think of it, I shudder. Why? I mean of all people! What had Henry got going for him? Studying that famous portrait by Holbein, we were all agreed that men with ginger hair were a turn-off for a start. Yet, almost every afternoon, we girls competed for his attentions like ladies of the Tudor court. Although none of us stood a chance against Marina.

Marina was still Henry's favourite. She was his 'Dark Maid', his 'Dove', his 'Black Lily'. Dead or not, the King hadn't lost his touch, he knew how to pull, all right. And Marina had taken on a kind of glow. Her cheeks were all flushed, her eyes bright. She washed her hair nearly every day, rinsing it in vinegar to bring out its shine. She was always whisking a mirror out of her bag, scrutinizing her face for a stray spot.

Actually, Marina's skin was pretty good, although she had more than her fair share of moles scattered about her chin and neck. Anne Boleyn was also a 'moley' person according to my project research, so it seemed Marina was in good company. Or bad company rather. Anyhow, if not for the fact that Henry was dead, I would have said that Marina was falling in love.

★　★　★

It was the Italian lesson that clinched it though, that showed me just how bad things really were with Marina.

We'd all signed up for this course, Parla L'Italiano! weeks before, long before Henry came on the scene. The local tech was running a course during the summer. It had been Lauren's Big Idea that we go along. Wouldn't it be utterly awesome, Lauren said, to have a working holiday in the land of pasta and Pavarotti after our A Levels? I wasn't sure about the Pavarotti bit, but chatting up the natives like . . . well, a native, had seemed like a good idea. Now, though, I had my doubts.

'It's just typical of Lauren,' I grumbled to Marina, as we took our places among the housewives and Tuscan villa-owner types. 'She talks us into this, then oh dear, she remembers she's got an urgent appointment at the Chinese Medicine Centre. Great!'

'We can manage without her, can't we?' Marina bestowed on me the pitying glance of the intellectually superior. Henry VIII himself, it seemed, had spoken several languages. Fluently.

'Henry was taught French, English and Latin.' She sounded as if she was reciting from a text book. 'He could understand Italian of course. Also, he regularly conversed in Greek.'

'Did he?' I didn't see what this had to do with us burbling phrase-book Italian, but too late. The scarily glam Signora Canciani was already clacking up the aisles between the desks in her vicious stilettos, teaching us how to say 'My name is Abigail Carter' in Italiano.

'*Allora*, we begin with some simple phrases, yes . . .?'

We began with those simple everyday phrases you never use in real life, like: *Will you accompany me to the cinema tonight?* Or, *My dog's name is Bobo.*

The idea was that the signora scribbled these riveting conversational openings on the board, and the class religiously copied them out into exercise books. Tedious, or what!

I whispered to Marina, 'Who needs this stuff? I mean, if we ever do get to meet any fit Italians, we're not going to talk about our pets, are we?'

But Marina ignored me. All around us, pens were scratching in the silence, Marina's faster than anyone's. Not that this surprised me. She was a natural at languages. Probably, she'd get an 'A' star for French GCSE, and I'd be lucky to get a 'C'.

'OK. Everyone got that down?'

I couldn't quite figure out what made the signora so scary. I mean, it wasn't even like she was a regular school teacher or anything. Maybe it was just that accent of hers. The kind you get in coffee ads, sexy and threatening all at once like the purr of a big cat. Even the Chianti-types seemed nervous, as they stumbled over the basics of how to order a meal, and ask if it was far to the Post Office.

'*Allora*, the two young ladies at the back . . .'

Damn! She'd spotted us. I cowered behind the wiggy hair-do of the woman in front. Please. Don't choose me. My prayer was answered.

'Let me see . . . Marina, isn't it? Marina, can you read to us what you've just written please?'

Scrape, scrape . . . the signora's heels approaching our desk. Scarlet stilettos, so narrow she must have required the services of a good chiropodist. Maybe I should give her my mother's card.

'Sorry, dear, I have your name right?' She consulted

her student list. 'You are Mees Marina Paulos?'

'Marina!' I whispered. 'She's talking to you.'

What was wrong with her? Marina's pen was still scratching away beside me, when everyone else had stopped. She wrote so fast, her pen practically skidded across the page. There was a breathlessness to it. An urgency.

'Marina!' I hissed, nudging her this time. But she felt closed off from me, from everyone, behind the dark curtain of hair. As if she wasn't really there, but in another room altogether.

Now the signora was standing right by our desk, wafting expensive perfume. I could feel the heat of her tawny eyes upon us. 'Marina . . . ?' Pink velvety lips smiled encouragement. '*Non preoccuparti*. Don't be embarrassed, eh? This is what we are here for, to learn. We are all beginners here. If you make a mistake, *non importa*, eh?' The signora shrugged.

By now, all heads had swivelled towards us. Still Marina didn't respond. My nudges seemed to have no effect either.

'Marina!' I tried a gentle kick on the ankle. Nothing. I was about to offer to read my own piece out, when the signora reached out with her scarlet lacquered fingernails and snatched up the exercise book with such a wrench, she almost took Marina with it.

'*Va bene* . . . I read it out, shall I, eef you feel shy.'

At last Marina sat up, blinking, smoothing her hair behind her ears. She looked bewildered for a moment, as if she'd just had, not a book, but a baby snatched from her arms. I held my breath as the signora read aloud in a perplexed, slightly irritable tone:

> '*There is written her fair neck round about*
> Noli me tangere, *for Caesar's I am*
> *And wild for to hold, though I seem tame . . .*'

'Well . . .' More shrugs of complete incomprehension this time. The signora gave us both an odd, not very friendly look. She slapped the book none too gently back upon the desk. '*No ho capito,*' the signora murmured as if to herself. 'I don't understand.'

You couldn't blame her for being mystified. These were not the words on the board. There was nothing about the dog Bobo or going to the cinema. Plus it was mostly in English. Or a kind of English.

'Perhaps,' the signora suggested, a note of sarcasm stealing into her voice, 'perhaps you have the wrong class, my dear. We are learning Italian today, *Parla l'Italiano!* I think you girls want the Creative Writing, or the Poets' Corner maybe?'

The Northgate Poetry Society apparently met on Wednesday evening. I tried to look grateful for this information as the signora turned away from us in some disgust. Meanwhile, Marina continued to gaze blankly ahead. *What was she on?*

I looked down at the page beside me. The four lines which the signora had read out stood out in a sea of loops and scrawls and twirls. Like that thing you do as children, 'taking your pencil for a walk'. For the past twenty minutes at least, Marina had been writing an entire page of complete and utter gibberish!

'So much for chatting up the Italian talent,' I said later, as we walked the few streets to her house. 'We won't be

42

going back there again. I nearly died of embarrassment. What was all that about anyway?'

'All what?' Marina stalked beside me, clutching her bag in front of her as if it contained the Holy Grail.

'Oh come on! The poetry, I mean. And all that gibberish. You were scribbling away like a demon. You should've seen that woman's face when she . . .'

'I'll tell you when we get home,' Marina said, and she smiled in that secretive, superior, maddening way of hers. A car slowed behind us at the lights, and the passenger leaned out to shout, 'Heh, like the wiggle! Going our way, girls?'

Whose wiggle he was talking about, we couldn't be sure. But Marina obviously took the credit, the way she tossed her hair back over one shoulder.

'Morons!' she declared, as we squinted, half-blinded by the trail of exhaust. 'Why is it, Abbie, that men are such total Neanderthals these days?'

I didn't say anything. But I noticed the way she emphasised 'these days', and I knew she was thinking of Henry.

'We can still play the Game if you want,' Marina said, turning the key in her door. We stepped into a dim polished gloom. 'There's no reason why it shouldn't work with just the two of us.'

'No . . . I mean no, I don't think we should. We need at least three. And maybe we should, sort of . . . I mean . . . give it a rest . . . just while Lauren's away. By the way, you haven't forgotten me and Lauren are going on holiday next week, have you, Marina? I was thinking, maybe we should leave it till after then?'

I'd agreed to go with Lauren and her mum to the south coast. She had this gran who lived by the sea. It didn't exactly sound like the holiday of a lifetime. On the other hand, anything was better than the annual week in Bournemouth with my parents.

Marina didn't seem interested in my holiday though. Dumping her bag on the floor she said, 'You're wrong about Henry needing three of us. He doesn't. He doesn't even need the Ouija board. He can come through in other ways . . .'

Other ways? That creepy goose-bumpy feeling took hold of me again. What did she mean, 'other ways'? She nodded her head at the stairs. 'I'll show you. Upstairs. In my room.'

I followed Marina up the stairs, barefoot as instructed. We were silent, creeping as if trying not to wake a baby. In her room, Marina had said. *What was?* My heart beat faint and quick. I was almost expecting to find Henry himself, the way she urged me to secrecy at the door.

'You won't say anything to anyone, even to Lauren?'

'My lips are sealed.' I made a zipping motion. What did she take me for? Wasn't I her most loyal, devoted disciple? As if I would gossip. Even if Henry *was* in there. But of course he wasn't. It was just Marina's room as usual, a bit over the top with frills and flounces, the filmy canopy over the bed, the gothic-style mirrors, and the enormous travel poster of Cyprus, all blue sky and glittering sea, forming a backdrop to the bed.

'Sit on the bed if you like,' Marina offered graciously. She peered critically in the dressing-table mirror. 'We're going back eventually,' she said, seeing me look at the poster. 'To Cyprus. When my parents have saved enough money.'

44

'For holidays you mean?'

'Not for holidays, for good.' She added scornfully, 'I mean Northgate . . . Cyprus – sorry, Abbie, but really it's no contest.'

'Yeah, well, it's beautiful and everything, but supposing you didn't fit in? I mean you go to an English school, your friends are English. You've lived here since you were three years old . . .'

'So what? England still isn't our home.' Perched on that quilted stool, tossing her hair siren-like, Marina looked as if her very beauty would lure mortal men to their deaths. Licking her little finger, she slicked her eyebrows into black crescent moons.

'Did you know Anne Boleyn's eyebrows were famous?' I said, mainly to distract her from the idea of going back to Cyprus and leaving me best-friend-less. 'They were known as the gift of Venus.'

Marina seemed to like the sound of that. In fact, she positively bloomed. 'The gift of Venus,' she repeated dreamily. Then, 'That reminds me, I must look up those lines . . .' She began scrabbling in her bag for the exercise book and repeated aloud the lines that Signora Canciani had scornfully intoned earlier that day:

> *'There is written her fair neck round about*
> Noli me tangere, *for Caesar's I am*
> *And wild for to hold, though I seem tame . . .'*

'Noli what's-it . . .' I said. 'Where did you get that from? It wasn't on the board, was it?'

Marina frowned. 'It's not Italian. I don't think Henry ever spoke Italian, although he could understand it. *Noli*

45

me tangere is Latin. It means . . .' She paused as if listening to some invisible translator. 'I think it means: *Do not touch me. Do not touch me, for I belong to the King.* It must refer to Henry and Anne Boleyn. Everything seems to lately.'

I was puzzled. 'You *think* it means? But, Marina, you should *know* what it means. You wrote it.'

Marina's eyebrows quirked up, aghast at my stupidity. 'I wrote it? I didn't write it, you clot!'

'Who wrote it then?'

'Well, Henry of course.' She waved the book at me. 'That wasn't me scribbling like fury this afternoon, it was Henry. Good grief, Abbie. You're the one that's so hot on the occult. I'd have thought you would guess. Haven't you heard of "spirit writing" before?'

Spirit writing. Of course. Now the elaborate scribblings made a kind of sense. There were even snatches of Latin among the scrawled gibberish. I was reminded of the way Henry sometimes resorted to gibberish during our Ouija board sessions. As if everything was in code, a puzzle, meant for us to decipher. I should have realized. Marina was right. It didn't resemble her hand at all. She had a very distinctive spiky kind of handwriting. The thought of Henry somehow manipulating her, his pudgy hand swirling her psychic fingers into a frenzied dance, made my throat go dry.

'That's . . .' I searched for the right words to describe it . . . 'That's . . . Marina, that's just so creepy!'

Marina rolled her eyes. 'Why? Why is it any more scary than a glass on a board?'

'I don't know. It just is.'

'Mediums do it all the time. You just let your mind go

blank and relax your hand, and let the spirits do it for you. And it's not just writing either.'

She fell to her knees suddenly, reaching beneath the bridal skirts of the bed and drawing out a roll of paper. The picture that unfurled before me was a pencil sketch, the lines wavery, as if sketched by a shaky hand. But it was clear enough who it was meant to be. A copy of the famous Holbein, the King in later life, so encrusted with jewels, he looked like an exotic beetle.

'A combined effort.' Marina spoke with that cool conceit that was beginning to irritate me. 'Mine and Henry's you could say.'

'Marina . . . don't you think . . . I mean, is this really a good idea?'

Even in these few rough lines, I could feel the force of the spirit's hand, the swagger and vanity; the mean eyes seemed to mock me before the picture furled itself back into a roll of old wallpaper.

'It's only a picture,' Marina laughed, though not very convincingly.

'It's hardly only a picture.'

'Well I didn't intend doing it. I was just sitting like now, with the paper leaning on a board on my knees, when the pencil began to move in my hand. Anyway, it'll be brilliant for my project. Henry coming to me like this, it's kind of a gift.'

She paused, as if waiting for me to congratulate her, to say, 'Hey Marina, that's really amazing,' but somehow I couldn't. I had that shivery feeling again, the same feeling I got in the lounge that time, taking the brandy glass from the cabinet.

'You've gone all quiet,' Marina accused me. 'This was

all your idea in the first place, remember?'

'Was it? Well, yes it was. The Ouija board was. But that's different. I mean, with the glass, we summon him up. We *invite* him. But this . . .' I nodded at the roll of paper. 'It's like he's looking for a way through. Like he's too impatient to wait for the Game. Maybe he's getting . . . I don't know . . . stronger . . .'

Marina didn't argue with this, because at that moment the doorbell rang. 'Wait there a minute,' she ordered, 'I'll get rid of whoever it is.'

This I could believe. The Pauloses rarely had visitors in the casual, just-popped-by sort of way.

Still, she wasn't getting rid of them *that* quickly. From downstairs I could hear the low rumble of a man's voice. Not her dad, I hoped – maybe he'd locked himself out? Spooked by that picture of Henry, the idea of being alone with his 'likeness', I crept onto the upstairs landing. Just below me, Marina's voice sounded lively, happy and utterly unintelligible, since she was speaking Greek.

I peered discreetly over the banister. Well. No way was that Marina's dad. The young guy was laughing, waving his arms about as he talked with so much energy you could almost feel the lightning crackle of it. I leaned further over, the knob of the rail pressing into my stomach until it hurt. What a laugh he had! Like warm honey trickling all over you. Greek mountain honey.

Marina was bowing her head, sort of mock-coy. What had he said? Who the hell was he? Should I go down? Make a grand entrance like one of those celebs on a talk-show staircase? Watch his face tilt towards me, his eyes light up?

I watched as he reached out and patted Marina's

shoulder, the brown hand bristling with rings. Oh jealousy! I'd never realized before how it could feel, like a snake coiled in your chest. Even such a brotherly kind of pat, for that's what it was surely, as Marina was seeing him to the door again.

At the door he turned suddenly, and looked straight up at me. I gulped. He was smiling. As if he knew I was there all along. As if he knew me. And this was the weirdest thing, I actually *felt* that smile, somewhere deep in the pit of my stomach, like a leaf unfurling.

'Who was that?' I ventured downstairs as soon as the door closed behind him. Trying to sound casual naturally. It wouldn't do to appear too eager.

'Only my cousin.' Marina looked a bit flushed.

'Your cousin?'

'Yes. He just dropped by to give me a message from my parents, as he was passing. They'll be home later than usual tonight. They have to call and see my aunty Rosa on the way home. I'd better get a move on.' Suddenly she was distracted. 'I must get that washing off the line.'

Washing to sort. Chores to do. Cinderella, wrenching her mother's delicate blouses, her father's shirts from the line.

I followed her out to the garden, and knelt on the grass, plucking the clover. The sun warmed my thighs like a dozing cat. I could still feel that smile, alight on my face. The flash of white teeth was blinding. Marina's cousin had the most snoggable lips I'd ever seen. If only I could ask about him without sounding too obvious. Instead, I began talking about the holiday. 'Why don't you come too? Lauren would love you to come, and her mum wouldn't mind.'

I tried to tempt her, telling her about the annexe cut off from the rest of the house, where, as I'd suggested to Lauren, we *might* throw a party or something.

'Her mum's really cool, and the granny's a bit ga ga, so Lauren says.'

But even as I invited Marina along, I knew it was useless. Her parents would say 'no'. They always did.

'Damn!' She was holding up her father's shirt, streaked with bird muck. A magpie chattered from the sycamore at the corner of the garden, as if owning up to the deed. It sounded evil. I thought of Anne Boleyn, DARKER THAN THE NIGHT CROW.

'Haven't you got some of that stain-remover stuff?'

'Not that, stupid. I mean, you and Lauren going off. We'll have to wait another couple of weeks now before we can play the Henry Game.'

It was no use. Marina was obsessed, in love. Her thoughts were all for Henry. As she heaved the laundry basket onto one hip, I got up to leave. Funny how, just for a moment, I'd been so busy dreaming of the handsome cousin, that I'd totally forgotten about Henry. Now the very mention of him gave me the shivers. Glancing up at the blank eye of Marina's bedroom window, I was glad suddenly to be getting away. The south coast, even some pebbly old beach with poor old Lauren and her nasal spray, seemed like heaven.

'Sorry,' I said. 'I feel sort of mean going off with Lauren, and leaving you here alone.'

I should have known better. If there was one thing Marina couldn't stand it was people feeling sorry for her. She gave me a challenging sort of stare as I brushed bits of grass and clover from my skirt.

'Go wherever you like. I can reach him by myself anyway,' Marina said with a toss of her hair. 'The letters and pictures speak for themselves, don't they? I'm not sure that Henry even *needs* the rest of you.'

Chapter Four

'*Well . . . it's a mar-ve-llous ni . . . ght for a Moondance . . .*'
Lauren's mum had a rubbish singing voice, even worse
than *my* mother's, and that was some achievement.

In the back of the car, Lauren was clutching her
stomach as if she'd just swallowed rat poison. 'For God's
sake, Mum, slow down! This is a thirty-mile-an-hour
zone in case you hadn't noticed. We just passed a speed
camera.'

Rummaging in her bag, Lauren offered me a
Fisherman's Friend. 'Want one? She knows I get car sick.
It'll be all her fault if I throw up all over the back seat.'

'Yeah, but can you, like, try not to?' I said, passing on
the Fisherman's Friend.

'*And wh . . .en, I . . . I . . . I touch you, it's just heaven
inside . . .* What's that, darling? Did you say something?'

Lauren clutched the back of Izzie's seat. 'I said, I'm
going to be sick if you don't slow down. And can't you
turn that racket down, Mother, puh . . . leeese? It's giving
me a headache.'

Really I was *impressed*. It was supposed to be the other
way round, wasn't it, parents shrieking at *us* to turn the
noise down. Lauren didn't appreciate what she'd got. She
didn't know how lucky she was to have a mother wearing combats and a T-shirt with *WHASSUP* on the front,
who told her friends, 'Call me Izzie, darling,' and sang

along to 'Van's Greatest Hits' even if she *was* crap at singing. At least it wasn't hymns, or Cliff Richard, which were my mum's favourites.

'She's a right old whinge, isn't she, darling?' Izzie changed gear, assorted bangles clinking down her forearm. 'I hope she's not like this at school, my daughter. I said, stop being an old whinger, darling. I'll get enough of that from your gran when we get to Ferring. Dear God, bloody Ferring, wheelchair riviera of the frozen south.'

'Sorry.' Lauren rolled her eyes at me. 'She can be dense at times. It's because she's in LURVE!' She gave the word mock emphasis. 'Lurve at her age. It's obscene.'

I smiled. I'd heard all about Lauren's mother's boyfriend before. Some bloke called Harvey, or 'Harvwit' as Lauren called him. From what I'd heard, Lauren was a bit cruel to poor old Harv-wit. I tried to imagine my mother with a boyfriend, but only came up with my dad. Even after thirty years of marriage, they still held hands in public. They even had *The Joy of Sex* on the bookshelves. But I tried not to think about that; some things the mind just reels away from.

'Only another forty miles to go,' Lauren said sourly. She fished her CD Walkman from her bag, and clamped the earphones to her head. Probably *The Dance of the Blessed Spirits* again. I'd forgotten to bring mine, so had to put up with:

'*Do you remember when we used to sing . . . da . . . da . . . da . . . dada dadada . . . da . . . da . . .*' and so on. We'd moved on to 'Brown Eyed Girl', which was really good in fact, if only Izzie hadn't sung along with it.

Only another forty miles. To begin with, I'd had high

hopes of this holiday. Maybe the sun and sand would do their stuff on Lauren, and she'd go all, like, *mellow*. Change character. Stop looking at any bloke who gave us the eye like he was something yukky she'd found in the plug-hole. The look she had now in fact, a sort of 'I'm going to throw up any moment' look. The day after we got back from Ferring would be my sixteenth birthday, the magical age of consent, and still there was no one to consent to. What a tragic waste of my nubile charms! (I'd heard them called that in a book I'd read, about some dirty old man who falls for the 'nubile charms' of a schoolgirl, and it'd become a kind of joke with Lauren, Marina and me ever since.)

Now though I had my doubts about agreeing to this trip at all. It just felt wrong to be leaving Marina alone for one thing. Also — I glanced out at the park-like land-scape of rural Surrey, sliding past us — what about Henry himself? In my mind's eye I could see him, piggy eyes glinting. It was a dead cert that we'd incurred the royal displeasure, deserting the court without permission. Leaving Henry to his 'Dark Eyed Dove' alone. And then . . . there was that cousin of hers . . .

'A pity Marina wouldn't come,' I said to Lauren.

But Lauren didn't hear me. She was staring into space, earphones clamped to her head, and a funny look of con-centration on her face, as if she was in touch with aliens or something.

Ferring, it turned out, was a bit of a let-down. The way Lauren had described it, it sounded a bit like *Baywatch*; all sun-bronzed surfers, and beach parties, and secret coves to get yourself ravished in. Obviously she'd lied, just to tempt me. In reality it was all funny little wooden chalets with names like 'Briny-cot', or 'Sailor's Rest'. There were no shops to speak of, not even a promenade to strut our stuff along. Nothing. Only a gorsey stretch of heath separating the houses from the beach, where people walked their dogs or steered their electric invalid-buggies. Hardly anyone looked to be under sixty-five.

'Well kiddies,' Lauren's mum said, unloading the boot. 'Here we are. Not exactly Benidorm I'm afraid. And if you find any talent, let me know. It'll be a first, believe me.'

Lauren and I exchanged 'looks'. Lauren's look said, *Excuse my mother, she's sex mad*. My look said, *Thanks a bunch for bringing me here on false pretences*.

Lauren's granny lived in one of the few 'proper' houses in Ferring. It had dark, seaweed-smelling rooms and a front gate that led directly onto the heath. There was a sort of tacked-on apartment once let to holiday-makers, but which Lauren and I now had to ourselves. Basically this was one large pine-panelled room with shower and toilet off it. There were a couple of canvas director's chairs, a plastic picnic table, and two lumpy futons which Izzie had lugged down for our benefit.

'Cute, isn't it?' Lauren said.

'Yeah.' I sat on one of the director's chairs. 'Your mum is brilliant, by the way. I suppose we could invite boys back here, do whatever we like, and she wouldn't even care.'

Lauren didn't look too sure. As I watched her unpacking her Scrabble board, my hopes of returning to London an experienced woman were further dashed.

'What's that for?'

'Well there's no telly. Something to do with the winds down here, poor reception or something. So I thought I'd bring some games, you know, in case we get bored in the evenings.'

'Bored? But you said there were clubs we could go to. You said your mum wouldn't mind.'

'Oh yeah, in Hastings I meant.' Lauren was folding her T-shirt nightie, pink with yellow teddy bears on it. 'Trouble is there's no bus back here after ten thirty. I'd forgotten about that. And my gran's got a thing about the doors being locked and bolted by ten o'clock, or she won't settle. That's because she was burgled last year. She probably needs counselling, that's my opinion anyway.'

'Ah.' I'd had enough of Lauren's opinions. And I didn't really see what her gran's burglary had to do with us going out.

It was the usual story of course. Outings with Lauren never lived up to their promise. I suppose we only put up with each other because Marina was practically in purdah. Now as I watched her arranging what looked like a complete medicine chest on the shelf, and enough sun-protection for a trek across the Gobi desert, I guessed that she'd invented her gran's ten o'clock curfew. She only wanted me along as a Scrabble companion, someone to huddle with on the beach and lecture about skin cancer.

'Hope you brought your malaria pills with you,' I said.

'Hah hah. Excuse me while I just die of mirth. It's not funny you know, Abbie. I can't help being allergic to everything.'

'Who's joking? Mosquitoes, you know. With teeth. They're, like, everywhere.'

'Well there aren't any in Ferring as far as I know.'

'No,' I said, looking miserably out of the window. 'They've got more sense.'

It seemed Izzie was right about the 'talent'. The only randy male on the beach next day was a Yorkshire terrier trying to hump a beach ball. We strolled the pebbly length of the shore, me trying to decide if it was safe to go swimming. Then Lauren noticed the turds bobbing about by the breakers.

'You'll catch some terrible disease if you go in there. It's absolutely disgusting!'

'Maybe you're right. Never mind, we'll just sunbathe.'

No way, Lauren said, would she expose herself to UV rays. Was I mad? Did I want crocodile skin before I was thirty?

'Not really, but hey, sometimes you have to live dangerously. Lauren . . . what the hell are you doing?'

'What does it look like I'm doing?'

It looked like she was setting up a massive beach umbrella, as if the hat wasn't enough. To be truthful I was a bit embarrassed to be seen with Lauren. Firstly there was this floppy great straw hat rammed on her head, and a long floaty dress that looked like a bedspread. The only part of her exposed to the air was her toes, poking out of her flip-flops. Probably well-smeared already with Factor 25 if I knew Lauren.

'You're not going to sit under that thing all day?' I wriggled out of my sarong.

Lauren squinted at me. 'Looks like you've grown out of your bikini, if you don't mind my saying. It's a bit . . . brief, isn't it?'

'All the better to show off my nubile charms, my dear.'

Since no one else was looking, I did a little dance just to annoy her.

I decided to ignore Lauren's health warnings. Stretched out on a towel on my front, I closed my eyes. Already, the sun was hot on my back. The waves had a soothing sound, like the wind in the trees. If you didn't open your eyes, you might be anywhere; some Greek island perhaps, with Marina's cousin mending his fishing nets and smiling that wicked smile that made leaves unfurl in your stomach.

'Haven't I seen you somewhere before?' this cousin would say.

That was as far as the conversation got unfortunately, as Lauren screamed suddenly. 'Oh gross! My mum's given us cheese in our rolls!' She dangled a plastic lunch bag in disgust.

'So? What's wrong with cheese? I like cheese. Did she put chutney in as well?'

'How should I know? They're not passing my lips. You have them.' She chucked me the packet. 'I can't believe my mother. She knows that cheese is poison to my entire system.'

'Well, if you're sure . . .' I began munching. At the same time, I decided to scribble a postcard to Marina:

Weather hot enough for Cyprus. Haven't come across any Greek heroes yet, but if I see Adonis, I'll let you know. Have you done any more you know what?
P.S. Hope Henry isn't missing us too much.
Love Abbie.

'What's "you know what" supposed to mean?' Lauren peered over my shoulder.

I shrugged. 'Oh, the Game, I meant.' I didn't want to tell her about the spirit writing, when Marina had sworn me to secrecy. Although the urge to do so was strong. I'd brought my project book with me, *The Pleasure of Kings*. Last night, reading propped up on my knobbly lonely futon, I'd come across the verse '*Noli Me Tangere*' and found it hadn't been written by Henry after all, but Thomas Wyatt, supposedly Anne's lover. I couldn't wait to tell Marina.

In fact . . . why not tell her right now? I released my mobile from its nifty holder, one of those plastic things with arms and legs waving about. 'Actually I'll call her. What's the sense in sending a mouldy old postcard?' I punched out Marina's number. The number rang and rang. 'Where the hell's she got to? Marina's never out.'

'Helping in the shop perhaps,' Lauren suggested. 'And you shouldn't hold that thing so close to your ear. Think of your brain cells.'

But I was thinking of Marina. What was she doing all by herself? Actually I hoped she was working in the shop. At least that would get her away from Henry for a while.

Suddenly we heard a voice screeching from along the beach. 'Hen . . . reee! Hen . . . ree . . . come here at once, you naughty boy!'

We both jumped. The Yorkshire terrier left humping the beach ball and went scampering to its mistress, an elderly woman in a fuschia pink tracksuit.

'Henry,' I said. 'That's a funny name for a dog, isn't it?'

'Not round here — you'd be surprised what they call

them. It's just a coincidence.' Lauren sounded as if she was trying to convince herself.

'Suppose so. Anyway this'll make you laugh. Did you know Henry's pet name for breasts was "ducks"? I read it in *The Pleasure of Kings* last night. It says in here –' I flicked open the pages – 'Letter from Henry to Anne Boleyn, *I can't wait to kiss your pretty ducks. Ducks!* Jesus, her boobs must've been, like, *really* weird.'

A breeze blew off the sea, flipping the pages of my book. It opened at an early portrait of the young Henry, admired, according to the text, as a golden youth throughout Europe.

Damn Henry. Henry was spoiling my cheese sarnies. I slammed the book shut. Why was I even thinking about Henry again, when we'd only just got away from him?

Perhaps it was a good thing, I realized suddenly. Henry's 'maidens' dispersed, apart. Marina in the shop, Lauren and me at Ferring-by-the-sea. Without us, Henry would grow bored. He would find some other more experienced medium to communicate with. Some mystical creature who would go into a trance and manifest great blobs of ectoplasm, and speak with Henry's own voice. 'All sweet ladies take my fancy.'

'Ducks though!' Still musing on this description, I frowned at the horizon. 'I mean, did they have feathers on them or what?'

Lauren's mother was on her hands and knees when we got back to the house. She was cleaning out Gran's fridge, which was growing several kinds of fungi, she said.

'Don't exaggerate, dear.' Lauren's gran was sorting

various pebbles, arranging them in a pottery dish. She was nothing like I'd imagined, with her softly curling grey-blonde hair and green kaftan. She was quite beautiful actually, as she smiled at us. 'Nicely toasted already I see, Abbie.'

'More like frazzled, actually,' Lauren said smugly. 'I told her to stay out of the sun.'

'What a dull time you kids have nowadays,' said Gran, 'Back in the sixties we roasted ourselves to a crisp without a thought. First chance you got, it was off with the clothes, imagine, dancing at festivals without a stitch.' She flung out her arms, as if she might shimmy out of the kaftan and reveal to us the ravages of the sun. It struck me suddenly that Lauren's gran was about the same age as my mother. It seemed incredible.

Izzie struggled to her feet, wash cloth slopping down her trousers. She stood observing us wryly. 'Well, you two are a pair of dark horses, aren't you?'

'What are you talking about?' Lauren was raiding the cupboard for something wholesome and additive-free. 'You put cheese in my rolls by the way, Mother.'

'Sorry, I forgot. Anyway, we had a phone call while you were out.' Izzie tossed me a Coke from the fridge. She wore a sly, lop-sided smirk on her face. 'Does the name . . .' She paused. 'Does the name *Henry* ring any bells? Uh huh! I see from the looks on your faces it does. Oh sorry, love,' as the malty froth of my Coke slurped out of the can and down my new skirt. 'Your lovely skirt, what a shame.' She dabbed at my hip with the fridge cloth. 'So who is this guy Henry then? He must be hot stuff, making Abbie jump out of her skin like that.'

I glanced at Lauren, her face mirroring my own. We

must have looked ghastly. I could actually feel the colour draining away beneath my tan.

'What did he say, Mum?'

'Not much. Just asked for Mistress Abigail and Mistress Lauren.' She rolled her eyes. 'Very posh. A right Hooray Henry I'd say.'

Lauren's gran rolled pebbles in her palm. 'Stop teasing them, dear.' She added soothingly to the girls, 'It's none of her business anyway, is it, who this Henry of yours is? My goodness, *she* had enough secrets as I remember, when she was your age.'

'*If you please, Madam*, he says to me.' Izzie frowned recalling the conversation. '*I wish you to inform these young ladies, that their presence is much missed at court.* Court! What's he on about? Is this guy a basket-case or something? To tell you the truth, he sounded a bit too old for you two. Kind of wheezy, breath all squeaking, you know, as if he was asthmatic or something.'

Noticing our dumbstruck expressions, she broke off. 'Oh oh . . . what's all this about? You look like you've seen a ghost both of you. What's going on, Lauren? You know I always say we should talk about it. You're not getting into any weird cults or anything? Oh damn . . . maybe that's him again . . .'

The telephone was ringing in the hall. We all looked at each other. 'What shall I say?' Izzie panicked suddenly. 'Shall I tell him to get lost? Look, don't worry, leave it to me.'

I wanted to slam my hands over my ears. I wanted to run. But where? It couldn't be true, could it? That it really was Henry, on the telephone? I couldn't bear to look at Lauren; we just stood, holding our breath, straining to make out Izzie's response. Then, ah, the relief, as she piped, suddenly shrill and girlish, 'Oh, it's *you*, Harvey!'

'Harv-wit,' Lauren murmured. 'Thank God for that.'

From the look of relief on her face, I doubted she would moan about the attentions of 'Harv-wit' ever again.

'It's got to be some kind of joke,' I said later. 'Somebody's pretending to be, you know, *him*, and having a great laugh at our expense.'

Lauren's mother had brought in cod and chips. We ate ours in the chalet, hunched in the director's chairs. A funny thing about being terrified out of your wits, it makes you hungry. Even Lauren was cramming her mouth with chips, straight out of the newspaper, without a single mention of additives or what the fish batter was made out of.

'Nobody knows about it though,' she said with her mouth full, 'unless you've been talking . . . Anyway, my mum said he sounded "wheezy", remember? Who do we know, who does impressions of wheezy old men?'

I shrugged. She had a point.

'OK, OK. I'm just trying to think of something. I mean what else are we supposed to think? That the spirit of Henry the Eighth is somehow connected to BT? Or that he's crammed his great bulk into a phone box to give us a call? Or that he's just coming through any way he can, by whatever means?' I shuddered. 'I mean it's just too, too . . .'

'Too much,' she finished for me. We both sat staring at the remains of our fish and chips. I waited for her to come up with something, but all she said was, why not have a game of Scrabble before we went to bed?

I nodded. Funny, I never dreamed I'd be glad of that silly Scrabble board, but now it seemed a comforting sort of thing to do. The board was spread on the picnic table between us, Lauren turning over the letters, shuffling them about, as darkness rolled like a wave at the window. It was quiet. Only the roar and hiss of the ocean outside. A friendly sound. Like a great animal breathing gently, snoring close by.

Cosy almost. Well, I was trying hard to convince myself. Willing myself *not* to think of the other kind of board, the letters, the glass.

'I'll start,' Lauren announced, as if she was about eight years old again.

'OK.'

It worked. At first, anyway. Twenty minutes into the game, and we were arguing over whether FART counted as slang or not. Still, at least we'd forgotten about *him* for a moment or two. Almost. We slapped down the letters and totted up the score as if it actually mattered, hunched over the picnic table like big-time poker players. Everything was all right until Lauren suddenly slapped down the word NIGHT. This wouldn't have meant a lot. It wouldn't have mattered, if I hadn't immediately followed with CROW.

'What made you put that down?' Lauren stared accusingly at me.

'I don't know. It just fitted. I had the right letters. Or the wrong letters, rather.'

It was true. Pure accident. Now the phrase NIGHT CROW dominated the board, and the hiss of the ocean outside the window was no longer a friendly presence, but somehow menacing, as if it was trapping us inside with him, with Henry.

'It's him!' I whispered. 'He made me put that. He's playing too. He wants to come through.'

We stood up together, both of us with one thought, to get out of that room, anywhere, to get away from Henry.

'I er . . . why don't we just pop next door to see how my gran's getting on?' Lauren tried to sound cool, but I could see the goose pimples creeping up her arms. The patch of eczema she got around her nose flared bright red suddenly. She began scratching it. 'Don't want my gran to feel hurt or anything . . . think we're ignoring her . . .'

Next door, Izzie was stretched full-length on a sofa reading a paperback, while Lauren's gran poured them a glass of wine each. Gran had changed into a floaty violet dress, and her grey hair was fixed up with a comb that looked like a clam-shell. She seemed surprised to see us.

'What are you two doing here? You should be out, enjoying yourselves.'

'This is *Ferring*, Mother.' Izzie spoke without looking up from her book. 'Enough said.'

Lauren squirmed a bit. 'We thought we'd come and have a cup of cocoa with you, before you go to bed, sort of . . . didn't we, Abbie?'

'What? Oh yes, cocoa . . .'

Lauren's gran gave us a long searching kind of look. 'Well that's very sweet of you, girls, keeping the poor old dear company. Tell you what, why don't you have a drop of this stuff instead, and while you're doing that, I've got something for you.' She wagged her finger at Lauren. 'I'll just go and get it.'

Minutes later she returned with a clock, a very old looking clock, and held it out to Lauren with both hands, as if it was precious, as if she was making a presentation of it.

'I was going to leave this to you in my will, but since I don't intend to pop my clogs for a very long time, you might as well have it now.'

Izzie sat up, laying the book on her knees. 'Oh, not *that* clock. I used to hate that clock, it used to have this horrible tick, like it was haunted or something. And anyway, are you sure you want to part with it, Mum?'

'Of course I'm sure. As long as it stays in the family. It's a German bracket clock in fact, rather valuable. It's been in this family for years. Anyway, it's for you, darling, my only granddaughter.' Lauren's gran reached out and tucked Lauren's floppy hair behind her ears. 'I want you to have it.'

It was all a bit embarrassing for me, standing there sipping the wine while Lauren pretended to be excited about an ugly old clock. When all the time, like me, she was trying not to look at the phone, to ask if that 'Henry fella' had rung again.

From the sofa Izzie yawned loudly. 'So anyway, what have you two been up to all evening?'

Since she was looking at me, I shrugged, and said not much. 'We were having a game of Scrabble actually.'

Lauren's gran threw up her hands. 'Scrabble! So that's what you girls get up to nowadays. How quaint! I haven't played Scrabble for years. Lauren, sweetie, why don't you bring it in here, and we'll all have a game?'

'No!' We both shouted out together, then looked at each other in horror. Then Lauren said she thought we'd just go back to the annexe and have an early night. 'We're both a bit tired actually, aren't we, Abbie?'

I nodded, pretending to stifle a yawn.

'Yeah,' remarked Izzie, 'it's hard work lying on the beach all day. You must be absolutely knackered.'

'Thanks, Gran, for the clock I mean,' Lauren said. 'I promise I'll take really good care of it. I'll treasure it for, like, my entire life. And I'll pass it on to my grand-children and everything. That's if I have any . . .'

'What sensible girls!' I heard Gran say, as we shuffled through the door. 'Cocoa, Scrabble . . . so . . . mature. I must say, Izzie, Lauren doesn't take after you, not a bit.'

But all Izzie said was, 'Hmmmm . . . I wonder. I wonder who that *Henry* character was this afternoon?'

Chapter Five

'You can have a party if you like,' my mother was saying. 'Me and Dad won't get in your way. You won't even know we're here.'

'Er . . . no thanks, Mum. I'm not bothered really.'

A party at no. 62 Smedhurst Road? The idea was laughable! Any more than four people at one time in our flat was a crowd. Then there was Mrs Croop downstairs.

'Have some consideration for Mrs Croop downstairs,' my parents cried whenever I played my music at a volume just about detectable to the human ear.

'Are you sure?' my mother said now. 'I mean, sixteen! It's an important landmark, sixteen.'

Too right it was. 'I'm glad you realize that, Mother,' I said. 'After all, I could be married, couldn't I? Not that I *want* to be married.'

'I should hope not, dear. Anyway, sixteen is far too young for that kind of thing.'

'Oh I don't know. Just think of Catherine of Aragon. She was only nine when she was betrothed to Henry the Eighth's older brother, Arthur.'

'I thought she married Henry.'

'Yeah she did. Arthur snuffed it young so they just passed her on to Henry and he got her up the duff in no time.'

My mother thought this disgusting. In my mother's

opinion, twenty-five was about the right age for what she called a 'relationship'. 'That poor little Catherine, just think, still with the cradle marks on her bum. And having to go with that fat old man.'

'Well he wasn't old or fat then, Mum. He was seventeen. In fact, Catherine was six years older than him. Practically an old crone by Tudor standards.'

'Was she? Well, I suppose that was the olden days for you. By the way, Marina Paulos rang here while you were away. Said she'd forgotten when you were getting back. Why don't you invite her over, to share your cake at least?'

'Nah, it's all right, Mum. I'm going over there in a minute. To Marina's.'

I'd only got back from Ferring the night before. My one thought this morning was to get to Marina's house, to tell her about Henry's phone call, and the 'Night Crow'. But first, I had to go through the birthday ritual, unwrapping my presents, while Mum looked fondly on. Ten knickers in a pack. Giant ones. Giant knickers with an all-over pattern of rosebuds.

'Lovely, Mum, I mean useful. Thanks.'

Dear God! What did she think I was! Didn't she know that lacy thongs were more the thing? It got worse. Next came the cardigan, knitted by my mother's own fair hands in pukesome last-season pink.

'Mmmm . . . nice colour, Mum. Thanks.'

After that came the medical dictionary. Er . . . medical dictionary?

'They're always useful,' Mum put in quickly. 'And if you ever decide to take up medicine as a career . . .'

'How is a girl who can't even stand the sight of other

69

people's feet going to poke about in their insides?' I couldn't help pointing out. 'I mean please, Mother, get real!'

'There's a shortage of doctors,' my mother insisted. 'And you never know, what with your father's and my own medical interests.' (The fact that my dad was an ambulance driver, she meant, that and their addiction to the hospital soaps on TV.)

I gritted my teeth and smiled. After all, I could always give it to Lauren; she could select her next disease from the comfort of her own armchair.

Lastly there was a nifty pedicure set in a furry pouch that looked like a dead hamster. Wow.

'I kept the receipts in case you want to change any of them,' Mum said nervously.

'Change them? Nah, they're brilliant, Mum. Thanks.'

Well I couldn't hurt her feelings, could I? Not when she'd probably spent hours agonizing over what to buy. Trouble was, there was so much stuff I needed. I'd had my own secret list of birthday 'wants'. It went something like this:

Mirrored bag from Monsoon, and harem-style cushions for bed, moody blue lava lamp (like the one Lauren got from the Gadget shop), giant quartz cluster (for warding off evil spirits, i.e. Henry) and Madonna style Crucifix (for same purpose), and one genuine crystal ball (for practising my future career as fortune-teller to the stars).

The trouble with my mother was, she had no imagination. Not like Lauren's mum. No way would Izzie Alexander present Lauren with giant flowery knickers and a puke-pink cardie. Oh well. Poor Mum. She meant well. Now she was crashing about in the kitchen

70

finishing my cake, the usual chocolate sponge thing she always made with butter-cream filling.

I left her to it and went to get dressed, wiggling into my denim skirt and black halter-neck top. It was still scorching. Outside my window the plane trees were full of chirping sparrows. I held my palm up to the light and checked out my child-lines beneath my little finger. I had three. This was kind of reassuring. Not that I wanted kids particularly. It was just what you had to do to get them that interested me. Or rather, who with. Perhaps today would be my lucky day? Though I couldn't think how. I would go to Marina's and Marina would want to play the Henry Game and that would be the height of it.

In Marina's garden the roses were all out, hideous pinks and oranges and yellows that reminded me of my knickers.

'If you know anyone who weighs about twenty stone,' I said, 'let me know and she can have them.'

Marina smiled. 'Never mind, I made your card myself, with my own fair hand.'

She handed it to me, a cartoon crab for my birth sign, Cancer: a crab with goggly great eyes and massive pincers. A very ugly and crabby-looking crab, which I couldn't help feeling she meant as an insult in some sly way.

Inside, in her best italic script, was the Cancerian personality in a nutshell. This concentrated on all the negative traits, like 'grasping' . . . 'moody' . . . 'introverted' . . .

'Thanks, Marina. But what happened to all the other stuff?'

71

'Other stuff?'

'You know, like, "artistic", "creative", "perceptive". What happened to them?'

She sighed. 'I couldn't get *everything* on the card, could I? Here's your present by the way.'

'Thanks.' I smoothed out the roll of paper, and there was Henry. A youthful, handsome Henry this time, very like the illustrations in *The Pleasure of Kings*.

'It's another self-portrait you could say. We did it together. I asked Henry, and he didn't mind you having it.'

'Oh. Thanks.' It was hard to look grateful. The last thing I wanted in my house was one of those creepy spirit-pictures. In this one, young Henry looked studious, even a bit swotty, as he twiddled thoughtfully with the ring on his little finger. But I wasn't fooled.

'Generous of Henry,' I murmured.

There had been messages too, although Marina was reluctant to say what they were.

'If you got a love letter, you wouldn't show it to anyone, would you?'

'Probably not, but . . .'

'Well then, it's private.' She added mysteriously, 'I *can* tell you that he has a way with words. He's a real poet actually. A musician too. Did you know it was possibly Henry who composed "Greensleeves"?'

'"Greensleeves"? Oh, you mean . . .' I couldn't resist singing in a silly falsetto voice, '*Al . . . as my lo . . . ve you do me wrong, to cast me off so . . . so, oh yeah . . . dis . . . courteously . . .*'

'Yes thank you, that one.' Marina smacked her hands over her ears. 'You sound like a deranged choir boy.'

'Funny, I learned to play that on my recorder in primary school. Year six, Mrs Hodgkiss. She used to sing along to it, in this terrible creaky voice like . . .'

'Don't!' Marina winced. 'The thought of you and Mrs Hodgkiss trashing Henry's beautiful song on your recorder is just too much to bear.'

Marina rolled onto her stomach with a groan, as if this was the end of the conversation. She swung her legs behind her, bare feet crossed at the ankles. There was a touch of the harem about Marina today. Toenails painted as if she'd dipped her feet in raspberry jam, the chink of silver at neck and wrists. I could smell her perfume, musky like roses, and a flirty slip of a dress riding up over her thighs, which I was sure her dad wouldn't approve of. There was a red blotch on her calf, I noticed, where she'd probably nicked herself shaving.

'I wonder what they did about hairy legs in those days?' I said.

'They wore about six layers of ankle-length skirts, in case you never noticed,' Marina said in a withering tone. 'So it hardly mattered. And trust you to think of something like that.'

'They tell you about skin creams and everything, how they whitened their skin with arsenic, but come on, Marina, it's important. I mean, Anne Boleyn was really dark, and she didn't go to bed in her farthingale, did she? Henry would have wanted a good look at her pins. Knowing him, I shouldn't think he was all that gone on body fur.'

Marina stroked her calf with the opposite foot, as if checking for stubble. 'Maybe they used honey or something. They probably had some secret recipe. Why don't you ask Henry about Anne's legs when we call him up, if you're so interested?'

'Nah. If they were that hairy, he'd probably have them chopped off along with her head.'

'Actually . . .' Marina rolled over onto her back, and gazed dreamily up at the sky, 'it's *eyes* that Henry likes. The windows of the soul. You should read what he says about mine. Except you won't of course, 'cos it's private.'

'Oh yeah?' I was treated to the full-no-holds-barred eye-flutter, lashes sweeping her cheeks like plushy paint brushes. It was quite *sickening*. If she was this swollen-headed over a few spirit messages, think what she'd be like with a real lover! 'Long as he doesn't admire your pretty ducks,' I said.

'My what?'

'Oh nothing. He's probably mixing you up with Anne Boleyn again. They were meant to be her great asset, her dark sparkling eyes. Until he went off her of course. Then he blamed her eyes for bewitching him. A wonder he didn't have them gouged out, he was such an old sadist.'

Sick of Henry squinting at me, I allowed the portrait to furl back up into a roll of paper. 'Marina . . . there's something I've got to tell you. When we were in Ferring, Lauren and me, something happened.'

'Oh don't tell me . . . you met some boy?' She said this in a weary indulgent way, as if she was a woman of the world, beyond mere boys, entertaining kings of the spirit realm.

'No. No such luck. Although we did have a phone call.' I paused. 'You'll never guess who from. Henry.'

That did it. Marina sat up, legs curled to one side. Her eyes fixed suspiciously on me. 'You're joking.'

'No, I'm not.' I told her then, about Lauren's mother taking the call. How Henry requested our presence at court. 'Mistress Abigail and Mistress Lauren he called us. Very posh, Izzie said, a right "Hooray Henry", she said. And wheezy, you know, like, short of breath. Henry the Eighth doing a heavy-breather, it's just so freaky! Every time the phone rang after that, well you can imagine, poor old Lauren and I practically jumping out of our skins. But it didn't happen again, thank God.'

'No.' Marina regarded me, slowly shaking her head. 'No, it couldn't happen. Henry coming through without me. He *needs me.*'

I wasn't about to let her get away with that one. In fact, I was just about to tell her about the Night Crow, when there was the sound of the front door crashing shut, and voices from inside the house.

'My parents!' Marina was tugging down her skirt, acting all guilty, as if she'd been caught at something terrible. 'I wasn't expecting them. You'll have to go, Abbie, and head off Lauren. I don't want her showing up now.'

'OK, OK, give me a chance. What d'you want me to do, climb over the fence, or dig a tunnel or something?'

Too late anyway. For there was Marina's father, Mr Paulos, standing on the concrete patio outside the French windows.

'Marina! Eh . . . Marina!' He was waving his arms, excited, gesticulating towards the house. They had visitors. This much I could follow. Unexpected visitors. The house was filling up with family, faster than I could scramble to my feet.

I'd encountered Marina's father only twice before. Both times he had ignored me. This time he gave a sort of nod in my direction, more of a head-butt really. He was a short, stocky man. Handsome I suppose, if you liked old men. Smart – I mean, crisp shirt and baggy stylish jacket. And hands waving towards the house as he let out a stream of furious Greek. At least it sounded furious. I imagined he was angry with Marina again, for sprawling about the garden with her English friend. Like Hermia, goddess of housework, deserting her hearth-side.

Marina answered back in Greek, quite coolly. I guessed she was talking about me. Making some excuse. Telling her dad that we were working on a project for school probably, the way she waved the rolled up paper with Henry's portrait. Ah yes. The history project. Well it was true, in a way.

Her father grunted. He had small hands, I noticed. The hands of an unevolved type; a primitive, even a murderer according to Cheiro. I slipped on my shoes. Marina's dad was no killer, but he was bloody rude to her friends.

'I'm off then!' I hissed at her. A black-haired toddler stumbled out onto the patio and peered at us between Mr Paulos's legs. Marina's father whisked him up into the air and carried him shrieking with delight back into the house.

'My aunt and some of my cousins are over from Cyprus,' Marina said. 'We weren't expecting them today. They were going to stay with my grandmother, but she's not too well. Look, I've got to go inside.'

She turned her back on me then, and stalked across the grass, the back of her neck scorched brown and

76

vulnerable where she'd put her hair up. So that was it. I'd been dismissed.

Sneaking back through the house like a banished servant was humiliating, but there was no back way out. Not unless I scrambled over the garden fence, and that was out of the question. Imagine if I got stuck halfway in my short skirt! Brushing bits of dead grass from my legs, I made for the kitchen. It was hard, though, not to sneak a quick look through the French windows into the lounge. I had a glimpse of Marina, crushed to the bosom of a voluptuous woman in a *Dynasty*-style suit, while Mr Paulos, merrier than I'd ever seen him, was pouring drinks and slapping shoulders.

Would he use the glass? I wondered. Henry's own special glass? Would Henry, deprived once more of his 'maidens', sulk and turn the sherry sour? Go for it, Henry! I found myself thinking nastily. Turn the sherry into frogspawn, and ruin the party.

In the kitchen, the toddler was gorging on a slice of my birthday cake which I'd brought to share with Marina. He laughed up at me, mouth sticky with chocolate. I glared back until his mouth crumpled. 'You'll get sick,' I said quietly, in my meanest voice.

I had a good mind to wrap up the last of my cake and smuggle it back out. Instead I snuck out into the hallway, into the fug of perfume and cigarette smoke. Laughter gusted from the lounge. Someone had put some music on. It sounded like people were dancing. At least Marina's relatives knew how to have a good time.

I felt like an outcast as I reached for my bag on the hat stand, concealed now by a flutter of scented silk scarves and expensive-looking jackets. While I was fumbling there, scarves fluttering as if from a conjuror's hat, I heard the stairs creak behind me.

'*Kali mera!*' The voice made me jump. I turned. '*Sas lene?*'

'What?'

It was him again. That cousin, leaning against the banisters watching me. *Woooh!* My heart leaped into my throat, as this vision of unsurpassable hunkiness wafted before me. Close up he was even better, if that was possible. I hadn't noticed his eyes from the landing; now I saw they were like that dark, luxury chocolate that tastes of violets. These, combined with a lean hungry look, made me think of a character from a Mafia movie, dealing cards beneath some vine-covered terrace. His shirt-sleeves were rolled up, and I noticed the skin of his forearms, like melted toffee against the white. His hands bristled with rings, a heavy silver chain at his wrist.

'I don't . . . I, er, don't speak Greek.'

Or anything else for that matter. Words scrambled in my head, like a muddled-up Scrabble board. Even English. Suddenly I couldn't even speak my own bloody language. What was going on? My tongue flapped uselessly in my mouth.

'Hey, you're English!' He made to slap at the side of his head, grinning at his mistake. 'Friend of Marina's, right?'

'Mmmm . . . right.' I nodded. I could feel his eyes on my bare midriff. Damn! I'd forgotten to hold in my stomach. I edged towards the front door. Better to get out before I made a fool of myself. And anyway, Marina's dad wouldn't be too pleased if he found me chatting up one of the precious family. Somehow I knew this, without being told.

'You live round here?'

'No, no not really. I'm from school, I mean, we go to school together, me and Marina. Anyway, I was just . . . going.'

He was at the door before I could fumble with the catch.

'Oh. Thanks.'

'No problem. See you again some time, eh?'

I might have mumbled something in reply. Afterwards I couldn't remember if I had or not. Just as well. If *I had* said anything, you could bet it was truly cretinous.

'Hey, Marina!' I could imagine him saying as the front door closed behind me. 'Who's the dopey friend? Bit of a thicky, isn't she? Couldn't string two words together.'

And then he would kiss her. A big smacking cousinly sort of kiss on each cheek, folding Marina into his arms, their dark heads meshed together. Imagine having a cousin like that, imagine!

It wasn't until I reached my bus stop, though, that the irony of the situation hit me. Like, how could Marina gibber on about that repulsive ginger-haired, piggy-eyed Henry so much, when she had a cousin who looked like a sex god? I mean, Henry VIII versus Adonis. No contest!

It was no accident, perhaps, that the instant this traitorous thought occurred to me, my fingers happened to brush against Marina's present as I rummaged for my purse. She must have stuffed the roll of paper into my bag before joining her family. Now here was Henry, twiddling with his rings and fixing me with a cold, intense look. Almost as if he was dreaming up some kind of punishment. What though? My head? The rack?

Something even more mind-bogglingly cruel and disgusting?

'Sorry, Marina,' I mumbled under my breath. 'Not that I'm ungrateful or anything.'

The bus stop was one of those with a litter bin attached. Into this bin, along with the burger cartons and ice-cream wrappers, and what looked and smelled like a baby's disposable nappy, went my unwanted gift. Henry ripped into a thousand tiny pieces. There! That fixed him. Dusting off my hands, I tried not to look in the bin, just in case one of those eyes had miraculously stayed intact. It would stare up at me from the dirty nappy, accusing, vowing some terrible vengeance. But this was stupid. It was just a picture, that was all, a picture that Marina had copied out of her project-book.

On the bus I thought of the cousin instead, his hands as he held the door for me, oblong-type with long strong fingers. The hands of a warrior-hero. The hands of the lover, according to Cheiro. Funny how thinking of his hands chased all pictures of Henry from my head.

Chapter Six

Marina kept Henry waiting for another whole week. Or rather her relatives did. I could just imagine him twiddling his pudgy thumbs, pacing the shadowy corridors of his palace, or wherever it was he lived, on the other side. Or maybe Marina scribbled late at night, in the privacy of her room, Henry composing sonnets and letters in Marina's own fair hand. MY DARK EYED DOVE, YOU ABOVE ALL OTHERS ARE MY OWN TRUE MAID YOUR OBEDIENT SERVANT, HENRY TUDOR.

Marina must have been just as impatient as Henry was, for the minute the relatives flew back to Cyprus, she was on the phone to me:

'Come round about three. I've got the house to myself, and we're playing the Game.'

It didn't occur to her that I might have a hot date. OK, I didn't, but that was beside the point. These days with Marina it was *Be here, or else*. Kind of a royal summons, you could say.

'What took you so long?' was how she greeted me later. 'Lauren's already here. We've been waiting for you.'

'Traffic,' I said. 'The bus took for ever.'

She seemed to forget that I lived further away than Lauren. It was no fun in this heat either, lurching along in a smelly old bus, half crushed to death by the fat woman next to me. And me, boiling in skin-tight jeans and one of those slash-necked T-shirts you can't wear a bra with, which made my breasts feel like two steamed puddings. It was one of those warm sticky days when the sun doesn't shine, and the air feels like poison, and everyone's scratchy and in a bad temper.

It was all right for Marina, I thought, coolly preparing herself for her visitors; gold hoop earrings today, and a swishy wrap-over skirt, which her aunt had brought her from Cyprus, rustling down the hall before me.

I followed Marina, glancing up at the stairs as I did so. Only a week ago, *he* had been leaning there, the cousin. Where was he now? I imagined him mending his fishing nets on a stretch of white sand, chatting up some half-naked beach-babe.

'Did you see this, by the way?' In the kitchen Marina held up her arm and rattled her new charm bracelet at me. 'Like it?'

'Gorgeous. Is it real silver?'

'Of course it's real,' Lauren put in. 'Can't you tell? You don't think Marina would wear the fake stuff, do you?'

'My aunt gave it to me.' Marina sounded smug as she twirled her arm, admiring the sparkle of tiny stars against her skin.

'Cor, it's all right for some people,' I said enviously. 'Why can't *I* have a rich aunt who lives in Cyprus?'

Then I forgot to be envious. Because I'd just noticed something about Marina's palm as she turned it to the light. Surely that hadn't been there before? A massive great cross on her head-line. A bad omen if ever I saw one. A cross anywhere was bad. It meant misfortune, self-sacrifice, fateful accident. On the head-line, it could mean getting your head bashed in, or going crazy, or anything. It could mean 'losing your head' like Anne Boleyn.

If only I could whizz back in time, to read Anne's palm. Hold that hand with the six witchy fingers in my own. What Cheiro said about extra fingers, I had no idea, but at least I could warn her about the cross if she had one. Forget Henry, I'd tell her, he's a right pompous old bastard. Stick to that nice Thomas Wyatt who wrote you the poem, and don't tell him to *noli me tangere* this time.

OK, I couldn't give Anne the benefit of my advice, but I could warn Marina. I was about to mention the cross, when the telephone rang. She went to answer it.

'Hallo?' Silence. Then . . . 'Who is that?' Marina was never chatty on the telephone; she had a kind of regal frosty tone like you might imagine the Queen would have. Now, though, her voice was different, a bit shrill and panicky. 'Listen, whoever you are, you might as well give up because you're not scaring me. Actually I think you're a very sad person! And perhaps you'd also like to know that my father has reported you to BT, and they're having these calls traced.'

Behind her back, Lauren and I exchanged glances. It wasn't . . . *him* again . . . was it?

But whoever it was, Marina didn't want to discuss it: 'Look it's just some sad old pervert. Let's get on with the Game, shall we? Henry's waited long enough.'

Marina's word was our command. We all went about our usual tasks. Marina pulled down the blinds, Lauren lit the candles, while I arranged the letters in their circle.

Funny how this time I really didn't want to play. And maybe Henry didn't either, because the glass moved sluggishly at first, as if it couldn't be bothered.

'Henry's forgotten how to spell,' I murmured, as the glass spelled GEEKWAJ, then OWAZINGGGG. 'Hey, Marina, is Henry speaking Greek?'

'Quiet,' Marina hissed. 'It's coming now, the message . . . look!' Slowly, as if teasing us, the glass spelled out TICK–TOCK . . . TICK–TOCK.

'Tick . . . tock . . . ?' We searched each other's faces for clues. The glass tried again: TICK–TOCK MISTRESS LAUREN.

'Tick-tock?' Lauren mumbled. 'What's he talking about?'

I attempted a joke to reassure her. 'He probably means, "Long time no see". You know like . . . "It's been a while, baby".'

But the glass continued: GRANDFATHER INSIDE CLOCK . . . TICK–TOCK . . . MUST BURN . . .

Lauren stared at me. 'My clock. He must be on about my clock. The one my gran gave me.'

'That old thing? But why should he care about that?'

'Would someone mind telling me what this is about?' Marina demanded irritably.

Lauren began to explain to Marina about her gift, as the glass repeated itself. You could almost feel Henry inside it, getting a bit tetchy, as if he'd really like to smash his fists on the table to get our attention.

In fact, all the while Lauren was doing her *Antiques Roadshow* bit, I became aware of a change in the atmosphere. The day had been heavy, almost becalmed. Now it seemed shot through with some strange

84

uncomfortable energy; a charge, a kind of electrical buzz, that had nothing to do with the rumbling freezer, or any of the other kitchen appliances. Whatever it was, was invisible. I shuddered, for no particular reason, the way people do when they talk about 'someone passing over their grave'.

Lauren must have felt it too. She halted mid-sentence as the glass spelled out suddenly: BURN CLOCK FREE SPIRIT.

'Burn . . .? Burn my clock? Oh no. Uh uh,' shaking her head emphatically. 'This is *not happening*. This is some kind of joke, right?'

At this, the glass fairly whizzed across the table: MISTRESS LAUREN I DO NOT JEST.

Two rosy-pink spots bloomed on Lauren's cheeks: 'But he's . . . why? Why my clock? It doesn't make sense.'

'Well nothing he says makes a whole lot of sense, does it?' I said.

'But what am I supposed to do? Abbie, you know how precious that clock is; it's been in my family for years. You heard what my gran said. I can't just burn it because of a stupid . . .'

Perhaps she was about to say 'spirit', I don't know. But anyway Henry didn't care much for her attitude. The glass whisked our fingers around the circle at once.

BURN BURN BURN, Henry said. I could imagine him stamping his foot, if only he'd had one to stamp. BURN BURN BURN. As if he was mixing up Lauren's clock with the heretics sizzling at Tyburn. As if he would see the clock on a spike at Traitor's Gate. I had to admit it seemed unreasonable. It didn't make any sense at all.

Marina, though, thought otherwise. She began to lecture us in her lofty, know-all way. Henry knew best. This was a message from the spirit realm for goodness' sake, and we should listen to it. 'If he says your clock is haunted, Lauren, then it is. He's only trying to help us. It's for your own good.'

'Well I just don't believe . . .' Lauren began. But . . .

TICK–TOCK . . . Henry teased, placated. TICK–TOCK . . . GREEN GROW HOLLY O. Now that he'd had his fun, and scared the wits out of Lauren, he began to change the subject, and we were back to Henry the ardent suitor. You could almost see him, chasing Marina around the maze at Hampton Court, crooning the honeyed words . . . MY DARK MAID . . . MY DOVE . . .

After the excitement of Lauren's haunted clock, it seemed a bit of a let-down. While my finger swept along with the glass as usual, my mind began to wander to other things. *Other things* meant Marina's cousin of course. The cousin I hadn't dared ask her about, the cousin I'd been thinking of all week. The way he smiled, and his smell as he'd opened the door for me, like clean sheets blowing in the wind, and old leather jackets, and after-shave; a lovely man-smell.

It was only as the others gasped aloud that I bothered to follow Henry's spelling. The glass was moving at furious speed.

Marina interpreted, spelling it out. ROGUE ROGUE ROGUE . . . PRITHEE REMEMBER MISTRESS . . . NO HEAD IS TOO FAIR . . .

'I hope he's not talking to me again,' Lauren said miserably.

BURN BURN CHOP CHOP CHOP . . . NO HEAD IS TOO

FAIR, the glass repeated.

'It's OK, Lauren, it's not you this time,' I assured her. '"No head is too fair" was a warning to the courtiers, when they were gossiping about Anne Boleyn. It was a warning of the Tower, the axeman's block.'

Lauren shivered. 'You mean, no head was too pretty for the axe. Eugh.'

'Question is,' I said slowly, 'what's it to do with us? Why is he warning us about heads and axes and stuff?'

'He's upset,' Marina said quietly, 'I know it. Look at the glass.'

We looked. The glass began rocking beneath our fingers as if some invisible creature was trapped inside. Lauren swiftly withdrew her finger. 'Can't help it.' She fussed with a tissue. 'It's the pollen count.'

'Never mind the stupid pollen count, put your finger back on at once!'

Even as Lauren obeyed Marina's order, the glass bucked, skittered. Then came to a sudden halt in the middle of the circle. It wasn't so unusual for the glass to pause for thought, but this was different. As if Henry himself declared the seance over.

I glanced at Marina. 'Was it something we, like, *said*?'

Marina answered me with a black look: 'There's something . . . something with us. Here, in the kitchen. Can't you feel it?'

'Yeah. I can. I'm trying *not* to feel it, actually.'

Whatever 'it' was. A presence. An invisible force. Dark and angry and old. Stealing between us and the outside world like a shadow. The usual summer sounds of children playing, birds singing, the rumble of lawn-mowers, now seemed muffled and remote.

All I could hear now was breathing. Hard to say whose breathing. My own, probably, the way my heart was pounding. Or Lauren, panting like an old war-horse, gasping in between breaths, 'What was that? What was it?'

The crashing sound, she meant. Coming from the other room. We all stood up at the same time, nearly knocking over the table.

'Take it easy,' Marina said. 'There's no need to get hysterical.'

Still, I could see that even *she* was a bit shaken, as Lauren and I followed her into the lounge. At first we couldn't see anything wrong. The lounge looked as it always did, fusty and undisturbed and smelling of lavender polish. Then Lauren cried out, 'The photograph!'

Marina stooped by the urn of pampas grass, turning over the fragments of glass in her palm. She looked vaguely stunned, like someone on an archaeological dig, who finds bones where they're least expected. 'It *would* be that one,' she murmured. 'The family group at my grandmother's birthday, all my cousins and everything.'

Thinking of her parents, I felt sorry for her suddenly. They wouldn't understand that the photo had just jumped off the mantelpiece, would they? Or, maybe . . . supposing it had been thrown off, in a fit of temper. A royal fit of temper.

'But how did it happen?' I rubbed my bare arms. 'I mean, things don't just jump for no reason.'

Rubbing my arms was like reading braille, so patterned were they with goosebumps. Yet it had to be nearly thirty degrees outside. Outside. Suddenly that was

88

all I wanted to do. Get out into the sunlight. But how could we desert Marina now?

'Could it be a draught or something?' Lauren suggested.

But Marina shook her head. We all knew there *was* no draught. The front bay-window was closed as usual, the curtains drawn half across to protect the furniture from the sun. Overlooking the garden, the French windows were fully-glazed and sealed tight.

'Marina, haven't you got another frame you can put it in? Then your mum and dad need not know.' I was squinting upside down at the photo, trying to figure out who all the cousins were, if *he* was among them, the cousin, when the sound of glass smashing, from the kitchen this time, made Lauren cry out.

Not again! For a moment we all stood, looking at each other; Marina's eyes like dark pools you could drown in, Lauren biting her lip until it bled.

Lauren clutched hold of Marina's arm. 'Could that be your . . . cat . . . Marina?'

Marina shook her off. 'I haven't got a cat, stupid.'

We were creeping now towards the kitchen, all three of us in a kind of cowardly huddle. No one wanted to be first. Perhaps we were all afraid of finding him there. Henry, enthroned on the kitchen stool, tapping his ringed fingers on the marble work surface.

But, to our relief, the kitchen was empty. It was just as we'd left it — except, that is, for the brandy glass. The glass had exploded, the way a light bulb does, littering the table-top with splinters. Most of the letters were on the floor.

'It's him.' I stood in the doorway. I looked at Marina.

'Marina, it's him. It must be Henry. Oh God. What do we do now?'

Nothing much, was the answer. Perhaps we might have stood there for ever, we might have gone on gibbering like hysterical monkeys, if the doorbell hadn't rung at that moment. It was one of those doorbells that chimes a stupid tune. So stupid I wanted to laugh. What better to chase away the ghost of Henry VIII than 'My Bonnie Lies Over the Ocean'? Henry, with his fine ear for music and his 'hey nonnies' and 'green grows the holly o'.

'Who's that?' Marina seemed to come out of a trance. She looked annoyed, as if the bell had interrupted something really good.

'You won't know until you answer it. Look, I'll clear up the glass while you go to the door.'

Having watched Hermia at her housework so often, I knew exactly where the cleaning things were. So it was that when Marina opened the front door to her totally gorgeous cousin, there I was on all fours, bum sticking out of the broom cupboard. I didn't know it was the gorgeous cousin at first, of course. Not until I emerged with the dustpan and brush. When I saw him, eyes gleaming at me over Marina's shoulder, I nearly lost my balance, only just managing a clumsy froggy-hop back to the safety of the kitchen.

'Who is it?' Lauren wanted to know.

'Family, I think.' I concentrated on sweeping up the glass.

'There's more under there.' Lauren pointed her toes in the direction of the fridge. Chinks of glass glittered in the sunlight, as she pulled up the blind and snuffed out the candles. It was almost back to normal again. Perhaps Henry had worn himself out with his tantrum, retired to his chamber to sulk, to plan his next attack. Poor Marina. I wouldn't have been in her shoes, not for anything.

Then again . . . it sounded like Marina and her cousin were going into the lounge, talking loudly. Or the cousin was doing most of the talking, Marina laughing. That reluctant velvety chuckle that made you want to entertain her, to tell her jokes, to stand on your head like the court jester, just to hear it. No doubt the cousin felt the same. And what was he doing here anyway? Why wasn't he in Cyprus?

The front door slammed shut again, and Marina came back into the kitchen, looking kind of evasive and weird. Almost embarrassed, I'd say, if I didn't know Marina better. If I didn't know that Marina was far too cool to get embarrassed.

'Only my cousin, Nikos. He left something here the other day, belonging to my aunt Rosa.'

I looked at her. Her pupils glittered black.

'I thought your relatives were back in Cyprus.' I tried to sound casual, as if I wasn't really that interested.

'They *are*. Nikos doesn't live in Cyprus. He only drove the others over from the airport, that's all.' Marina gave me that devious look she always did when questioned about family. End of subject.

Lauren stood chewing her fingernails, a habit she was supposed to have given up *months* ago. 'But what about the glass?' she said. 'Marina, you don't think this could be, like, some kind of mass hysteria? I read about it once. It used to happen to girls of our age, especially in convents.

They used to run about screaming, and tearing their clothes off, and . . .'

Marina turned coldly on her. 'Are you trying to say that Henry doesn't exist? That we caused all this damage ourselves?'

'No but . . .'

'Yeah, come on, Lauren. I mean we're not exactly tearing off our clothes, are we? Well not yet anyway.' I tugged at my T-shirt, which had slid right down over my shoulder, what with all the crawling about with the dustpan and brush.

Marina twiddled vaguely with a gold hoop earring. 'You know what I think? I think it's all to do with Lauren's clock.'

'My clock? But . . .'

Marina spoke in her sternest voice. 'Henry was trying to warn you, Lauren, and we didn't show the proper respect. It's clear what we have to do, we have to burn your clock, like Henry says. Then everything will be under control again.'

Poor Lauren. You could almost feel sorry for her, sneezing all the way back down Arcadia Avenue. Grass mowings and traffic fumes probably. Although Lauren reckoned it was partly emotional. After all, she was really fond of her grandma, and the thought of burning the clock was a kind of sacrilege. Also, Izzie had recently had the clock valued, and it was worth hundreds, apparently.

'It's got sentimental value.' She blew her nose hard. 'It's not the money I'm thinking of.'

'Yeah, your gran's really nice.' I had to agree with her.

'But, you don't think, I mean, maybe Henry's right and your grandfather's spirit is really inside it? We'd be doing him a favour, wouldn't we? It can't be much fun being trapped inside an old clock for eternity.'

Lauren shook her head. 'It's just a clock. Why would a spirit live in a clock? Oh I don't know. I'm so *confused*. You don't think . . .' Lauren continued wretchedly, 'you don't think Marina's going over the top with this stuff? She's different somehow. She's getting a bit . . . well . . .'

'Bolshie?' I finished her sentence for her. 'Yeah, I'd noticed. Marina was always a bit on the bossy side, but she used to care about other people, you know, show an interest. I reckon it's this Anne Boleyn thing. She thinks we're like her ladies in waiting or something. Everything she says is like a royal decree.'

I couldn't say any more. Because it felt disloyal to gossip about Marina this way when she was, after all, my best friend. I just had to remember the old, pre-Henry Marina; how we'd shared our secrets, our ideas; nattered about everything from mascara to the Meaning of Life, until we were hoarse. Poor Marina. Imagine her now, alone in the silent house.

It was strange, the sense of freedom I always felt, stepping outside into the street, leaving Hermia at her hearthside, where the smithereens of glass still lay.

At the bus stop we parted as usual, Lauren still fretting about her clock. Across the road, from Bromfield Park, the sound of children squealing on the swings drifted across to me. Nice, everyday, normal sounds. Usually everyday, normal sort of stuff just bored me rigid. But now I was doing my best to think of anything but the seance, the haunted clock and exploding brandy glass. If I let myself think of all that, I wouldn't be able to stop. I didn't want Henry following me home, back to Smedhurst Road. I didn't want Henry haunting *me*.

I was trying so hard *not* to think of Henry, I only vaguely registered the car pulling up at the stop. A convertible, shiny lipstick red, with the top down.

'Hey! Marina's friend! Want a lift somewhere?'

It was him. Marina's cousin. He leaned across to open the door for me. 'You waiting for the 127, yeah? Well hop in then, I'm going your way.'

'Oh I . . . no, no thanks. It's OK. I'm getting the bus.'

Why? The words flew out of my mouth before I could stop them. When really I wanted to cry, YES YES! and leap in beside him before he could change his mind. Then again, what would Marina say? Me accepting a lift from one of the family? It was unheard of. Unknown.

'You'd rather take the bus?' He held up his hands in disbelief. 'Come on. I don't charge no fares you know.'

I stared into the distance. There was a sort of yellow-ish, poisonous-looking heat haze hovering, and no sign whatsoever of the 127. Perhaps, if it had loomed into sight at that moment, I might never have taken that lift. Things might have turned out so differently. But there was no sign of any bus, just the cousin, leaning over to open the door, grinning at me.

'Lucky I came along eh?' he said, as we streaked away from the stop. 'Those buses, filthy! Never come on time, do they? You could've got heat stroke standing there all day, know what I mean? Strapped in properly?'

He reached out to check my seat belt. 'That's it. Don't want you coming to any harm, do we?'

From deep in my leather seat, I must have smiled. For how could I? How could I possibly come to any harm, with Marina's cousin beside me?

Chapter Seven

I decided not to tell Marina about her cousin. I just had this gut feeling that she wouldn't be too delighted about the lift. And anyway, there was nothing to tell. True to his word, he had driven me straight home. The car pulled up right outside our shared front porch, and I prayed Mrs Croop wouldn't come out to inspect. It was one of her annoying habits, noting down numbers of unfamiliar cars, checking out the neighbours' visitors.

'Tell me, what were you kids doing this afternoon then?' Marina's cousin had switched the engine off. He sounded intrigued. I could feel his chocolatey eyes on my face, and wanted to hide. You know how the two sides of your face are different? I read about it in a magazine. And it's true. On my right side I'm like Quasimodo, and on the left, well there's just a touch of Kate Winslet there, if you sort of squint your eyes. But no, as fate would have it, Marina's cousin was copping the full glory of my Quasimodo side; the way my nose went all blobby at the end, and the spot next to it, which was turning into a whitehead.

'Doing?' My voice came out all squeaky for some reason. I tried to lower it. 'We weren't doing much. We just meet up at Marina's house sometimes, that's all.'

He made a tutting sound: 'Yeah yeah, I know. Naughty girls eh? Raiding my uncle's drinks cabinet, yeah? Having a bit of a party behind his back.'

'No, no . . . we don't drink. Well not much. At least I don't. We weren't doing anything wrong. You won't say anything, will you, to Marina's dad? He's not keen on her having us round you see.'

Was this what the lift was all about? I wondered. Getting me to *sneak* on Marina? Reporting us all to her dad, so he could have her swaddled in black robes and carted back to Cyprus? It was so unfair. It was medieval in fact.

The cousin was tapping the steering wheel, as if considering. As if not telling was a real moral dilemma. He whistled through his teeth. 'That's a tricky one. After what I saw and heard, you know? Someone screaming, glass smashing . . . looked like you girls were up to something to me.'

'Screaming?' I frowned. How could he have heard that, without listening at the letterbox? 'Oh, that must've been Lauren you heard. She saw a spider, and knocked the glass off the table. She's like that, you know, phobic. About spiders and things.'

This was silly. I wasn't going to sit here and be interrogated. I was about to get out of the car, when he started to laugh. 'So your mate Lauren, she's scared of spiders, is she? What about you then? You got any phobias I should know about? I mean you're not phobic about men or anything?'

'Men? Course not, why should I be?'

I turned and gave him the full frontal, praying that Kate would have the edge over Quasi, that Beauty would overcome the Beast.

'You seem a bit jumpy, that's all. Thought I was

serious, didn't you, thought I was giving you the third degree? Don't look so worried. No one takes anything I say seriously.'

I was quiet, distracted for a moment by Mrs Croop. She'd just come scuttling out with her milk bottles. She looked just like one of those gingery spiders you find in the bath, as she bent down to one of those tray things that has a wipe-on/wipe-off message for the milkman. When she straightened, the sun must have shone directly in her eyes, for she didn't notice me; just blinked and went back inside.

'I'm Nikos by the way.' He said this as if his name was a secret to most people, as if it might have some special magical power when uttered aloud, like Rumpelstiltskin. *My name is Rumpelstiltskin!* 'Most people call me Nick. I don't know your name, do I?'

'I'm Abbie,' I told him, ashamed of its homely innocent sound.

'Abbie.' He seemed to ponder it, to taste my name on his tongue. 'How old are you then, Abbie?'

'Sixteen. It was my birthday last week.'

Almost at once I regretted telling him that. It sounded so childish. And now he was going right over the top, acting like it was some great achievement, like winning an Olympic gold medal.

'Last week? I'll have to get you something, won't I? Belated birthday present.'

'Oh, that's all right.' I was fumbling with the seat-belt, feeling a right prune. I'm one of those people who gets stuck in automatic doors, or push instead of pull doors, catches, exits, entrances — they always seem to unnerve me.

'There you go.' Reaching across me to free the catch, his arm brushed my chest, so light and casual it *might* have been accidental. On the other hand he couldn't fail to notice that I wasn't wearing my bra.

'Tell you what, Abbie, do me a favour eh? Don't get in any more cars with strange men.'

'Thanks. For the lift and everything.'

I was out of there like a shot. I didn't look back, even to wave, just let myself into the flat and pounded up the stairs with no regard whatever for Mrs Croop's head. I ran straight to the front-room windows, sneaking a look behind the net curtain. The car was gone already. Just an empty space that Cara, the West Indian girl next door, was trying to reverse into. Suddenly I felt abandoned. Why had I behaved like such a prat? Why couldn't I think of one witty remark, instead of sitting there like a gormless idiot. Well, it was too late now. He'd gone. 'I'll get you a belated present,' he'd said. Would he? Just to *see* him again would be present enough.

Luckily for me, Mum hadn't see the car pull up. She was in the living room dusting what she called the 'dado'.

'Oh, it's you, dear. I didn't expect you back so soon.' She paused, duster in hand. 'Actually, I was thinking, Abigail, they've got a card up in Victor Values. Students wanted for shelf-stacking. Well, it's no use looking like that, dear. It's better than mooning around the house for the next six weeks.'

She didn't understand that 'mooning around' was just what I wanted to do. Mooning and dreaming of

Marina's cousin, and practising my Winslet smile in the mirror.

'Haven't you got any toenails to cut?' I asked Mum. I couldn't imagine Izzie Alexander, who had just taken up belly-dancing according to Lauren, dusting dados.

Mum said she was having a day off to catch up on housework, if I didn't have any objection. What with the heat making people's feet swell up, she'd been scuttling round the neighbourhood with her little black bag all week. 'It's all right for some, who have nothing in the world to do. You know what they say . . .'

'No, Mother,' I sighed, 'but no doubt you're going to tell me.'

'*The devil finds work for idle hands.*' She gave me one of her *funny* looks then, which made me wonder if, boring and down to earth as she was, my mother might just have psychic powers after all.

Anyway, she couldn't accuse me of being idle exactly. I had business to attend to, didn't I? The very next evening, in Lauren's garden. A little matter about a clock. Marina had called to say the deed must be done as soon as possible.

'It's only fair,' Marina said, 'because if Henry wrecks my house again, then it'll be all Lauren's fault.'

Lauren's garden was large and neglected with withered fruit trees and massive rhododendrons you could practically camp under. The garden was protected from nosy neighbours by a high thorny hedge. Oh, how I envied her that hedge, thinking how it would frustrate the likes of Mrs Croop pegging out her drawers and looking for someone to talk to.

The bonfire threw out showers of sparks. A dark plume of smoke billowed up into the sky, drifting towards Highgate Heath. The light had almost gone, leaving a streaky pinkish-violet. A blackbird sang for its life nearby. The flames zipped and crackled. It was madness really, to light a fire in this heat wave, but it must be done. Lauren's clock must be consigned to the flames this very night, according to Marina.

For a start, Izzie was conveniently out for the evening.

'She's got her belly-dancing class.' Lauren hovered uneasily at the edge of the flames. 'And she always goes to the pub afterwards with her mates. It's just the people next door I'm worried about. They're absolute fanatics about the ozone layer and everything. They sold their car, and now they cycle everywhere with face masks on.'

'Be thankful you don't live next door to Mrs Croop,' I said, thinking how good it would be, if *she* wore a face mask.

'Who on earth is she?' Peering anxiously up at the next-door's windows, she said, 'I hope they don't mention it to Mum.'

'Say you were having a barbecue, trying to cook some sausages or something,' I suggested. I couldn't help feeling sorry for Lauren, dithering about by the fire, making those little whinnying noises like a horse, to clear her sinuses. 'Hey, d'you think *I'd* make a good belly-dancer?' I began strutting about the lawn like a demented stripper, twirling the chain-belt which hung from my jeans. 'You have to do a sort of pelvic-thrust, don't you, like this . . .' I demonstrated.

The idea was to make Lauren laugh. She just stared at me in disgust. 'It's not funny, Abbie. She's only doing it to get Harv-wit excited. Can you imagine, old women shaking their flabby old bellies about? All those stretch-marks and cellulite and stuff. It's totally obscene, that's my opinion.'

From the other side of the fire, Marina cleared her throat. She'd been standing quietly, staring into the flames. Dressed in her long swishy skirt and silk embroidered shawl, and decked out with enough charms and chains and jewellery for a warrior-queen's burial, she had a noble sacrificial look.

'When you're quite ready. If you remember, this is *meant* to be a ceremony. I mean, if you want to strut your stuff, there are better places. Remember what we came here for? What Henry told us?'

Ouch! Marina's reproachful glare was like a rap on the knuckles.

'Sorry.' I stopped gyrating at once. 'What do you want us to do then?'

'Just concentrate, and draw as close as we can to the flames. Ready then, Lauren? I don't want to hurry you, but I've got to be home by ten.'

Lauren hugged the clock to her chest. 'It's no good. Now that we're here, I can't bring myself to do it. I feel as if she's watching me. I feel so ungrateful!'

I squeezed Lauren's arm. 'Don't worry. She won't need to know, will she? It won't mean you don't care about her or anything. And anyway, she's kind of hip, your gran, maybe she'd even understand.'

Marina sighed, exasperated. 'Look, give it to me then. I'll do it.' Marina wrested the family heirloom gently from Lauren's grasp. 'You don't have to watch if you'd rather not.'

As she held out her offering to the flames, Lauren put up no resistance. She stood, gaping pathetically at her heroine. 'Don't you think, Marina, I mean, is it really necessary? You don't think it might have been a mistake, a joke?'

Poor Lauren. I got the feeling that she would have done anything for Marina, jumped into the flames herself if Marina so commanded.

'Think of it as an exorcism,' Marina said. 'You'll feel better once it's gone, believe me. It might even cure your hayfever.'

Now that was stretching it a bit far, I reckoned. What had clock-burning got to do with the pollen count? Lauren looked doubtful too, but she followed Marina's lead and closed her eyes. We both copied Marina, holding out our arms as if we were conjuring some great unseen power from the sky. It was so quiet you could hear the clock ticking. Quite a friendly sound really. What had Henry got against it? I wondered. Unless it was just a way of testing us, testing our loyalty. He was making sure we would follow his orders without question, no matter what. Tonight it was just an old clock. What next? What would Henry ask us to give up next?

'We should say a few words,' Marina said. 'Witness this, our Lord, as we commit this trifle to the flames.' Wow! Impressive stuff. I half-squinted at her through the smoke. She was fantastic. Head thrown back, voice ringing across the garden. 'Let the grandfather of Mistress Lauren join the Light.'

I watched, slightly appalled, as the clock was tossed into the heart of the fire. I expected something dramatic to happen, a banshee wail, or thunder-clap, or maybe the smoke would take on the form of Lauren's ancestor, heaping curses upon us and our descendants. Luckily, none of that happened. Just the sound of someone practising the violin (badly), the notes floating through an open window, over the leafy gardens, trembling in the dusk like a dirge.

There were tears in Lauren's eyes as the flames swallowed up her precious heirloom. Although that might have been the pollen of course.

'If my gran finds out . . .' Lauren sounded shocked, as if she couldn't believe what she'd just allowed to happen. 'My mum's bound to ask where it is . . . they'll think I've gone mad.' She looked pathetic, like a little kid standing there in her natural cotton-weave shift, spaniel-ear hair tied in bunches, and chewing on her thumb.

'I don't see why they should think anything.' Marina tossed back her hair, as if the effort of clock-burning had exhausted her. 'It was your property, Lauren.'

I helped Lauren to put out the fire with the garden hose and shovelfuls of earth. Now that the ritual was over, Marina was impatient to leave. She stalked on ahead of us back to the house, urging us to get a move on.

'How much did you say that clock was worth?' I asked Lauren as we turned our backs on the dying embers.

She sighed. 'I don't know exactly. There weren't many of them made.'

104

'So it could be worth hundreds?'

'Don't rub it in, Abbie. Anyway, what would you have done? It's all right for you, Henry hasn't picked on you yet. Supposing he asked you to burn that precious palmistry book of yours?'

'Supposing he did? Supposing he told *you* to jump in the fire with the clock? Would you do it?'

'Don't be stupid.'

'It's not so stupid. What about those people who commit murder and blame the voices in their own heads? It's not so different when you think about it.'

'Well, I'm hardly going to murder anyone, am I?'

Lauren had one of those huge mirrors in her hallway, the kind with an elaborate gilt scrolled frame that must weigh an absolute ton. Perfect for Marina to preen herself in, brushing the black river of hair, eyeing her reflection as if it was a work of fine art.

My own reflection next to hers spoiled the effect. I had two huge smuts on my nose from the bonfire. 'Look at that. Thanks a bunch for telling me, you two. I might have gone out like something out of *The Hundred and One Dalmatians*.'

Marina smiled as she pencilled black lines round her eyes. Other people's afflictions always made her titter. Especially mine. 'Honestly, Abbie, you look as if you've been dragged from a burning room.'

'Sorry,' Lauren said, 'but I've got more important things to worry about than your nose. I wish I hadn't done it now. I really wish I hadn't.' Her voice had that panicky sound, verging on tears.

Turning reluctantly away from the mirror to face her, Marina said in her stern but kindly, mother-knows-best voice, 'You know, Lauren, you're well-rid of that clock. I just know that Henry meant it for the best. He'll be so pleased that we carried out his orders, honestly.'

Orders? So Henry was giving us orders now! As I followed Marina out into the night, I nearly said something. I mean, girls didn't take orders from men any more, well only their dads perhaps, or their teachers, but even then not without a fight.

I had a horrible creepy feeling suddenly, when Marina got on the bus for Northgate. I wanted to tell her to be careful, that perhaps we should leave Henry, now that we'd had the grand burning ritual. But all I actually said was, 'I'll see you tomorrow then.'

Marina looked doubtful for a moment. 'Not sure. I *might* have to work in the shop. If not we'll play the Game.'

'Oh yeah,' I said. 'Cool.'

Which was stupid, because 'cool' was a word I never ever used. Usually.

Chapter Eight

'What was that thump just now?' My mother opened the living-room door and shrieked along the hall. 'You'll bring Mrs Croop's ceiling down, dear, if you're not careful. A thump like that. It could give her a nasty shock.'

I snorted to myself. Hah! If only my mother knew. If what I suspected was true, Mrs Croop would have more than a shock. Mrs Croop was in for a lively old time if a poltergeist really *had* come to live at no. 62 Smedhurst Road, although God forbid it had.

The book, *Poltergeists — An examination of the phenomenon*, was the size and weight of a tombstone. Last night, nodding asleep over page 398 at some unearthly hour, I'd somehow kicked it to the foot of my bed. Now I wasn't sure if my foot waggling had knocked it to the floor, or if it had been hurled by some unseen spirit-hand, Henry's perhaps?

The book glared up at me from where it had fallen, spine open. It was *terrifying*. No wonder it had been tucked away in the psychology section of Northgate library, looking like no one had taken it out in a million years. Not that it was gory or anything; no spectacular green vomit, or blood dripping from taps, or any of that. It was written in a scholarly style by some professor, which made the descriptions of the case-histories all the more frightening.

'Turbulent spirits', as the professor called them, were no respecters of property. Whole dressers of crockery had been smashed, bedclothes stripped from the victims as they slept, people forced from their homes, driven out of their minds.

'Don't you dare move,' I said to the book. 'Don't even think about it!'

Since yesterday's phone call, and that day at Marina's house when the glass had smashed, nothing seemed certain any more. I mean, Rule of Life, objects don't dance about by themselves. They just don't. Well wrong! *Sometimes* they do. And according to the evidence, I was at just the right age for a dose of demonic possession. There was nothing the spirits liked more, so the book said, than a nice adolescent girl. Or rather a nasty one. The nastier the better. Spots, and periods, and *lusting* after boys, and threatening to kill yourself because nobody understands you . . . wow, they just couldn't get enough of that stuff!

I suppose you could understand it. I mean if *I* was a spirit, doomed to walk the earth for all of boring eternity, I'd be looking for a bit of action frankly. It wouldn't be much fun haunting some old couple like my parents for instance, and watching them dunk digestive biscuits in their cocoa every night.

I wouldn't have taken the book out at all, if not for Marina. Yesterday morning, the morning after the bonfire, she'd called me up. 'Sorry, but you'd better not come over for a bit. It's my parents. The bus got held up last night, and made me late.'

She told me the story in a strange dull voice. How her parents had got home earlier than usual and were furious to find her not there. How her dad refused to believe she'd been at the late night library opening, doing research for her project. How he had demanded to know who she'd been with, what was the boy's name? Who were his family?

Usually I didn't comment on her parents. This time I couldn't help it. 'They treat you like a servant, Marina. I mean, this is the twenty-first century for God's sake. Why do you stand for it?'

Marina snapped at me then. It was natural for parents to worry, she said, and anyway they were tired and hungry, and had a right to expect some help with meals and so on. 'You wouldn't understand. You're just spoilt. And anyway, I didn't ring to tell you about the row, it's what happened afterwards . . .'

It was then she told about the biscuit tin, the tin we kept the letters in, diving from the top of the fridge for no apparent reason.

'I know this sounds strange,' Marina said. 'But I think it was Henry's way of protecting me, sort of sticking up for me, you know. When the tin just sprang off the fridge like that, it stopped them shouting. They were so surprised.'

'I bet they were. Gallant of Henry. Coming to your rescue like that.'

'It won't be so easy to play the Game now. My parents want me to work in the shop for the rest of the holidays.'

'What? But that's so unfair! How can you work in the shop, and do all the housework, and the cooking, and do your project stuff and . . .'

'It's not so bad. I'll only be at the shop until about three. Look, why don't we meet outside there tomorrow? I need to buy new shoes, and we can talk about . . . you know . . .'

So, I said yes, OK. There was no point going on about it. If there was one thing Marina hated, it was sympathy. To salvage her pride, I knew she would make out that working in the shop was actually fun.

For now, I picked the book up and dusted off the cover. Later, when we met up, I'd lend it to Marina. Maybe reading about the 'turbulent spirits' would convince her to give up the Game, to give up Henry before it was too late.

The area where the Pauloses had their shop, at the lower end of Commerce Road, was like a scene out of one of those street-wise vampire movies. All boarded-up windows, ripped posters and drifts of rubbish. The few shops that were open for business had wire grilles at the windows, like cages.

It was so hot, it felt like everything would just peel back, and curl up like a banana skin: the tar on the road, paint flaking from doors and windowsills. Because of the heat, I'd swapped my jeans for a dress and now regretted it. It was one of those strappy, flimsy things that look more like underwear.

'Going out in your petticoat, I see,' my mother remarked when she saw me leave the house.

'It's a *frock*, Mother,' I had to remind her. 'And no one wears petticoats these days. Oh by the way, can I get you anything from the shops while I'm out?'

110

I had to add this, because I'd just remembered about the turbulent spirits. I imagined them whirling in dark clouds like tornadoes, or swarms of mosquitoes scenting blood. Perhaps if I made an effort to be nice to my mum, they'd back off.

'From the shops?' Mum blinked in amazement at my simpering smile. 'No I don't think I want anything, dear. But it's nice of you to offer.'

Actually, she had a point about my get-up. Skimpy dresses were fine on starved-looking models, but they looked tarty if you had bouncy bits, and had to run for a bus. Undoubtedly Marina would have something to say about my outfit. I could just imagine her, surveying me with that superior smirk of hers.

Marina. Where was she? The scent of spices and garlic wafted from the Cyprus Mini-mart. Marina would be sitting in there, straight-backed at the checkout, tapping at the till with her psychic fingers, shaking out her hair over a nylon overall.

'Meet me at two,' she'd instructed me. 'But keep out of sight of the shop, where my dad won't see you.'

As if I needed reminding!

I looked at my watch. Ten past. Trust her to be late. Just down the street, two Asian women sauntered out of Marina's shop, flamboyant in glitzy saris, behind them an old man mumbling and spitting onto the kerb. Charming! I wandered up the street a bit. The travel agent's looked like a safe place to loiter, there was the same poster of Cyprus in the window that Marina had on her bedroom wall. I pretended to stare at it with serious intent, when a voice from behind me said: 'Planning your holidays, eh?'

He was leaning against a grubby transit van, smoking, watching me. I didn't recognize him at first. He was just a bloke in a Gap T-shirt and combats, and mucky old trainers, chocolatey eyes concealed behind sunglasses.

I didn't answer of course. My experience of men wasn't that great, but I *did* know that if you fancied a guy, the thing was to look at him like he'd just crawled out of a drain or something.

'Hey, remember me?' He gestured at himself. 'I gave you a lift home, remember?'

Marina's cousin! My heart did a quick flip, like a tossed pancake.

'A bit more style than this heap of junk, yeah?' He thumped the side of the transit, explaining that he was just making some deliveries for the shop, to help his uncle out. 'Thought it must be you. You waiting for Marina to finish, or what?'

'We're going shopping,' I said. 'Marina wants some shoes.'

'What time you supposed to be meeting?' He looked at his watch.

'Two. She's a bit late. Are they busy in there?'

'You've got a long wait then, love. Her dad's unloading out the back, and her mum just popped out to see her aunty down the street. So she's holding the shop.'

'Oh.' I tried to look cool about it, as if waiting there half choking to death in the traffic fumes, in about forty degrees was no problem. In fact I was furious. Why couldn't Marina just tell her parents that her friend was waiting? Why couldn't I just go and sit at the back of the shop until she was finished?

112

Nikos removed his sunglasses and wiped his forehead with the back of his hand. 'Tell me something, why don't we have siesta in this country? You know, no one should have to work in this kind of heat. It's not natural. Even lions, right . . . they do their hunting at night, don't they? Tell you what, why don't I buy you a cold drink or something? There's this place I know, just round the corner.'

'Well . . . Marina . . .'

'She won't be finished for half an hour at least. You'll be melted, the time she gets out.'

'Your work though . . . ?' I hesitated, looking at the van.

He laughed. 'This? This isn't my real work. You're a right little worrier, aren't you? Like I told you, I'm just helping my uncle out for the day. Got to take a break now an' then, otherwise you know, too much work . . .' He tapped the side of his head. 'Bad for you, that is.'

'I don't know . . . well, just a few minutes then, in case Marina comes out and wonders where I am.'

I glanced towards the shop. Supposing she should come out right now? That would spoil everything.

'No worries,' Nikos said with a shrug, as if he himself didn't have a single worry in the world. 'Nice cool drink and you'll be back in two shakes.'

He took hold of my arm, just above the elbow, like we were old friends. I allowed him to steer me gently up the street. Not that there was any need for steering, because right at that moment, I would have followed him anywhere.

★   ★   ★

I was expecting he'd take me to one of those mysterious dark little bars, where old men with huge moustaches sat playing dice all day. A Greek sort of place. Instead we went to a place called The Gallery, some kind of art gallery-cum-Bar, with cool vanilla-ice walls, chunky blue sofas, and paintings that looked like cosmic explosions.

I was hoping we'd sit on a sofa, but Nikos made for the bar stool, which meant I had to balance my poltergeists book awkwardly on my knees.

Nikos smiled at me. 'Nice place, yeah? It's just opened. Owned by a mate of mine, Stefan. Hoping to attract the arty-farty crowd.' He leaned closer and whispered suddenly in my ear, 'Reckon he's picked the wrong location myself.'

'Oh . . . do you?' The way he leaned over me, I thought he was going to whisper something about how beautiful I was (not that I was, it was just the look in his eye that made me think that).

'Yeah. That's why I brought you here. Swell the numbers. You look the artistic sort, yeah, am I right?'

'Hmmm . . . well sort of . .' I tried to look enigmatic. Enigmatic. Mysterious. Like Marina. Problem being, it was hard to look enigmatic with a massive great tombstone of a book sitting on my bare thighs. Still it seemed better to leave it there. Propping the wretched thing against the stool was risky. Nikos might notice the title, and think me some kind of screwball. He didn't look the type to believe in spirits.

'What can I get you then? Pineapple juice? With ice? You sure that's all?'

'Yes, thanks.'

While he ordered drinks, I glanced around. The customers were a mixed bunch. A man in a violet shirt, with a scary haw-haw sort of laugh, was feeding bits of cheesecake to a girl young enough to be his grand-daughter. A couple of Goths hunched gloomily at one end of the bar, and a girl with masses of chestnutty hair and a minuscule black dress sat cross-legged on one of the sofas. She was reading a newspaper. Or pretending to. Every now and then her eyes would flick over the top, as if to check whether Nikos had noticed her yet.

Well it was only a matter of time before he did. Their eyes would meet over the headlines and that would be IT. I mean, chestnut hair girl and me, there was no contest. But she might just have been a stick of furniture the way Nikos's eyes slid dismissively over her. His gaze settled on me instead, like I was the only snoggable girl in the entire universe, let alone The Gallery.

'What's this, another day off, Nick?' A balding pony-tailed man emerged from a back room. He loomed over us. 'Well, come on. Aren't you going to do the intros?'

Nick grinned reluctantly. 'Stefan, say hallo to Abbie.'

I couldn't say I liked this Stefan much. Mainly because in my opinion, old men over thirty look stupid with pony-tails, like they think they're rock-stars or something. So I wasn't very happy about him taking my hand and kissing it.

'Abbie . . . short for Abigail, am I right?'

I nodded.

'Enchanted to meet you, Abigail.'

'Yeah, yeah, just put her down.' Nikos slid his arm

about my waist. 'And tell us what that load of old junk's about, over there.'

The sculptures he meant. There was an exhibition in one corner. It consisted mainly of headless dummies in various poses, and broken furniture, like the old chair with three legs.

Stefan laughed. 'Does this young lady know about you, Nick? What a complete *philistine* you are? What does it say to you, ask yourself that?'

'It says, don't sit on this chair unless you want to fall on your arse.'

Pony-tail raised his eyebrows at me. 'Abigail? What does it say to you?'

'Well . . .' I began, feeling myself go hot in the face, 'the dummies make me think of Anne Boleyn . . .' Immediately I wanted to kick myself. Why did I have to say something so utterly totally dorky?

Nikos and his friend looked a bit blank, as if they didn't know who Anne was.

'She er . . . got her head chopped off,' I reminded them. 'By Henry the Eighth.'

'Nice fella,' Stefan said smoothly. 'Bit of a dog, was she? Couldn't he just have stuck a paper bag over her head?'

'Listen, haven't you got any glasses to polish or something?' Nikos said. He was stroking my shoulder, as if he sensed how awkward I felt. Which made me feel really grateful to him.

Stefan said he paid someone else to polish the glasses, thank you, but he could take a hint. 'I'll leave you two "love-birds" alone then. And get yourselves another drink, eh, on the house.'

'Actually, I'll have to go in a minute,' I blurted, as Stefan turned his attention to the girl on the sofa.

'What's the panic?' Nikos wanted to know. 'You only just got here. Don't mind him, he's all front.' He ordered himself a coffee, then swivelled round on his stool to face me so that our knees brushed. He scratched his head, as if he was puzzled. 'Tell me something, you and Marina, you're good friends, yeah?'

'Yes, we are. Best friends actually.' I watched him heap three teaspoons of sugar into the black coffee, stirring endlessly. 'Well, we're in the same classes for most things, at school.'

'That right? And you tell each other everything, about your boyfriends and that?' The chocolate eyes drifted over me, and my heart did that pancake trick again.

'Not *everything*.'

His knees pressed closer. I couldn't move though, not without sending *Poltergeists* smashing to the floor. Perched on my stool, I could feel myself growing rigid and red in the face, with the effort. My knees began to tremble. I wasn't going to fall into that trap, tell him I *had* no boyfriend. Also, I didn't want him to think of Marina and me as a daft pair of girlies, twittering on about clothes and make-up all day. I decided to put him right.

'We talk about all kinds of things actually,' I said. Then stopped. What did we talk about? Henry mostly. The spirit world. Here, in The Gallery, it was hard to imagine there *was* a spirit world at all. 'I mean, books, and history, and art and stuff, and well . . .' I finished feebly, draining my fruit juice, 'You know, life.'

'Life, eh?'

Now that I had started talking, I couldn't stop. 'We're both, well actually, we're both a bit psychic. So we . . .'

Oh God, I couldn't believe I'd just said that, about being psychic. It was a known fact that men didn't go for that stuff. He would think I was some kind of head-case, for sure. But no. He was nodding at me, like I was some kind of really impressive genius.

'You know,' Nikos said, 'I really go for intelligence in a woman.'

Intelligence, he said! Woman! Suddenly I was a *woman*! So chuffed was I, to be promoted to womanly status, that I forgot all about the book and crossed my legs. The idea was to elicit a seductive swish of skin, and flash of knee as I did so. Instead of which, that great door-stopper tome, *Poltergeists*, slithered straight off my lap, wham on the black-tiled floor. Worse, it wedged itself right beneath the stool of a scornful-looking blonde in leopard-print sandals. To reach it, I had to grovel about beneath her legs, muttering, 'Excuse me,' and 'Sorry.' Imagine the total humiliation, when the blonde nudged the book with her elegant pointy toe into, not mine, but Nikos's outstretched hands.

'I think this is yours.' She didn't merely say these words, she *purred* them. Also she had the cheek to smile right at him with her velvety, rose-petal mouth. Her lips were all squishy, like one of those carnivorous jungle flowers that swallows insects whole. I expected that Nikos's eyes would pop out on stalks, how could they help it? But all he said was, 'Cheers, love,' and turned to me.

'What's this you been carrying around with you then? Don't tell me you've read all this? Take you a lifetime that would.'

I almost cringed then, as he read the title aloud. 'Poltergeists? That's "things that go bump in the night", right? You believe in all that stuff?'

'No I . . . I, er, I got it out of the library for someone. A friend. Can I have it back please?'

'Yeah, take it easy, course you can.'

'Sorry. It's just that it's overdue, you see.'

Nikos handed it back to me. 'There you go. No problem. Listen, Abbie . . .' He was scratching behind his ear, as if it helped him to think better. 'I was wondering. All these books . . . well, a girl should have some fun sometimes, right? What about I call for you tomorrow night? We'll get out of town, go for a run in the country, get some fresh air away from this stink-hole. What d'you say, Abbie?'

Nikos's face was close to mine. His voice was so soft, persuasive, you could almost *feel* it, like silk against your skin. 'I'd really like to see you again,' Nikos said. 'In fact, I'd like to see a lot more of you, Abbie, because I reckon you're something special.'

'Yeah, OK then.' Just like that, I said it. Really casual. When all the time, such a turmoil was going on inside me, heart-flips, stomach-flutters, stuff he could never guess at in a million years. But the turbulent spirits could. The turbulent spirits, attracted by lust, would be swarming around me in no time.

'And, er . . . leave that book at home tomorrow, eh?'

I nodded.

Outside on the pavement, Nikos reached out and

caught my chin between finger and thumb. 'You can find you way back to Marina?'

'Of course.'

He looked a bit worried suddenly. Better, he said, if I didn't say anything to Marina about us having a drink together. 'For a start, I'm supposed to be doing this bit of work for her dad. And my uncle's a bit old fashioned, you know, strict with her. What with her not getting out much and that, she might be upset. It's the way it is in our family.' He shrugged apologetically.

I nodded. 'I know how it is. I won't say anything.'

'Tomorrow then.' Nikos tilted my face towards him, as if to kiss me. But then the fingers let go, his hand moving slowly down my throat like a spider dropping from a web. I swallowed. Never had my throat felt like this before: a hot spot, an erogenous zone, as if he'd touched me in some private, forbidden place.

I felt his eyes on me as I strolled back to the corner. It was a bit unnerving. I tried to make like I was some cat-walk model, hips swaying, really cool, until I turned and saw he'd vanished into the bar. Only then did I break into a gallumphing run, book gripped beneath my arm, skirt flipping against my thighs. I ran all the way back to the high street, where Marina stood glaring into the stream of traffic.

'Where the hell have you been?' Marina wanted to know. 'I've been waiting ages.'

Chapter Nine

Nikos negotiated the choked roads of outer London, as if he was steering a ship in a storm, one hand on the wheel.

'Comfortable?' He glanced at me. 'Not too draughty for you? Don't want you catching a chill or anything.'

I shook my head. 'I'm fine. Really.'

'Fine' was a bit of an understatement. What with the wind in my hair, moody jazz in the background, and the sex god beside me, I might have just died and gone to heaven. I might have been Anne Boleyn on her wedding day, sailing down the Thames, attended by a Cleopatra's fleet of barges; flags fluttering, bells chiming, cannons booming.

'Good to get out of the smoke, yeah?' Nikos said. Although we weren't. Quite. He waved a hand at the suburbs flashing past. 'Be with nature, you know . . . trees, birds 'n' that. I'll be buying a place out here one of these days, like my mate Stefan has. Bit of space, fresh air. I want my kids to grow up with roses in their cheeks, know what I mean?'

Kids? Whose kids? Mine and his, did he mean?

'What about you, Abbie?'

'Oh me too. I mean, I like the country too.' Liar! Fields and cows and all that stuff bored me rigid. It would be all right with Nikos though. Both of us knee-deep in some buttercup meadow, with skipping golden-haired children. 'Actually, I was just wondering . . . you saying you like the country . . . did you use to live in the country, back in Cyprus?'

Uh oh, stupid question. And where did I get that lisp from? My voice sounded like it belonged to some other girl, some dumb girl who didn't know anything.

'Cyprus?' Nikos laughed. 'I don't remember that far back. I was a babe in arms. You'd have to ask my mum.'

Oh, yes please! I'd like to have heard more about his mum and Cyprus, but his mobile rang and for the next ten minutes he was having what seemed to be a riveting conversation in Greek. Whoever was on the phone must be a right comedian. At one point Nikos laughed so much, I thought we'd have an accident and I had to cling on to the seat.

By the time he'd finished we were pulling into the forecourt of a pub, one of those Georgian coaching inns, with millions of hanging-baskets out front, and a plastic tree-slide in the garden for the kiddies. The car park was crowded with flash, shiny cars like the one Nikos drove. The owners sat at trestle-tables, bronzed by a setting sun, shrill blondes and men in their summer casual-wear.

'Here we are then. Bit crowded for a Wednesday night, must be the weather, making everyone thirsty.' Nikos slipped his arm about my waist, leading me to the seat furthest away from the kids' slide. 'Not that I don't like the little brats, but I'd rather talk to *you*, know what I mean? What can I get you then?'

Bacardi Breezer was considered a cool drink at school. I nearly asked for one, then opted for Coke instead. Alcohol made me giggle in a hee-haw-haw sort of way, like a demented donkey, as Lauren had once kindly pointed out to me at a party.

While Nikos was gone, I angled my Kate Winslet side so that he'd get the full benefit. Hopefully the rosy sun would show up my new copper-blonde highlights, straight out of a packet that very evening. I had to look totally gorgeous, to make up for being so dumb.

I tried desperately to think of something riveting to say, as Nikos crossed the grass towards me, carrying our drinks. Obviously the latest hot news from the spirit world was out of the question. What then? It didn't help that he looked so, what some of the girls at school would have called 'well-fit', in the black T-shirt and jeans. I wasn't the only one that noticed either. A girl at a nearby table was having a sly ogle over her boyfriend's shoulder. In fact her tongue was practically hanging out. Honestly! I glared back at her.

Nikos seemed not to notice. Maybe he was used to girls drooling over him all the time.

'You're looking great, Abbie, you know that?' He sat down opposite me, our knees instantly brushing. 'Like the outfit. Can't stand those baggy great jeans you schoolgirls wear nowadays. They don't do a girl any favours, know what I mean?'

'Don't you think so?'

Phew! A narrow escape. I'd nearly chosen my favourite baggies and crop-top for tonight, and changed my mind at the last moment. I'd settled instead for an off-the-shoulder T-shirt dress. A bit girlie, but I had this feeling Nikos was the sort of bloke to like girlie stuff (on girls that is).

'Let's have a look.' He was peering hard at me, as if I had a smut on my nose or something. 'Yeah, that dress matches your eyes, sort of turquoise, aren't they? Beautiful.'

I blinked. No one had ever called my eyes beautiful before. Marina's dark eyes were beautiful. Now my plain old blue eyes were suddenly turquoise. This was impressive, a man with colour sense!

Probably it was something to do with Nikos's line of business, as he called it. He began telling me about his father's clothing factory. 'We're expanding, you know? Getting in new designers. Going for a younger age-group. That's my job, you know, the networking part. Contacts, all that.'

'Really?' I tried not to look as impressed as I felt.

'What's this?' He leaned forward suddenly to inspect the giant crucifix, which I'd rushed out to buy at the time of Henry's last phone call. Nikos held it reverently in the flat of his palm. 'I didn't know you were religious.'

'Oh, I'm not. Not really. It's just . . .'

My cheeks burned like electric hot-plates. How could I tell him the truth? Oh well actually, I'm being stalked by Henry VIII. I'd be dumped on the spot!

'Don't tell me, it's to keep the old vampires at bay, right? Just in case I turn out to be Count Dracula, and take a little bite of you round about midnight.'

He lunged at my throat, with a mock growl. I

shivered as his teeth grazed my neck. Not that they were anything like Dracula fangs whatsoever.

'How did you guess?' I said. 'I was going to try the garlic, but . . . can I have my crucifix back, please?'

Nikos tucked it back inside my dress where it nestled, cool in my cleavage.

'Talking of midnight snacks,' he said, 'what time are they expecting you back home tonight, your mum and dad?'

I rolled my eyes. 'Eleven. Sorry about that. They're a bit old fashioned.'

'No worries. You'll be home on the dot, no problem.'

Surprisingly he seemed to respect their entirely unreasonable attitude, going on about how it was right for parents to worry, only natural and all that. I began to think that maybe he'd be glad to get rid of such a tongue-tied dud. Why couldn't I be witty, and arch, and provocative, like Anne Boleyn when she was ensnaring Henry? Or enigmatic, like Marina?

But then he started talking about a couple of dresses he might have for me, from his factory. 'Sometimes the girls don't put the buttons on right, nothing wrong with the stuff, all quality stuff, but the shops won't take them. What are you . . . ?' He ran his eyes over me. 'A size twelve, right? I'll bring one to show you, you can try it on.'

'How do you know what size I am?'

'It's my business to know these things. I've got a trained eye, you know.'

'You mean you're good at sizing people up?' I ventured.

He laughed. 'How old did you say you were again?'

'Sixteen. How old are *you*?'

'That would be telling. Older than your boyfriend, I bet, older and wiser.'

Of course I didn't intend to blurt out the embarrassing truth, like what boyfriend? I *have* no boyfriend. But something in my face must have given me away. That kind of smile I have, catching my lower lip with my teeth, looking away.

'What's his name then? Your boyfriend?'

'Well, actually, I'm not with anyone just at the moment. I've got a lot of studying to do and everything.'

'Sensible girl. Do well at school, eh, and stay away from the boys.' He stood up with a kind of sigh. 'Come on then, finished your drink? We'll go for a bit of a drive.'

Back in the car, he was quieter than before. The car put on speed, neat fields and knots of woodland flashing past. After about ten minutes, Nikos pulled off the main road and drove along a tree-lined lane, past some riding stables, and a place called Hampney Manor, which was actually a health farm, Nikos said, but looked like a palace out of Disneyland. As we left the houses behind, the trees thickened. The sky looked like velvet does when you ruffle it the wrong way, a sort of greyish-violet. We pulled in suddenly at a lay-by on the edge of the wood. I could just make out tracks, scarring the shadows between the trees. The air was tangy and pine-scented.

Nikos folded his arms and stared at me. 'You know

what? You surprise me . . . no boyfriends. A girl like you.'

I wasn't sure what he meant by a 'girl like me'. How did he know what kind of girl I was? I didn't even know myself.

'Of course I've had boyfriends,' I said, thinking he must imagine me to be a right saddo. 'I meant, just not at the moment.'

Boyfriend. Could you call the likes of Leon down the road a boyfriend? Leon was seventeen, an apprentice mechanic, and considered himself an ace stud. After Leon the First, there had been a stream of one-off dates, with Leon-type clones, best forgotten about. Then there'd been Ben Hinkley from the sixth form at Bromfield, whom my mother greatly approved of. But then she didn't have to suffer his wet kisses, or listen to him talk about his 'Fantasy War Game' strategies for hours on end.

Nikos reached out and brushed something from my cheek with his finger. What was it? Hopefully not a splodge of Mum's cottage pie, which she'd insisted I eat before going out.

'That's better,' Nikos said. 'Just an insect or something.'

'An insect!'

'Don't look so worried. It's the heat attracts them.'

I ran my hand through my hair feeling itchy suddenly. Trust me to get a squashed fly on my cheek. I mean it was hardly romantic.

But Nikos was smiling. 'Some blood-sucker thing probably. Can't really blame it for taking a fancy to you, when you're so tasty.'

I searched desperately for something interesting to say, to distract him. But all I came up with was, 'You know, I think Henry the Eighth used to go hunting round here. It was one of the royal forests. I expect it had deer then, and wild boar and . . .'

'Yeah? I'm a bit of a wild boar myself,' Nikos said.

Later I learned that neck-kissing was his speciality. He was an expert. It was like being lightly tickled with palm fronds until you thought you'd just die on the spot from sheer pleasure. When we finally got round to the full-scale snog, I felt like one of those headless dummies in the gallery-bar, as if my back-bone had turned to jelly and all the stuffing had gone out of me. If not for my mum's cottage pie earlier, I might even have fainted!

'All right?' Nikos said, drawing away from me at last.

'OK . . . fine.'

'We'd better get you back home then,' Nikos said, which kind of spoiled everything, and made me feel about six years old, not sixteen, 'otherwise your parents won't want you going out with me again.'

He turned the ignition key and the engine purred into life. Again? My heart soared as we drove back towards Northgate. There was going to be an 'again'.

'Next Wednesday then,' Nikos said at my front door. I nodded. It wasn't really a question. He took it for granted that I'd be waiting, just like Marina when she issued her commands. Be there or else. I supposed it must run in the family.

Going out with a sex god is all very well, but it's not

much fun unless you can brag about it, and watch your friends go green with envy. I wanted to shout it from the rooftops: 'I'm going out with a sex god. Yeah, *me*, Abigail Carter, with the blobby nose and the brace!'

But I couldn't, of course. What with Marina being so secretive, so private about her family and everything. I just knew she'd hate me going out with her precious cousin. I couldn't brag to Lauren either, because I knew for a fact that no sooner had I sworn her to secrecy, than she'd be on the phone to Marina like a shot.

How I longed to tell her though. 'Hey, by the way, Marina, I was out with your cousin last night.' *That* would stop her in her tracks, I thought, as she stalked a little bit ahead of me through the park. *That* would give her something to think about.

Marina's short legs snipped like scissors. The new ankle-strap sandals made a slow scraping sound on the tarmac path. How was it she managed to look so elegant, when she was at least five centimetres shorter than me? Her hips switched in the denim skirt, dark hair streaming down the perfectly arched dancer's back. The look in her eyes could have withered marigolds in their beds, sent ducks to the bottom of the lake. Marina was *not* in a good mood.

'I haven't got long,' she snapped over her shoulder. 'I only came to give you back the book, as it's overdue. I can't see what it's got to do with Henry, to be frank. Henry is hardly a poltergeist.'

Poltergeists — An examination of the phenomenon was the reason for me straggling along behind. The book weighed a ton in my bag.

'I thought you should read it though,' I called out behind her. 'I mean, the glass and the photograph, and the tin and everything. It could just be the beginning.'

Marina halted impatiently for me to catch up. 'I wish you'd stop trying to imply that Henry is evil. If he was evil, don't you think I'd be the first to know about it?'

'Well if he's such a saint, why isn't he in heaven, or Nirvana, or some higher spiritual plane? Why is he earthbound, Marina? Think about it.'

A woman trailing two whining toddlers gave us both a funny look. Probably thinking that if she'd been young and free again, she'd have better things to talk about.

Bromfield Park was only a short walk from the school gates. It had everything, the kiddies' playground, an old man's bowling green and a tiny old-fashioned museum with cased butterflies and a stuffed fox. At the far end of the park, a tarmac path veered past an aviary of chirruping budgies to a secret walled garden, where the dead of the First World War were commemorated.

We often came here to the Garden of Remembrance. It was the kind of place you could scheme in, tell secrets in. Confess. Now Marina and I wandered along the stone-columned arcade, beneath the lilac wisteria, the clambering roses like clots of dark blood about our heads.

'Marina, is something wrong? Has something happened again?'

I caught her up at the lily pond. The water glistened emerald in the sunlight. Goldfish slid about beneath the lily pads. Marina and I sat on our usual bench by the pool.

'There's nothing wrong. I told you, I haven't got much time.' She glanced at her watch. 'I've got to be at the shop at three. My mother's hurt her back; she can't lift, or stack shelves, so they really need me.'

'I suppose they do.'

'I don't mind. It's just frustrating, not having time for the Henry Game. He'll think we've deserted him.'

'Nah,' I tried to reassure her. 'Think of it this way, Henry's waited nearly five hundred years. A couple of weeks won't make any difference. Anyway, it'll do him good. About time he learned some patience.'

He could wait another couple of hundred years for all I cared, be cast out for ever into dark eternity. It was hard to understand why Marina wanted to carry on with the Game anyway, with her house slowly turning into a scene from *Poltergeist II*.

'You're going off the idea, aren't you?' When Marina was angry, her eyes grew twice as big. They were a different kind of brown to Nikos's eyes, I noticed. More milk than dark chocolate. I hated it when they got like that, all suspicious and accusing, as if she'd been betrayed, as if I was unworthy to be her friend. 'It was you who started it all, remember? *Let's have a seance*, you said. You were the one who set it in motion.'

'Yeah, "motion" being the right word. How did I know things would start walking and jumping all over the place? Look, I'm not backing out. We'll play the Game again, when you've got time. I'm up for it. Just say when you're ready.'

'Maybe you've found something more interesting to do?' Marina said slyly. She sounded so suspicious suddenly, my heart gave a jolt. She didn't *know*, did she?

I spent the next ten minutes convincing her of how boring life was while she worked at the shop.

'My mum keeps going on about me getting a job in Victor Values. Honestly. Have you seen their red overalls, and the caps? I'd rather die. And I'm completely skint, of course. Oh, I did go with Lauren to her Chinese Medicine Clinic the other day, and afterwards we went to see this incredibly boring French film, called *Les Enfants du . . . du . . . what's-it*". Anyway Lauren didn't enjoy it much, because she was feeling sick after this icky green stuff she had to drink. Mind you, she made a miraculous recovery when we bumped into Andrew Warrender in the foyer. You know, Andrew Warrender? In our year? Skinny. Looks like a prime swot. Anyway, he asked Lauren if she'd like to see this totally naff production of *Macbeth* next week which the Northgate Players are putting on, and she said she'd think about it!'

Marina was staring at me in a funny way, the way you look at someone when a wasp is crawling in their hair.

I patted my head automatically, 'What's up? Have I sprouted horns or something?'

'No, but you've dyed your hair.'

'Have I? I mean, I haven't. It must be the sun.' I ruffled my crop with my fingers. She was right, of course. My efforts to beautify myself for Nikos had gone a bit wrong. The bottle had promised sun-kissed highlights, but I'd left the stuff on too long.

'You look like a dandelion,' Marina said, never one to

mince her words. 'I hate to say this, but it doesn't match your eyebrows.'

Whenever Marina said, 'I hate to say this,' you knew she actually relished saying it. Marina loved pointing out other people's faults. She always did it as if it was for your own good, and she was doing you a favour. Funny, just lately I didn't even *like* Marina much. Yet she was still my best friend. And you had to make allowances. After all, if it had been *me* stuck behind the check-out all day I'd have been in a permanent strop too.

'Oh well, perhaps the sun'll bleach *them* too,' I said.

She began in a different tone, 'By the way, I saw Hannah from our English group the other day, when I was at the bus stop. She said she'd seen you in a car with some dark-haired guy . . .'

'Did she? Hah, I should be so lucky.'

'That's what I said. If Abbie'd found herself a boyfriend, I told her, don't worry, we'd all know about it.'

For the first time that afternoon she laughed, as if the idea of me whizzing about town in a fast car with a handsome stranger was frankly so ridiculous, she couldn't help herself. I could feel myself gripping the edge of the bench. How I'd love to tell her, wipe the conceited smile from her face! But all I said was, 'Funny. It must have been my double or something.'

'If I were you,' Marina said, as we began walking up the steps that led from the pool to the gates, 'if I were you, I'd tone my hair down a bit with some of that Ash-toner. You don't mind me telling you?'

'Actually it's cool to look like a tarty blonde these days.' I decided to stick up for myself for once. 'Who's that actress with the black roots? Can't think of her name now, but—' I stopped, catching my breath. 'Listen! What's that?'

Something, or someone, was moving, just out of the corner of my eye. We'd reached the entrance which led back out to the main park. To the right of the gates, which were elaborately scrolled, the pergola stretched invitingly into deep violet shadow.

'What?' Impatiently, Marina followed my glance.

It was hard to say *what*. Some faint discordant strumming, blown on the air. The mournful tune of the wind in telegraph wires. Except there *was* no wind. The air was so still, you could feel the weight of it, like water.

'That wisteria,' I said to Marina, pointing to the far end of the arcade. 'It's moving, look, as if someone just brushed against it.'

Marina was unimpressed. How could anyone else be in here, when we'd been talking for the past half hour and the gates hadn't clanked open once?

'Harlot,' Marina mused, fiddling now with the catch, and pushing the gates wide. 'You talking about tarty black roots reminds me, that's what Henry calls Anne when he's in a bad mood: *That cursed harlot.*'

'Does he?' I didn't want to hear any more about Henry. Couldn't we just get off the subject for once? Supposing he was here, now, with us? Lurking behind some bush in true dirty-old-man style, watching our every move. Yet, when I looked back at the garden, there was no one there. There was only the shimmer of water, the cool stone and swaying greenery, glimpsed through the black iron curlicues of the gate.

'By the way,' Marina went on, 'Henry wrote your name last night when I was doing the spirit messages. He wrote your full name – *Abigail*. He wrote it twice actually.'

We had reached the main gates of the park by now. Marina stood back, watching my face for a reaction. I tried not to let her see how this information frightened me. I mean why *last night*? I'd been out with Nikos last night.

'Why should he do that?' I said innocently.

'I'm not sure. Either he wanted to speak to you directly, or maybe, he wanted to tell me something about you.'

'About me? Like what for instance?'

'Well how should I know? Maybe he wanted to tell me you'd dyed your hair.' Marina tittered nastily. 'I mean there's not much else to tell, is there?'

I shrugged agreeably. 'No. Absolutely nothing to tell.'

'Well don't look so worried then. I'll call you when I get a chance.' She turned to cross the pedestrian crossing outside the gates. 'If I get anything in the messages tonight, I'll let you know.'

'Thanks.'

Waiting for my bus, which would probably take until 2010 to arrive, the poltergeist book in the bag on my back, like Quasimodo's hump, I found myself wishing Marina hadn't told me that, about Henry. It gave me a hunted feeling. What was Henry up to? What was he trying to tell her about me? Imagine if tonight, when Marina was up in her room scrawling her spirit messages, imagine if Henry came up with the name *Nikos*. And supposing the names were somehow coupled together . . . Abigail and Nikos? That would be enough to . . .

what? Send us both to the Tower? Or to Tyburn, our heads on spikes like kebabs, crows plucking our eyeballs out.

I shuddered all over. Maybe it was just that 'thing' in the garden that made me feel spooked. That mournful strumming sound, which I was sure had something to do with Henry.

I prayed silently, 'Stay out of my life, Henry. Get yourself reincarnated. Find your own girlfriend. *Noli me tangere*. Listen, Henry, get a life why don't you!'

Chapter Ten

According to *The Pleasure of Kings*, Anne Boleyn had kept Henry waiting not for weeks or months, but *years* before giving herself to him. Giving herself in body and soul, that is. How on earth had she managed it? I wished I knew her secret. Nikos was already impatient after only four dates. Now, whenever we pulled into what I'd come to think of as *our* lay-by, the smoochy clinches had given way to a kind of exercise in the martial arts. Nikos would make a move and I would counter it with some nifty hand-movements.

'You got to trust me, Abbie,' he would croon in my ear over and over. 'You're a very special girl, you know that? I'd never do anything to hurt you.'

Had Henry said something like this to Anne? I wondered.

'I will have no other mistress but you,' Henry had sworn to her in his letters. And maybe, nuzzling that swan-like neck of hers, he also gave her the line about, 'Trust me, for I am the King.'

Or something like that.

On those days, those long hot idle days, when Marina was working in the shop, when I wasn't actually seeing Nikos, I'd lie on my bed and try *not* to think about my exam results which were surely going to come plopping through the door any day now. I'd think about Anne instead. I'd lie there with cucumber slices on my eyelids, and Dead Sea Mineral Balm setting like concrete on my skin. I'd think about Anne making her own beauty preparations for Henry. She would lighten her swarthy complexion with saffron, she would slick her eyebrows into silky crescents. I would think of her permitting small 'liberties'. The glimpse of an ankle, an ear to be nibbled, and on very rare occasions when Henry had been especially good, a peck of the 'pretty duckies'.

When finally he got his own way, Henry must have been beside himself with gratitude. He lavished Anne with all the treasures of the kingdom: gold, servants, jewels. At her coronation, it was said she wore 'strings of pearls, bigger than chick peas, around her neck'. Did she know then, I wondered, when she bent her head to be crowned that soon, all too soon, she'd be bending it to the sword?

It was hard not to think over and over of Nikos, and Anne, and Henry, as if somehow they'd all become tangled up in my head, like a kind of horrific eternal triangle. The worst thing was, I couldn't talk to anyone about it. Lauren was away for a couple of days with her mum, and Marina seemed to be working every day now at the shop, often returning home late with her parents. A couple of times I called round to the house in Arcadia Avenue, hoping to catch her in.

'Marina, you there? It's only me!' I'd yell through the letterbox. I didn't like to ring the doorbell. The sound of it playing that silly tune in the empty house made my stomach turn. It was weird to think of the silent kitchen, the biscuit tin poised on the fridge, the glasses sparkling in their cabinet. How must Henry feel, abandoned like this? Was he still in there, strutting about the gloomy hallway? A cold presence, an indefinable smell, a draught that comes whipping out of nowhere.

Then there was one afternoon, when my heart almost stopped on the spot. I'd done my usual howling through the letterbox bit, when for some reason I decided to peer through the front-room window. The curtains were half-draped across as usual, to protect the furniture. Through the gap I could see the green sofas, with the cushions plumped up, and a glimpse of the reclining leather armchair that Marina said cost a bomb, and that her father always sat in. And there he was, sitting in it now. Or someone was.

At once I jerked out of sight, my back flattened against the knobbly pebble-dash, feeling like a criminal; a peeping tom, a burglar. Supposing he'd seen me? How would I explain my nose flattened against the window-pane? It only occurred to me then, Marina's dad at home in the daytime? Reclining? It was unheard of. He never had a day off, had to be persuaded not to work on Christmas Day, Marina said.

Well then, who? Somehow I braced myself for another peep. Yes, someone had been in the chair. It was swivelling from side to side, as if some heavy-weight occupant had only just eased himself out of it.

Stumbling down Arcadia Avenue, my heart thumping, I had the mad idea that it was Henry back there. Henry swivelling in Mr Paulos's recliner as if by royal right, his ermine-trimmed cap propped against the head-rest, picking his nails with his hunting-knife. Waiting for Marina to come home.

A furious, love-struck Henry.

'My lady, I am struck by the dart of love – your obedient servant, Henry Tudor.'

'Hope you've got a good appetite,' Nikos said, 'cos this place is a bit classy. They all come here don't they, celebs and that. Bit on the pricey side, but then,' he shrugged as if money was nothing to him, 'we're celebrating, right?'

My GCSE results, he meant. It was now late August. The holidays were nearly over, and I'd just heard a few days back that I'd got five passes. Nikos seemed to think this made me some kind of amazing genius. Flattering though this was, I felt I should put him straight.

'Actually, five passes isn't much to boast about,' I admitted as he pulled out a chair for me, with a kind of gentlemanly flourish. 'And the only "A" I got was for English. I mean, I could have done better if I'd worked harder. There are girls in my class who got eight. Nine, even.'

I was thinking of swotty Clementine Bradley who got straight 'A's, six of them starred. My one comfort was that Marina and I had drawn even, while Lauren beat both of us with six.

'Yeah, well, exams aren't everything,' was Nikos's response to this. 'I mean you can't be stuck with your head in a book all day long, can you? Anyway,' he rubbed his hands briskly together, as if he'd had enough of exam-talk, 'so what do you think of this place, eh?'

'Oh, it's nice. We could've gone somewhere local though, I wouldn't have minded.'

Somewhere Greek, I meant really, somewhere his friends and family might hang out to eat dolmades and play dominoes. Somewhere dark and intimate where we could huddle together in the candlelight and tell each other our deepest, most personal secrets.

This restaurant, Swanks, was one of those scarily modern places, with great expanses of metal and flying saucer lights, the kind that illuminate pimples and other deformities in day-glo colour. Like the spot just below my nose, which was throbbing like a volcano. Something I put down to exam-result stress. Among other things.

Nikos looked a bit offended. 'I thought you'd like this place. They do all this arty stuff, you know, everything piled on top of the other. You have whatever you fancy because . . .'

'Because I'm worth it,' I tittered, then wished I hadn't. One thing I'd noticed – Nikos didn't seem too keen on my jokes. OK, my jokes weren't hilarious exactly, but they weren't that bad. Maybe he thought that being funny wasn't, like, feminine or something. That was the other old-fashioned thing about Nikos I'd discovered. He was always on about how he *liked a woman to be like a woman*. I'd never been quite sure about that one. I mean, how could a woman be otherwise? It was all so confusing sometimes.

Nikos studied the menu. 'Of course you're worth it, clever girl like you with qualifications and that. That goes without saying. I mean that we took a good order last week, at the factory. So I'm feeling a bit flush. Why not take Abbie out somewhere special, I said to myself, celebrate her success? By the way, the Thai chicken and cous-cous is good. I had that last time I came here.'

'OK, I'll have that,' I said feebly, mainly because I didn't recognize anything else on the menu.

'I suppose you eat Greek food at home mostly,' I said, half an hour later, as the waitress brought my chicken and Nikos's pie, the pastry perched on top of the meat like a jaunty tombstone.

Nikos shrugged. 'Me, I eat anything. I'm not fussy, know what I mean?'

'But what about moussaka and that?'

'Yeah, it's all right.'

I sighed. It was hopeless trying to get Nikos to talk about his life, his family, any of that stuff. What he talked about mostly was films, telly, celebs and how much money they made. He talked a lot about money, and all the stuff he was going to have when he made his first million. Not that there's anything wrong with having ambition. But what did I really know about *him*? I wondered.

All I knew was this: He was twenty-one, he ran a small fashion business and helped with deliveries to the Mini-mart, oh yes, and he had the kind of dark smouldering looks to turn heads, churn stomachs, and weaken the knees of any female within ogling distance. And he was Marina's cousin of course. Still it wasn't enough.

'Nikos?'

'Hmmm . . . ? What d'you want for afters then? Pavlova, I bet. They do a great pavlova. All girls like pavlova, don't they?'

'Nikos, what date is your birthday?'

'What do you want to know for? Gonna buy me a present, are you?'

'I might.'

142

He smiled craftily. 'I don't know if I can wait till my birthday. April . . . that's a bit of a long wait.' He turned to call over the waitress.

In profile, his nose was hawkish. I remembered Marina telling me how a lot of Greeks had Roman blood. Oh yes, I could see it in Nikos suddenly, the cruel nobility of the centurion. Here he was, the blood of a conqueror surging in his veins, and nothing to conquer. Except . . . well, me, perhaps.

Our puddings arrived, a whole mountain range of meringue, enough cream to cause a spontaneous eruption of my pimple. Damn. I could even feel it throbbing in anticipation.

'April,' I said, really casual like, chinking my spoon through the meringue. 'What day in April would that be?'

'The ninth.' Nikos grinned at me. 'Put a ring round it on your calendar. As for the present, no need to wrap it up, eh? Look at you. Messy girl. You've got cream all round your mouth. I'll just have to lick it off, won't I?'

With that, he leaned across the table and very lightly flicked his tongue around my lips, which was just about the most romantic thing ever. One look into those chocolatey eyes, and I got that weird sensation in the pit of my stomach again, like leaves unfurling in a speeded up nature film. I totally forgot for a moment what sign the ninth of April actually was. Taurus? Pisces? My mind did a quick whirl of the zodiac before I worked it out.

'Oh, you must be an Aries then?'

'Aries . . . yeah . . .' He was pulling out his wallet now. I noticed he only had to nod at the pretty young waitress for her to come scurrying with the bill, fast as her kitten heels would carry her. 'If you say so,' Nikos said. 'Aries the Ram. Not that I believe in any of that rubbish.'

As soon as I got home that night, I scribbled Nikos's name in my birthday book, under *ARIES the Ram*. Aries, the me-first sign of the zodiac.

'Well?' My mother stuck her head round my bedroom door.

'Mother! Can't you knock? Aren't I entitled to any privacy in this house?'

Really it was too much. She was always waiting up for me, while my dad snored, ready for his early ambulance-shift. I thought I'd got away with it tonight, creeping past the kitchen while she rinsed out her cocoa mug. But no such luck. Here she was in her Marks & Sparks dressing-gown and furry mules, her library book tucked under her arm, ready for bed.

'Well, where did Jack-the-lad take you tonight then? I must say, he looks much too old for you, Abbie. I'm surprised you can't find a nice boy at school to go out with.'

'I don't want a "nice boy from school", thank you, Mother, and another thing, where do you get those antique expressions from, like Jack-the-lad? I mean, what is that supposed to mean exactly? No, on second thoughts, don't tell me. And now I'd like to sleep if you don't mind.'

'Well, if you don't want your message, that's fine with me,' she said, all sniffy. I knew how she longed to sit on my bed for a heart-to-heart, but I wouldn't give her the chance. If only Izzie Alexander were my mother, she'd toss me a packet of condoms and invite Nikos home for a belly-dancing demonstration.

'What message, anyway? Did Marina call?'

'No, she didn't.' Mum tied her dressing-gown belt tighter, as if girding her loins for an argument. 'It was a man actually.'

'A man?'

'He didn't give his name, just wanted to speak to Abigail.'

'Abi . . . gail?' I pulled the duvet up to my chin. Oh God, 'Abigail'. There was only one person (apart from that creep Stefan and Mr Purviss at school), who called me 'Abigail'.

'Or should I say, *old* man,' my mother said. 'I thought maybe you'd gone after a holiday job, and it was the manager at Victor Values, but I knew it couldn't be him, because he doesn't speak like he's got a plum in his mouth. "Are you from my daughter's school?" I asked him. "Are you one of her teachers? Because if you'd like to leave a message," I said . . .'

'Oh Mum, you should've just put the phone down. It must be some pervert or something, I don't know any old men with plums in their mouths.'

'So you say. *Mistress*, he called you, *Mistress Abigail*. Now Abbie, I want a straight answer, do you know this person?'

'I er . . . I think I might,' I said, trying frantically to think up a story, before my mother called the police. 'It's not a person exactly. It's people. Kids I mean. Some of the boys in my class, there's this little gang of them with this, like, totally juvenile sense of humour, and they ring the girls up, you know, and pretend to be dirty old men. For a joke. Hah!'

145

'I don't know.' My mother was not amused. 'That's not the sort of thing you'd expect from Bromfield boys, surely?'

'Hah, you'd be surprised, Mother.' I shook my head darkly. 'They are totally pathetic! Well, now you see why I don't go out with any of them.'

'Hmmm . . . you'd think they'd have better things to do.' Mum didn't look very convinced as she turned to go.

'Mum?' I called her back.

'Yes?'

'He didn't say anything else, did he? The boy who was mucking about, I mean.'

He didn't get a chance, my mother said. 'I put your dad straight on, and that seemed to scare him off.'

It seemed unlikely. My dear old dad wouldn't have scared a fly, let alone the ghost of a Tudor king.

'Stay out of my life, Henry,' I whispered into the shadows.

The thing to do was not to let him spook me. To think of other things. Nikos for example. Only Nikos, it seemed could banish the vision of a fat jewel-encrusted king, wheezing into the telephone.

The Arian lover will sweep you off your feet – my book said – *And when you touch the ground again, you may feel a little dizzy.*

Too right, I felt dizzy. I ran my finger over his name in my birthday book, then I placed it beneath my pillow. It was kind of comforting somehow.

Chapter Eleven

Now that Marina was never at home, we had to make do with meeting at Lauren's house. Or rather her bedroom. The rest of the house had been taken over by the kind of music that charms snakes from a basket, and enough belly-dancers to fill the harem of the richest sheikh in Arabia.

'They're supposed to be practising,' Lauren grumbled. 'She's got absolutely no consideration for my project-work on the Virgin Queen.'

'Did you tell her that?' I asked her in my best sympathetic voice. I was in a 'be-kind-to-Lauren' mood today. After all, I could afford to be extra-nice, having a boyfriend as handsome as Nikos, when poor Lauren's only admirer was swotty old Andrew Warrender.

'Of course I told her. D'you know what she said? Life is short.'

'Life is short?'

'No, to be precise, she said, "Well, Lauren, sweetie, life is short." Then she said I could try cotton wool in my ears.'

'Seems a bit harsh,' I murmured. It was difficult not to smile though, with Lauren looking so outraged.

'Yeah, well, she's annoyed with me, because of this.'

She hunkered down on the floor to roll up her rug. Lauren was lucky in some respects. She had this huge attic bedroom, all clean and light, Scandinavian style. Lauren didn't go for clutter, because of being allergic to the house-dust mite (which is a bit like a head-louse under the microscope, only uglier, Lauren says). So instead of some smelly old carpet like my own, she has this really cool stripped beech flooring, and dhurries scattered about.

Or at least, she *used* to have stripped flooring. I stared at the design she'd painted on the boards, in bright blue and orange.

'What's that? Lauren, what have you done?'

'It's a five-pointed star of course, a pentagram. What does it look like? I copied it out of a book. It's for protection,' she explained. 'Against the spirits.'

'Oh yeah, but, not that I want to scare you or anything, but wouldn't you have to be, like, a really *feeble* spirit to be scared of some old star-shape?'

'Well don't ask me how it works, it just does. You have to sit inside it, like this . . .' Lauren demonstrated, clumsily squatting in the denim ankle-length skirt with its giant front pocket (handy for her inhaler). She took up her position, ankles crossed, arms folded over her chest.

I tried to look impressed. 'I suppose it might work, if you had a crucifix as well.' I fingered my own, remembering how it had lain so recently in Nikos's palm. 'You know, the crucifix, the Bible, the strings of garlic. I reckon you'd need the lot to keep Henry out.'

Lauren frowned. 'Trouble is, my mum's being totally unreasonable about it. She started going on about how I'd have to scrub it off with white spirit and wire wool because I'd totally ruined the floorboards. It's weird, she's not usually so uptight about things like that.'

'But why did you paint it? You haven't had any more phone calls, have you? You know, from a *certain person*?'

'No. But ever since the thing with my clock, well sometimes I just get this feeling.' She glanced over her shoulder. 'Like somebody's in here with me sometimes. Just breathing. Maybe you should have a pentagram in *your* room, Abbie?'

'Yeah, I wish. But I'd have to roll the carpet up, wouldn't I? And since the bed takes up most of the room, I'll just have to manage without one. Anyway, a pentagram wouldn't stop him making those phone calls, would it?'

I told her about the latest call. It pained me to leave out the bit about being out with Nikos at the time, but no way could I trust her not to tell Marina.

'My mum was all for calling the police,' I said. 'What really got her was the "mistress" bit. Asking for Mistress Abigail.'

Lauren shuddered. 'Well he hasn't rung here again, thank God. Not that he'd get a chance, the way my mum hangs on the phone to Harv-wit all the time. It's a wonder Andrew ever managed to get through. He rang to ask me again about, you know, going to see *Macbeth*.'

'Oh yeah? How thrilling. Out damned spot! That's about all I remember from Year nine Shakespeare.' Automatically, I checked out the pimple under my nose. Still there. Must be the super-long-life variety.

Lauren said smugly, 'Actually, Andy's really, like, *cultured* and *interesting* when you get to know him. I might just go with him. And there's no need to make that face, Abbie, just because I'm not into the muscle-bound moron sort you like.'

Muscle-bound moron, she said. Cheek! Nikos wasn't a muscle-bound moron. And anyway, Lauren didn't even know about Nikos. It was a bit of a waste really. If only they could have seen me now, Nick's arm around my waist, as he steered me through a hallway hung with those cosmic explosion pictures I'd seen in The Gallery.

'You wouldn't believe it, would you?' Nikos said. 'Bloke who painted them must be worth a fortune. Wouldn't give them house-room myself. Looks like a four-year-old kid did them, you ask me.'

Earlier, pulling up the gravel drive, I thought for a moment he was bringing me to meet his family. But the house in Cockfosters was empty. Apparently it belonged to the bar-owner Stefan, who was away for a few days. Stefan had left the front-door key with Nikos, to check on the cat.

'You come all this way, to feed the cat?' I said in amazement, for Nikos didn't strike me as a cat-lover exactly. I was touched. Sometimes blokes are a bit embarrassed about showing their sensitive side. But here was Nikos crooning in this really sweet (and quite sexy) way: 'Pusspussspuss . . . here, Athena . . . here, baby . . . come and see your uncle Nick.'

The Siamese came slinking from the kitchen, a bell jingling at its neck.

'Here's the little pussy, here's Athena. Little beauty, eh?'

The cat waved its tail in his face, arching its back as

150

he bent to stroke it. For a moment I was almost jealous, watching Nikos caress the cat, with those long heavy sensuous strokes. Then, quite suddenly, and for no apparent reason, Athena lashed out with a crafty left-hook.

'Argh! Little . . . devil!' He reeled back, clutching a hand to his cheekbone.

'Are you all right? Looks like it's drawn blood.'

'S'all right . . . just a nick, that's all.' Nikos shrugged off the wound, as the cat fled yowling to the door. 'Never mind that thing, what d'you think of the place then? Done well for himself, Stefan has.'

Nikos was strutting about, examining ornaments, patting the snowy sofas as if he owned the place himself. 'Real leather, that is, none of your plastic garbage. Stefan knows how to put things together, yeah. You got to hand it to the man, he's a bit of a poser, but he's got style.'

'It's nice.' I tried to look impressed. Actually it looked to me like a showroom from World of Leather, all smoky glass-topped tables, and floor-to-ceiling mirrors. My reflection caught my eye at every turn, as if it was trying to tell me something. The girl hovering awkwardly in the slip-dress, one strap sliding over her shoulder, looked kind of dazed and lost.

Why Stefan's house? That was what I was thinking. Why not Nikos's own place, or rather the room in his parents' house, where I could listen to his CDs, browse through his bookshelves, nibble his mum's sweet pastries and stuff in the kitchen? That would have been much cosier.

Nikos crept up behind me, lacing his fingers about

151

my waist. 'Penny for them. You're thinking again, aren't you? You should give that up, you know. It's bad for you. Gorgeous girl like you, you'll get wrinkles.'

'Aren't you going to feed her then?' I asked him.

'Who?'

'The cat of course.'

'After what she just done to me? You kidding? Nah, she can wait a bit, can't she? Not going to starve to death in the next ten minutes, is she?'

'Suppose not.'

It was funny watching our reflections, framed in the mirror, as if we were two other people, and not ourselves. Nikos's dark head nuzzled in that hollow just above my collar-bone. It felt all tingly and shivery. His body pressed closer. I closed my eyes for just a second.

Afterwards I wished I'd kept them closed. Because when I opened them again, the strangest thing happened. There was Nikos's head still rummaging about my neck like some furry black creature, and *there* was someone else, another reflection shimmering in the background. My brain scrambled to make sense of this. It was Stefan perhaps? Stefan letting himself in quietly, creeping up on us.

I blinked hard. The way you do if you get spots before your eyes. Maybe it would just go away again? But no, there it still was, or rather *he* was. For now I could see him, plain as day. Henry VIII, standing in that famous pose of his, legs astride and chest thrown out, as if to say: *Well? Aren't I a fine fellow?*

No! I closed my eyes again. It couldn't be. How dare he? How dare Henry come here, to Stefan's house of all places? How dare he come between me and Nikos?

Please please go away, I prayed to whoever might listen. My greatest fear suddenly was that Nikos would see him. And then what?

I must have gasped aloud, because Nikos, mis-interpreting the sound, drew me closer.

'Mmmmm . . . you smell nice,' he murmured.

'Do I? I mean, thanks.' I wriggled. I couldn't stand it any longer, the shimmer of jewelled doublet, the flash of that knife, Henry cuckolded.

What have we here, Mistress? Out with this foul churl before I have his head on a spike!

Did he speak? Did Henry actually speak aloud? I was going mad, surely? Somehow I'd twisted round in Nikos's arms to face him, his chin resting on my head.

'Right little fidget, aren't you?' Nikos said.

'Sorry . . . I . . . I thought I heard something.'

I forced myself to look over his shoulder. And, oh blessed relief! An empty room. Only Athena, poised, growling, hackles raised by the door.

'Listen to that thing,' Nikos laughed. 'Thinks it's a bloody panther or something.'

Nikos hadn't seen anything. Was it just a trick of the mirror then? I had to tell myself that, or I'd shortly be taking the tablets. Pressure of exams, they'd say. Growing pains. Over-active imagination.

As Nikos settled his hands on my hips again, I grabbed one of them. It didn't seem right with Henry looking over my shoulder. Perhaps if I distracted him a bit?

'Can I see your hand?'

'What? Oh, the cat you mean. It got my face, not my hand. Don't you worry. I'll get my own back later.'

'No, I mean your palm.'

'My palm?'

'I read palms. It's kind of a hobby. I do it for all my friends.'

'Tell my fortune you mean?' He looked surprised, as if I'd thrown him off track. Then he ruffled my hair and said he'd get us a drink first, and then we could make ourselves comfortable. 'Then you can tell me if I'm ever gonna be rich, like my mate Stefan, OK?'

He went over to the bar in the corner, all lit up like a gaudy shrine.

'I think I'll have coffee if you don't mind,' I said.

The last thing I wanted was alcohol, when I was already quite woozy enough, seeing things that weren't, that couldn't be there.

'Sure? Coffee it is then. Don't go away.'

From the kitchen, Nikos sang as he rattled the cups: '*Whe . . . en . . . a ma . . . an loves a woo . . . man, can't think of nothing else . . .*'

Left alone, I checked in the mirror again. No sign of His Royal Highness, thank God. I sat on the edge of the couch. This was difficult. It was too low for perching upright on, a couch to sprawl on, all languid and gorgeous while your lover fed you peeled grapes, and fanned you with coconut palms. I had the certain feeling that if I ever lay down on this couch, then all would be lost.

'Guess what I found.' Nikos bustled back with a tray: thick black china cups, and a plate of Danish pastries, stuck with sultanas and oozing syrup.

'That Stefan,' he licked his fingers, 'he eats too much anyway. He won't miss them.'

Stefan must be a good friend, what with Nikos helping himself to the food and rummaging now among the stack of CDs.

' "Whe . . . en . . . a ma . . . an loves a woo . . . man." This is a good one, yeah? You'll like this.'

It was one of those compilations. *Music to Seduce Virgins By.* Barry White's 'Lu . . . urve Machine'. Oh dear.

The sofa sank lower beneath Nikos's weight, his thigh pressed against mine. 'I give you my hand!' Brushing pastry crumbs from his hands, he asked, 'Any one in particular? You will tell me good things, won't you?'

'Your right one is best,' I told him. 'That's where your personality is stamped. Your left one is the future.'

'In that case you get the left hand.' He laid it palm upwards upon my lap. 'I'm not interested in my personality. I know what I'm like. I live with myself; right. It's the future I'm interested in, the near future. Like tonight for instance.'

With his hand, warm, captive in my own, I felt tongue-tied again. The lines were strong and clear as if they'd been scored by a knife. It was the hand of a man who knew what he wanted, and usually got it. It was the hand of an Arian all right.

'Well . . .' I cleared my throat. 'You've got a strong Mount of Jupiter.'

'Sounds good. What's that mean then?'

'Usually it indicates financial success.'

'Yeah! Like it!' punching the air with his right fist, as if already bank notes were raining down from the sky.

155

'And you should live a long and healthy life.' I was trying to pitch my voice low and meaningful and witchy like Mystic Meg. Trying to impress him.

'That right? Well I'll need to, won't I, to enjoy all that money I'm going to make?' He gave me a sideways look. 'But what about love though? Makes the world go round, love does.' With his free right hand, he pulled me closer.

'You've got quite a short heart–line actually,' I said. It was hard to stay sitting upright the way he was pulling me.

'Is that bad? Give it to me straight.' He pretended to look brave. 'No need to spare me, I can take it.'

His tongue flicked in my ear. I jerked away slightly. 'Nikos, you're not taking this seriously, are you?'

'Of course I am. I'm deadly serious.'

Hmmmm. In fact, a short heart–line was a bad sign. Bad for me at least. It meant he was only interested in the chase. What was that Henry said? A foul churl! A rogue! Well what did Henry know? He was just jealous, that was all. And anyway, even the lines on the hand couldn't tell you the whole truth about someone. Nikos for instance, the sweet, sensitive loving side that lay beneath that blokey act of his.

'It's like an art, you know,' I told him. 'A lot of, like, really important people, film stars and presidents and oh . . . all sorts have their palms read.'

'I'm not saying they don't. I'm not taking the piss. Would I take the piss out of you, Abbie, when I respect your intelligence and everything? As if I would. It's just that all this future business is a bit irrelevant, know what I mean?'

'I hardly think the future's irrelevant,' I said, realizing at once how snotty that sounded. Actually I was thinking of our future together, tip-toeing through the buttercup meadow hand in hand, into the sunset.

Nikos just shrugged. 'We might all be dead next week though. We might all go up in smoke. Some dirty great big meteorite, right, whizzing out of nowhere. Bang! There goes the earth, and you and me with it. We should live in the present, that's my philosophy.'

I looked down at my lap. Nikos was stroking my thigh, the way he had stroked Athena a while ago. Suddenly I knew what he meant by 'living in the present'. A strange purposeful look had come over his face. A sort of 'Let's get down to it' look, an 'I mean business' sort of look. And we hadn't even talked properly yet, we hadn't even got beyond his Mount of Jupiter!

I could have just pushed him off of course, and bolted for the door. But that was too final. Perhaps, even flat on my back, I might strike up a conversation? But what? Before I could think of a subject, the word was out of my mouth, almost as if someone else put it there.

'Marina!' I blurted out.

It was as if Marina's name possessed some magical power. It worked like a charm. Nikos raised himself on one elbow and stared at me.

'Marina says that . . .' Well, what did Marina say? I stared. The couch was so low, he'd rolled right off it onto the creamy shag-pile.

'What are you talking about? Marina? She's not

157

here, is she? I thought she'd walked in the bloody door.'

Somehow or other his shirt had come out of his trousers. I felt almost sorry for him kneeling there, madly tucking it in, the look of a hunted animal on his face.

'I just wanted to ask you something about her,' I said feebly. 'It just came to me suddenly.'

'What about her?'

'Do you ever take her to the cinema or anything? Only she told me she sometimes goes with her cousins, at weekends.'

'No. As it happens, I don't. What is all this anyway?' He looked ruffled, confused. 'You and Marina . . . you've been talking about me?'

'Not about you. Only cousins generally.'

He stood up with a groan, as if his back hurt. 'You do pick your moments, don't you. You nearly gave me bloody heart failure, shouting like that.'

'Sorry.'

'Yeah, well, it's OK . . . one of those things.' He was looking in the mirror, smoothing the ram's curls with an offended, searching look. His tone was different. Cold. Nikos had got the hump.

'Ready?' He hardly looked at me as he said it, just twirled his car keys on the end of one finger, as if he couldn't wait to get rid of me. My heart felt weird suddenly. As if it had just shrivelled up, withered inside me like a sun-dried tomato. I'd blown it, hadn't I? I'd blown our future together, in some stupid panic.

We drove home in silence. Without the smile, and the

laugh-a-minute banter, Nikos's profile was cruel.

'About tonight,' I began. 'It's not that I don't want to, it's just that . . .'

'No problem,' he said, cutting me short. 'I don't have to force girls to do anything they don't want. They do it because they want to. Know what I mean? I don't need the aggravation. And anyway, we were only having a cuddle, weren't we? That was all. No harm in a cuddle.'

In Smedhurst Road, he parked some way away from my house, at the top of the road. He turned to face me: 'What you got to understand, Abbie, is I'm not one of your schoolboys, right? I'm not interested in a bit of a fumble. Either you want to go out with me or you don't.'

'Oh I do!' I almost cried. 'I do want to.'

The chocolate eyes melted just a little, then hardened over again. He reached in the glove compartment and handed me a card. A card! He wasn't even going to kiss me goodnight.

The card said – NIKOS ANDREAS FASHIONS – in gold lettering, with two telephone numbers beneath.

'That's my mobile,' Nikos said, pointing, 'You can always leave a message, you know, when you make up your mind.'

For a moment, maybe a couple of seconds, I sat there, the card in my hand, feeling stupid. What a fool I'd been. Had I really imagined that this was love? That Marina's cousin gave a toss about me as a person: my family, my ambitions, my fortune-telling abilities? There were tears in my eyes. I wasn't going to cry though. Not now. Not in front of him. I stuck the card on the dashboard.

'Keep your card. I've made up my mind already. Oh and by the way, that short heart-line on your palm, it is a bad sign actually. Really bad. You probably ought to give up smoking and watch your cholesterol.'

There! That would give him something to worry about. I was out of the car before he could say anything, and then I was running and sobbing, both at the same time, all the way to my own doorstep.

Chapter Twelve

It was almost too much, that week after Nikos dumped me. I could barely stand the sight of my parents. Their cosy evenings together, Mum doing her cross-stitch, while Dad tried to answer the questions on his favourite quiz shows.

'Come and sit down with us, love,' Mum would call from the sitting room. 'There's a nice costume drama on. Jane Austen. You did her for your exams, didn't you? And I was just going to make a cup of tea.'

'Don't want tea. I hate costume dramas anyway,' I'd shriek from my bedroom. The woman had no idea, of course, that I was dying from a broken heart. That I was far too busy studying the lines on my palm to watch a lot of simpering females in poke-bonnets and nightgowns waltzing with Mr Right. My palm gave me no reason for hope either. All those whiskery lines leading nowhere, the all-important heart-line, sagging towards the head.

Disappointment in Love, Cheiro said.

As if I needed telling!

Perhaps it was just as well that only a few days later we were back at school again. As the three of us walked to Marina's house, you could smell autumn in the air. When I was little I used to love the autumn, which seemed to smell of new shoes, and books with crinkly new pages, smoky and pine-scented. Now the air carried something else with it, something over-ripe and putrid. The smell of old fur coats, of something festering.

'Slow down, you two. Please!' Lauren lagged behind, hobbling like a ninety-year-old, groaning at every step. Apparently, hard though this was to believe, she'd dressed up in her mum's belly-dancing gear one afternoon when Izzie was out, tripped over her flowing veils and wrenched her ankle.

'Honestly, Lauren, you're such a hypochondriac sometimes.' Marina wasn't waiting for anyone. Now that term had started, she was in a hurry to get back to the Henry Game.

I hung back, waiting for Lauren to catch up. The look of agony on her face would have been hilarious if only I hadn't been feeling so miserable myself. Still, I couldn't help just a twitch of a smile.

'Sorry, Lauren, but I just can't imagine you belly-dancing. Be honest, it's just not *you*, is it? How did you manage to trip anyway? It's supposed to be all relaxed and sinuous, not like doing the Irish jig.'

'I told you why. Harv-wit was creeping around spying on me. I tripped over as I ran to slam the door in his face. I just knew he was some kind of pervert the moment I saw him, with those horrible little glasses and that phoney smile. But will my mother believe me?'

'I don't know. Will she?'

'Will she hell! Serve me right, she said, for nicking her stupid outfit without asking.'

162

'So Harvey, he was actually in your room?'

'No. Well I didn't see him exactly. There was just all this creeping and rustling on the landing. I heard it when the music went quiet suddenly, and then my door just clicked open.' She glared at me. 'Well it couldn't click open by itself. Although Harv–wit swears he was downstairs the whole time, fixing a curtain-rail or something for Mum. I mean. A likely story!'

'You didn't see anything, I mean anyone else?'

'Yes, Father Christmas, who d'you think?'

I decided not to say any more. The thing was, I had a pretty good idea who it was lurking outside her door. But how could I tell them what I'd seen in the mirror the other night? They'd think I was a complete screwball.

Maybe I was getting paranoid, for the moment Marina pushed upon her front door, I heard someone cough. A man's cough. Wheezy, bronchial, like you hear in a hospital ward.

'Your dad isn't home, is he?'

'He's at the shop, of course.' She bent to pick up a thick wad of circulars from the mat. 'He always is at the shop at this time of day.'

'Oh, yes, I'd forgotten. I thought I heard something.'

Marina gave me an odd look. Again I decided not to say anything. Marina had enough problems. Since I'd last seen her, a spectacular great mole had appeared on her left cheek, the size of a chocolate drop. When we were brushing our hair in the cloakroom at lunchtime, Lauren tried to kid her it looked like a beauty spot. But I could tell Marina was embarrassed

163

because she kept smoothing her hair forward to hide it.

Still, it would take more than a mole to shake her confidence. She still wore that secretive, superior look as she moved about the kitchen, making our pre-Game coffee, opening a pack of chocolate digestives.

'Abbie, are we playing this game or not?' Marina wanted to know. She and Lauren were going through the usual rituals: the tin, the candles, the incense. For the music, Lauren had decided on Mozart's Requiem, which, she informed us, he had composed upon his death bed. The combination of the music and the blind rattling down made me shiver.

I took a good slurp of the coffee Marina shoved in my hand, and said I would finish drinking it first, if no one had any objection?

Lauren raised her eyebrows; 'What's up with you? You're in a right mood today.'

'Look who's talking.'

'Well I have got an excuse. I'm in agony, in case you haven't noticed.'

'I'm not feeling that great myself,' I said. 'My period's coming on.' I felt a bit uncomfortable as their eyes fixed on me, but what could I say? I couldn't tell them I'd just been dumped by a sex god, that my pillow was soggy with tears, and my heart actually hurt so much, I thought I might be getting angina, like Mrs Croop downstairs. It would have been such a relief to confide in my friends. It might make me feel better. On the other hand, if Marina found out about Nikos, she'd never speak to me again.

'So you've got your period. It's hardly a tragedy, is

it?' Lauren went griping on. 'You should think yourself lucky, when here I am, practically a cripple. And then there's poor Marina, and her wart thing . . .'

Uh oh. Wrong thing to say. Marina didn't take this reference to her blemish kindly. '*It is not a wart*. And anyway, the doctor says they can laser it off if I want. But I quite like it actually. A mark is a sign of distinction.'

We were by now all sitting down at the table. It was four-thirty, still light. In a month or two it would be dark at this time, and we wouldn't need the blind down.

'Like a witch's mark,' I said. 'Like Anne Boleyn. She had a lot of moles, didn't she? I think she had one really big one on her face, just like that. They thought it was a sign of the devil, you know, like the extra little finger on her left hand.'

Marina sighed. She tapped her fingers impatiently on the glass, her nails making a chinking sound. 'I can't think why the subject of my mole should be so fascinating to everyone. Are we going to sit here all night or . . . or . . .' She broke off.

The glass was moving. With or without our fingers, the glass was moving by *itself*. I steeled myself for another smash. But all it did was skate gracefully towards the letter 'L'.

'Henry,' Marina whispered. 'Henry's moving the glass without us.'

'Yeah,' I said, sounding a lot cooler than I felt, because it frightened me, the way Henry seemed to be taking control of things. 'Patience never was one of his virtues.'

'Shhh . . . listen!' Lauren waved her hands at us both. 'The music, what's happened to the music?'

We sat for a moment in silence. We tried to make sense of it. What *had* happened to the music? Mozart's Requiem had given way to a high, wavery, horrible voice. A man's voice. A man trying vainly to hit the top notes. A man trying to sing like a woman. The words floated through to us from the other room:

> 'Yo . . .uth must ha . . . ve some dalli . . . ance
> of good or ill some pas . . . tance . . .'

'*Oh my God*. Marina, it's . . .' But that was as far as Lauren got.

'I *know* who it is.' Marina spoke as if through gritted teeth. 'Of course I know. It's one of Henry's very own compositions. He's singing it to *us*.'

It was incredible. Marina wasn't a bit scared. I noticed her eyes had this weird shine to them as the ghostly crooning continued:

> '*Co . . . mpany methinks then best*
> *All thoughts and fancies to digest . . .*'

The tension was almost unbearable. I had to do something, say something to break it. 'I don't think much of the lyrics, do you?' I whispered to Lauren. 'Henry must have been having an off-day when he wrote this one, I reckon.'

Lauren managed a nervy smile; 'It does rhyme though . . . best . . . digest . . .'

Encouraged, the warbler continued:

> *'For idleness is chief mistress*
> *Of vices all.'*

The 'vices all' bit was so high and shrieky I had difficulty keeping a straight face.

'Vocals are a bit rough,' I said. 'D'you reckon his pants are too tight, or something.'

Lauren didn't usually fall about laughing at my jokes. This time though she couldn't stop. It began with a kind of snort, then her whole body shook like she was plugged into the National Grid. 'I was just thinking . . . oh it hurts . . . imagine Henry joining a boy band! Or auditioning for that crap TV contest *Pop Idol*. Oh, Abbie, don't say anything else, please don't, my stomach hurts!'

Although I hadn't said anything else, I didn't need to. The music had stopped. That creepy voice gave way to silence. An offended sort of silence. I could even imagine Henry throwing down his lute or whatever in disgust. 'Hah, so you don't like my singing!'

'Now look what you've done!' Marina flushed with anger. 'You've upset him now. You've insulted him with your stupid childish behaviour.'

She began wittering on about the song, and what a great talent Henry had and so on.

'We are humbly grateful, Sire,' Marina said, 'that you should honour us with such a rare performance.'

This outrageous bit of flattery must have done the trick because the glass was on the move again.

LADIES SO GLAD YOU ARE COME TO COURT.

Henry had forgiven us, more was the pity. Thoroughly sobered by Marina's ticking-off, Lauren's eyes met mine. They had a pleading look. A 'we've got to get out of

167

here' look. I tried to smile, to reassure her. If we broke the circle now Marina would never forgive us. Just a few more minutes, I told Lauren silently, managing to squeeze her free arm beneath the table.

'Marina,' I said. 'Maybe you should just ask if he's got a message for us. I mean, time's getting on and that.'

'So what's your hurry?' Marina snapped, as our fingers slid back onto the glass. 'Have you got a hot date or something?'

Ouch! This was like a slap in the face. The empty pointlessness of life without Nikos, striking me afresh. I was almost grateful for the distraction of the glass, as it spelled out the words:

GREETINGS MISTRESS LAUREN.

'Oh, not *me* again,' Lauren protested almost tearfully. 'It's just so unfair. I'm not burning any more of my stuff, if that's what he wants. My mother was only asking about the clock the other day.'

But this time, instead of skidding straight towards the letters, the glass moved confusingly in a kind of Celtic knot-pattern, up and down, right and left.

'What's it doing now?' Lauren said, with a distrustful look.

'I don't know.' I tried a feeble joke. 'It looks a bit like . . . like line-dancing to me.'

But before Marina could tell me off, the glass swept our fingers to the letter 'D'.

DANCE, said Henry, pleased, it seemed, as if I'd guessed the answer to a riddle.

'Dance?' Lauren practically snapped at the glass. 'Is that all? Dance?'

'He's dancing, don't you see?' Marina said. 'Henry was

168

a great dancer when he was young. That's probably a galliard he's doing.'

'So,' I said, 'Henry was a bit of a mover. He's not expecting us to get on down and boogie with him, is he? Too bad if he is, because we never learned the galliard thingy, did we, Lauren? Lauren?'

Lauren was gaping stupidly at the glass. 'You didn't see. You're so busy gassing, you didn't catch what he just spelled out!' She intoned the words: ' "*Thy pretty dance pleaseth me greatly.*" That's what it said. Marina caught it, didn't you, Marina?'

'Yes, but it's *your* message, Lauren. He's talking to you.'

The glass continued: PRITHEE MISTRESS I BEG YOU TEACH THIS PRETTY DANCE TO THE LADIES OF THE COURT.

The belly-dancing he meant of course. I'd only just twigged. It was Henry who'd been spying on Lauren that day, not poor old innocent Harv-wit. I glanced sympathetically at Lauren. Poor thing. Lauren wasn't given to blushing particularly, but now she was positively on fire. If she got any hotter, she'd spontaneously combust.

WHAT SAY YOU MISTRESS? Henry wanted to know. The glass paused in the centre of the circle. Waiting.

'It wasn't Harv-wit after all,' Lauren murmured. 'It must have been . . . *him*, spying on me . . . when I dressed up. When I undressed rather. When I . . . oh my God!' She clapped a hand to her mouth. 'He saw me. He saw it all. Everything.'

'Yeah,' I whispered. 'He's a perv. Don't worry.' I patted her arm. 'He couldn't have seen you, you know, in the flesh. I mean, he just couldn't, could he?'

I held my breath. Just like before, the atmosphere

seemed to thicken about us. At the same time I noticed the smell. Surely it hadn't been here when we came in? As if something rotten had crawled into the room, something old and furry, and maggot-ridden, crawling into a corner to die.

'What's that niff? Marina?' I nudged her lightly. 'Can you smell it?'

Marina nodded. Our eyes fell to the glass again. Impatient for an answer, it slid towards the letter 'Y'.

YOUR BELLY MISTRESS IS FAIR AS LILIES.

But this was too much for Lauren. She seemed to come suddenly to life. 'Oh that's it! That's just too gross! You've been spying on me, you, like, totally disgusting, perverted . . .'

'You know your trouble, Lauren?' Marina coolly broke in. 'You can't take a compliment. Don't you realize what an honour it is for Henry to pick you out? And sit down, will you? Stay in the circle. He isn't finished yet.'

'Well maybe *he* isn't,' I said carefully, 'but I see what Lauren means. It's getting a bit *personal*. Plus, that stink is getting worse by the minute. It must be Henry. Maybe he has a personal hygiene problem or something.'

But Marina didn't care about smells. Marina was too far gone, demanding of Henry another message. Another message? Hadn't we had enough? There was an insatiable glint in her eyes. Of course, that was why she didn't want to break the circle. Marina was waiting for her own message. She was hungry for Henry to talk to her, to single her out like before, as his *dove*, his *duck*, his *dark-eyed Venus*. Marina was jealous of the attention Lauren had received for her belly-dancing, and now she would have her moment of glory.

170

But it seemed not. I felt myself grow cold all over, as the glass singled out MISTRESS ABIGAIL for his attention.

'Oh no . . . Marina, I . . .' I touched her arm with my icy fingers, and she shook me off with an irritable movement, as if I was a fly.

'Oh grow up, Abbie, for heaven's sake! I thought you understood these things. I thought you had a bit more spirit.'

In any case, the glass had already swept across the table, taking our fingers to the letter 'M'.

MASTER NICOLAS IS A ROGUE.

The glass paused again, as if waiting for the message to sink in. It did. Suddenly I had that vision of Henry in the mirror. So he had really been there! Watching us. Stalking us. I could feel the hairs on the back of my neck stand up. A new fear had taken me over. What if Marina realized? What if Henry gave me away?

MASTER NICOLAS IS A FOUL CHURL, the glass continued. Then, REMEMBER THIS MISTRESS NO HEAD IS TOO FAIR.

By now the smell was so bad, all three of us were holding our breath.

'This is just so putrid.' Lauren shook her head at the glass, as if she would no more touch it again than pick up a live scorpion. 'Sorry, Marina, but you'll have to do this without me. I just can't take any more. I'm not supposed to get stressed-out. The therapist at the allergy clinic, she said my eczema was stress-related, and—'

'You realize, both of you, you've completely blown it now? Just when we were getting some really interesting messages.'

'Sorry, Marina, but it's true, about being stress-related I mean . . .' Lauren wittered on. While she did so, I seized

171

my chance. In a cunningly swift movement, I shifted my elbow, and 'accidentally' brushed the letters off the table.

'Oh dear. Don't worry. I'll put them away.' Before Marina could protest, I began sweeping them into the tin, then replaced the brandy glass in the cabinet, knocking over a couple of tumblers in my panic. When I got back to the kitchen, the smell had eased up a bit.

Marina nodded in the direction of the garden. 'The smell's gone. Was that what scared you? It was only someone sticking horse-muck on their roses, for God's sake.'

Lauren and I looked at each other. Neither of us had the guts to say it didn't smell anything like horse-muck. That it wasn't nearly so wholesome.

'Well, I ought to get home.' Lauren glanced awkwardly at her watch. 'I would have had to leave early anyway, Andrew's taking me for a drink before the play. We're going to see *Macbeth*,' she explained to Marina. 'Not that I'm in the mood really. But it would be cruel and everything, to let him down now.'

'Andrew?' Marina made a face, as if the smell had come back again, 'Who's *Andrew*? Oh don't tell me, I know. What about your poorly ankle then? I suppose Andrew will have to carry you into the theatre. How romantic.'

'Marina, I . . .' Lauren looked upset at first. I could see why. Her loyalties divided between the blessed Aphrodite and Andrew Warrender. I mean, it was a toughie! But then she shouldered her bag with a decisive air, and said, 'Well, see you both at school tomorrow then.'

Marina and I were alone. She glared at me. 'I suppose you suddenly hear your mother calling too?'

'I hope not.'

'It's just too bloody bad.' She began crashing saucepans for the evening meal. 'I've waited weeks to get us all together again, to play the Game. Then when things begin to really happen, you all run scared.'

'I didn't run,' I reminded her.

'But you wanted to.'

I tried to reason with her. 'Yeah, I wanted to. Come on, Marina, you can't really blame Lauren. I mean, better if it was some dirty old man watching her, at least she could call the police and have him arrested. Henry . . . whatever it is in that glass, it's evil. Can't you feel it? It was horrible tonight, as if it was talking dirty . .'

'Stop calling Henry *IT*!' She twisted round at me, wagging the vegetable peeler in her hand. 'He's not "IT". And it's all right for you, you got your messages. I was waiting to hear what mine was. I needed to hear it. Henry wanted to talk to me.' She turned the knife on herself, making stabbing motions. 'You understand, *me*? He was only doing you lot first to get the boring bits out of the way. I'm the most important one to him. "I give up all other mistresses for you," that's what he told me, Abbie . . . he gives them up for me!'

I said nothing. Marina looked crazy. She sounded crazy. Her words chilled me. 'I give up all other mistresses for you.' That was the promise Henry made Anne Boleyn when he was trying to get her into the Royal bed.

'Marina, have you told your parents about this?'

Phew. Parents. The magic word. It seemed to bring her back again, the old, cool, contemptuous, self-possessed Marina. Reminded of her chores, she turned back to the chopping board and began to slice onions.

'Of course I haven't.'

'Why not? They might be able to help.'

'I don't need help.'

'Marina, I've got to say this . . . your parents keeping you prisoner and everything, is that why you keep on about Henry so much, because you can't go out and find a real boyfriend? I mean I . . .'

The knife clattered suddenly to the floor. Marina swivelled slowly round to face me. She seemed quite calm. 'Let's get this straight. One, my parents don't keep me a prisoner, as you put it. Two, I don't "keep on about Henry", and three, I'm not interested in boyfriends, especially not the nerdy Andrew-Warrender variety. And . . . four, what do you know about getting a "real boyfriend" anyway?'

This was my signal to leave. I grabbed my bag. 'I'd better go. I'll see you tomorrow.'

'No don't go yet.' She stood, blocking the kitchen doorway. 'Who is this Master Nicolas Henry was on about? We never did get round to that, did we?'

I blinked innocently. 'I haven't the faintest idea.'

'Haven't you? I mean really?'

I shrugged. 'I don't know a Nicolas.'

Well I didn't. Not any more. Gossip must be slow to filter through to the spirit world, because obviously Henry hadn't heard the latest. Nicolas Nikos, Nick, whatever name he went by, was in the past. Nikos was already history.

Marina smiled scornfully. 'Well whoever he is, Henry doesn't like him. He should watch out.'

'Yeah, suppose he should. Whoever he is.'

Marina stood aside. Perhaps she was a bit embarrassed

at losing her temper like that. She smoothed back her hair, with a hand smelling of onions, and I felt suddenly sorry for her.

'And I'm not a prisoner,' she said again, as I got to the front door. 'It's not like you think, Abbie.'

'I know. I'm sorry. I didn't mean *prisoner*, exactly.'

'They only want the best for me.'

I nodded. 'Yeah. Course they do.'

Anything to get out of her house, to breathe the air. Even polluted North London air seemed sweet to me.

One thing I knew, as Marina closed the front door on me, I would never sit down to play the Henry Game again. Not if she twisted my arm behind my back, not if she begged me on her knees, not if she tortured me on the rack. NEVER!

Chapter Thirteen

Some days you just know are going to be weird. You can tell the minute you wake up, even before you step outside. It's like everything's just pretending to be normal. As if even the weather forecast, which my mother insisted on listening to at breakfast, had some other, sinister portent.

'Looks like the heat-wave's broken at last,' my mother commented over her All-Bran. 'Thank heavens for small mercies. I've never seen so many cases of Cracked Heel as I have in the past few weeks.'

'Yeah,' I said, 'and heels aren't the only things that are "cracking", it seems to me.'

'What did you say, dear?'

'Nothing, Mother. Nothing of any importance.'

Another weird thing: Marina wasn't at school. Now this was really strange because Marina was never ever away, if she could help it. Why would she want to be, when school was her entire social life? Practically the only place, other than her own kitchen, that her parents approved of her going to.

'I'm surprised it's not *you*, bunking off school,' I said to Lauren. 'What with that shock you had yesterday, and then your ankle and everything.'

Lauren confessed she felt guilty. 'I was a total wimp, wasn't I? But how would *you* feel if your house was apparently haunted? You can't imagine what it's like. I can never take my clothes off again, not even to have a bath. Although it's a relief in a way to know that Harv-wit's not quite the creep I thought he was. What d'you think is wrong with Marina anyway?'

'I don't know, but it must be something serious to keep her at home. Remember that time when she was doubled up with period pains? She actually went green. She had to huddle over the cloakroom radiators all through lunchtime. I wonder if they've got anything on exorcisms in here by the way?'

It was our free period, and we were lurking about the history section of Northgate library. We were supposed to be researching our projects, but after the goings on yesterday, our hearts weren't in it.

'Do you think I should ask the assistant? About the exorcism, I mean.'

Lauren followed my gaze over to the desk: the library assistant had spiky hair and a voice that could cut steel. She shook her head. 'Not unless you want half of Northgate to know you're possessed by demons.'

'Suppose you're right. *Poltergeists – An examination of the phenomenon* was bad enough. And they never told you how to get rid of the flaming things. Except . . . I just remembered something in one of the case-histories, about spirits being proud. They get all huffy if you don't take them seriously apparently.'

'Well how can you take them any other way? They're not exactly a laugh a minute, are they?'

'No, I suppose they're not, but remember how the first time Henry came, I got the giggles when he called us "sweet ladies"? The glass just stopped, didn't it? End of game.'

Lauren wasn't convinced. 'I thought it was just my sneezing blowing the letters off the table. Marina was livid about that.'

'Maybe, but what about yesterday, when we were sniggering at his song? He got the hump over that, didn't he?'

'It didn't get rid of him altogether though, did it?'

'No, because Marina messed it up by giving him all that guff about his "rare talent" and everything. Oh I don't know. It's just an idea.'

We picked out two reassuringly boring-looking tomes on the Tudors and sat down at one of the tables.

'So how was *Macbeth* anyway?'

Lauren shrugged. 'All right. I couldn't really concentrate though. I told Andy I wasn't feeling too well, what with my ankle and so on, and he was really sweet actually, and sympathetic.'

'Oh. Nice.' I flicked over a page and read that Henry VIII could *throw a four-yard javelin, and draw the bow with greater strength than any man in England.*

'Listen, why don't we call round to Marina's at lunchtime?' Lauren said. 'I'm quite worried about her. She was so strange yesterday. We could take her some grapes.'

I had to think quickly. I needed to see Marina, but not with Lauren hanging on. Somehow I just knew it was better to discuss this whole 'Henry' thing between the two of us.

'That might not be such a good idea,' I said. 'She's probably in bed, throwing up. There's a bug going round. We don't want to catch it.'

The word 'bug' was enough to put Lauren off.

'Perhaps you're right. I said I might go with Andy at lunchtime, help him choose a birthday present for his mum.'

'Oh. Sweet.'

'You don't mind?'

'Nah, of course not. I'll just hang out here all lunchtime, you know, checking out the exorcism stuff. They probably have this secret vault with a locked cabinet, where they keep all these ancient manuscripts on demons and that, and you need special permission and a high-security pass for access.'

Lauren laughed. 'Honestly, Fab. What are you like? You and your imagination!'

The rain had stopped some time in the early hours. Still, a dense milky moisture hung in the air as I walked to Marina's house. If only the sun would come out, I might feel better. It was odd, this churning feeling I had in the pit of my stomach; a dentist's waiting-room kind of churn that made you feel empty and hungry all at once. Turning into Arcadia Avenue, it felt so bad I almost turned back. What if Marina really was ill? What if her parents had taken a rare day off work, in order to punish her, to sort her out?

The house, as I approached it, had an unwelcoming look. There was the lavender-painted front door as usual, the silly doorbell, the empty milk bottles sparkling on the step. But there was something else too, a kind of invisible barrier, as if someone had cast a 'Keep Out' spell, as if an invisible cross was slashed upon the door – *PLAGUE victim lives here.*

Marina took a while to answer the doorbell. The sight

of her gave me a shock. I couldn't help blurting out, 'What's wrong? Are you ill? I didn't get you out of bed, did I?'

Whatever had happened? I'd never seen Marina like this before, hair tied back, no make-up, and slopping about in one of those velour dressing gowns, a drab dried-blood colour, the kind that middle-aged women wear.

'I've got a headache,' Marina said. 'It feels weird, all muzzy and light. My neck too. My neck feels . . .' She gave it a tentative rub. 'It feels bruised, like someone tried to strangle me.'

Her voice was different somehow, like the dull plop of a stone in a well. Following her into the lounge, I saw the reason why.

'*Oh my God!*' I stood, taking in the devastation. 'What's happened here? Did your dad freak out or something?'

It looked like the place had been charged by a wild rhino. The carpet was littered with wheaty shreds of pampas grass, drawers were half wrenched out of the glass-fronted unit, lamps were overturned, light bulbs smashed.

Marina curled up in a corner of the sofa. She was hugging one of the velvet cushions to her chest, smoothing it in a rhythmic way, as if it was precious, a baby's head or something.

'You don't imagine my dad did this?' Impatiently she rolled her eyes. 'Don't be such a moron. Why would he trash his own house? It was like that time we did the bonfire at Lauren's house, only worse. It was him.'

'*Him?* You mean . . . ?'

180

I couldn't bear to say the name aloud. I didn't want to imagine Henry trashing Marina's house in the same fit of rage that saw monasteries wrecked, and heretics burned, and wives beheaded five hundred years ago.

'Henry was angry because Lauren broke the circle,' Marina said flatly. 'I knew he would be. I don't even blame him.'

'You mean it was like a gross insult to his precious royal person? Yeah, well he doesn't have to go, like, totally ballistic, does he?'

'My mother thought it was an earth tremor,' Marina went on, 'like they have back in Cyprus sometimes. This morning my dad was checking the walls for cracks. He thinks the house is subsiding, and now he's going to get a surveyor in, to check the foundations. I can't tell them what it really is. They don't believe in spirits. Ghosts are for superstitious old peasant women according to them. They've left all that stuff behind them now.'

A horrible thought had just occurred to me. 'Did this happen straight after the seance?' I asked her.

She frowned. 'About nine, I think. What's the time got to do with it?'

'Nine,' I said. 'Just about the time that Lauren and Andy would have been in the theatre, sharing a box of chocs . . . hmmm . . .'

Marina screwed up her eyes irritably. 'Hmmm . . . hmmmm . . . what are you "hmmmming" about. I don't see what Lauren's love life has got to do with anything.'

'Don't you? Supposing . . . supposing Henry was jealous? I mean only a few hours earlier he'd been raving on about her belly being as the lilies. Imagine, his

181

Vision of Loveliness being groped by handy Andy. He might have him hung, drawn and quartered for that. Instead he took it out on you, because you're closest to him. This . . . house . . . it's where he's strongest.'

Marina didn't care for this idea. Wasn't she Henry's chosen one? His dove? Why should Henry care what Lauren got up to? And as for Vision of Loveliness . . . Lauren? Oh come on! 'Don't you understand? He's in love with me. He did this because we insulted him, I told you.'

She glanced wearily around the room. 'I promised I'd have the place cleaned up before they got home. I wish my head didn't hurt so much.'

She looked so exhausted, I felt sorry for her.

'Listen, Marina, why don't I clear up for you? You go and have a lie down, you look terrible. It's only biology this afternoon. I can go in late, pretend I had to go to the dentist. You might feel better once the place looks normal again.'

Marina was doubtful at first about leaving me in charge, as if she didn't trust my house-keeping skills. 'Are you sure? I mean you're not exactly domesticated, are you? I've seen the state of your room remember.'

'Anyone can whisk a hoover round for God's sake. Marina, I'm not completely hopeless. Please let me do it. Go and lie down before you fall down.'

Finally she agreed, but not without leaving me with a confusing variety of polish cloths, and special dust-attracting dusters, and instructions on how not to wreck the Dyson.

I listened to her footsteps on the stairs, slow and dreamy as a ghost.

The first thing I did when Marina had gone was open the windows and let in the fresh air. Then I set to work. My mother would have been proud of me. Hands that had never before touched so much as a bottle of Lemon Squeezy, now dusting, polishing, tidying as if born to it. It felt good, being of real service to Marina at last. I was proud to think that she needed me at this moment, not Lauren who would have kneeled at her feet and peeled grapes for her, given half a chance.

But what were we going to do about Henry? I dreamed up various options as I scooted about with the Dyson, and plumped up cushions. We needed an exorcist, but where did you find one these days? They didn't exactly advertise in the *Yellow Pages*. And how could I persuade Marina we needed to act, when she seemed to be in love's sweet dream, and losing her entire reason?

There! That would do it. The Pauloses' living room restored to its usual immaculate, un-lived-in state. Feeling rather pleased with myself, I put the cleaning things away. I'd already decided to bunk off school for the afternoon. An emotional crisis after all, even if it was Marina's crisis, not strictly mine. And anyway, what with the events of yesterday, and now this, I did feel tired suddenly.

Why not rest for a minute? Plan what to do about Henry, and then wake Marina with a nice cup of tea? This seemed like a good idea. Mr Paulos's reclining leather chair looked inviting suddenly. Feeling all virtuous and worthy after my cleaning frenzy, I flopped into it with a sigh.

Then . . . ughhh! I was out of it again, in a second, as if I'd just sat on a live cobra. Something had groaned beneath me. I staggered to the window. Something was in there already. Someone was sitting in Mr Paulos's chair! No cool cushioned leather beneath my thighs, but velvet-sheathed muscle, bone, sinew, a whisper of ermine about my ear, of beard tickling my neck. I'd just sat down on a man's lap.

'By my soul, wench, but you are a lusty creature!'

So this was how Henry VIII looked, sounded! A voice like the rustling of dusty silks. A voice that once roared, bellowed, now hoarse with age and disuse.

'This would please me well enough, but for my leg. I fear a humour has fallen into it lately. A fall from my horse, my physician thinks may be the cause. But no matter, try me again, Mistress, that I may be *prepared* to receive you this time.'

The King settled himself again. I could barely take my eyes from him, the hands like jewelled exotic crabs, one of them, strangely, cupping what looked like an orange. He was just like in the portraits, emblazoned with gold, dripping with furs, the shapely calves in yellow stockings, the giant outrageous cod piece . . . ugh don't look at that.

My fingers clenched. *Don't worry, you're just hallucinating. It's just something in the water.*

So, if this wasn't real, but a hallucination, maybe I could fight it? 'That chair doesn't belong to you,' I said. 'It belongs to Marina's father, to Mr Paulos.'

Henry seemed mildly surprised. 'It is a goodly throne. I would have a throne like this at court, that other is a cursed thing. To sit astride my Flanders mare would bring more comfort. Where does this throne come by, Mistress?'

'MFI probably, and anyway you shouldn't be here at all.'

I wasn't going to sit about and discuss home furnishings with a demon, a ghost, a poltergeist, a tyrant like Henry. Where was my priest, my crucifix, my string of garlic or whatever it took to get rid of him? Unable to believe my courage, I forced my voice out of my mouth, 'Go! Leave this place. Go back to where you came from.'

This seemed only to amuse him. He laughed, hoarse as a desert wind. 'By my soul, Madame, this lamentation is not warrented. A King may rest his bones where he pleases, I think.'

'This is not your house.'

'Not mine?' More dry gusts of laughter, then, 'Madam, the entire of this realm is mine. I am the *King*, Madam. And you tell me I shall not sit in this goodly throne. For shame, Mistress, if you were not so pleasing to my eye, I would have you taken to the Tower.'

'You can't. You're dead. And the Tower isn't a prison any more. It's full of Japanese tourists. And anyway, Parliament makes the laws nowadays, not the King. The Queen I mean. The Queen just opens things, and shakes hands and gives a speech at Christmas.'

Was I so brave? If not for the wall, solid against my back, I might have been a quivering heap. Yet somehow I knew I had to face this thing. It had been me that called it up in the first place; it was my fault that Marina was nearly losing her mind, and her house infested by

185

the worst poltergeist ever. I'd cleaned up Henry's mess, now I had to cleanse the house of Henry himself. Pity I couldn't just suck him up the Dyson like so much dust!

Now he looked worried at least. 'What's this you say? Parliament makes the laws?'

I took a deep breath. 'That's right. That Divine Right of Kings doesn't count any more. One of your descendants, Charles the First, he thought it did, and they chopped off his head.'

'The King's Head? Ha ha . . .' Clearly Henry thought this ludicrous. 'Mistress, do not cozen me with your prattle. I do not like a scold. You are too young, too fair. You sound like that other scold, that witch, that Night Crow. I will not have that, Mistress.' He patted his knee, and said in a gentler tone, 'Come, Mistress, come and sit by your Sovereign Lord.'

The sight of his beady brown eyes fixed on me, the droplets of pearl and froth of lace at his neck, the red-gold beard, sparse like pig bristles was too much.

I folded my arms to show I'd have nothing to do with him. 'Hah! You've driven poor Marina mad, and now you try to pull her friend. Disgusting!'

This seemed to worry Henry not a jot. He merely played with the orange, tossing it from hand to hand like a tennis ball.

'The maid has but the sweating sickness, 'tis common in my realm. A man may shiver one minute and be dead the next. Yet do not fear for the maid. In women it takes a gentler course. The sweat is more lenient when lodged in females.'

Oh yes? I remembered from my project on Anne

186

suddenly, how she'd fallen victim to this mysterious plague along with half the nation. And what did Henry do? Did he sit at her bedside and soothe her brow? Like hell he did! Henry was off into the countryside like a shot, dosing himself with potions and going to church three times a day.

'I know something of these matters,' Henry went on boasting. 'My cardinal, Wolsey, doth swear by oranges to keep this plague at bay. I have myself devised a posset of herbs that shall bring out the sweat most profusely.'

'Thanks but we'll pass on that. Why don't you just go back to hell where you belong and take your mouldy old orange with you? We'll make you go, me and Marina. We'll bring a priest . . .'

Perhaps it was the mention of the priest that did it. At once Henry's mood changed. His chops (for there was no other word to describe his cheeks, which were long and fat all at once) quivered with rage.

'Do not threaten me with priests, wench. I care not about priests when I am Lord of Christendom entire. This is indeed a sorry spectacle,' he shook his head, 'that you should threaten me, who saved your very honour at the House of Mirrors the other day.'

House of Mirrors? It took me seconds to realize that he meant Stefan's house. The terrible apparition looming over our reflections. Mine and Nikos's. No wonder we had broken up. Henry's appearance had been the kiss of death on our relationship.

'*I* could handle that,' I told him. 'You just can't go interfering all over the place. Things are different now. Maidens, I mean girls, we can defend our own honour and that.'

There was a ponderous silence, then he said in a new, ominous tone, 'Methinks you would rather dally with the Greek, than serve your King.'

That did it. I felt my hands clench into fists. 'Yeah well, thanks to you, I'm not "dallying" with Nikos. I'll probably never "dally" with him again, because he's dumped me just the way you dumped Anne, OK? Happy now? And anyway, and anyway . . .' I took a deep breath, 'it's none of your business who we see, or what we do. Nikos is alive, and you're dead! And in case you didn't realize it, you've been rotting away in your horrible tomb for nearly five hundred years!

It was a bit of a shock to his system, I imagine, to be told he was like, DEAD. But then something changed in the room, as if that milky fog outside had fingered its way through the window, and slithered down my neck. The recliner chair swivelled horribly to face me.

I took a step back as Henry levered his great hulk out of it, groaning as if with the effort. As he did so, he let forth a series of high piping farts, trilling like wind-borne sparrows. The idea of a ghost with wind was so extraordinary my terror seemed to evaporate. A ghost with gas! Henry, the foul old windbag, letting one rip in Marina's living room.

Oh dear. I could feel the laughter bubbling up inside me, that pressure that makes your throat ache. I cupped my hand to my mouth. Too late. The giggle trigger had been pressed. It was one of those situations, the more you try *not* to laugh, the more utterly convulsed with laughter you become. That such a pompous, all-powerful king could produce such a squeaky little noise from his backside, seemed to me the most hilarious thing ever.

'You dare to mock me, girl?' Henry's voice was reedy, tremulous. 'To mock a king is treason. Know you the pun . . . ish . . . ment for . . . ?'

But my eyes were so full of tears Henry seemed a bit blurred suddenly. I blinked, and in blinking the tears from my eyes, I seemed to blink Henry away with them.

Afterwards, I could hardly remember which came first, Henry vanishing or Marina screaming out from upstairs. Marina, who never screamed, or squealed, or even giggled much; Marina who just wasn't the screaming, squealy sort.

I must have taken the stairs three at a time, because in the same instant I was there, in her room. Marina was standing on her bed, alone, thank God. No sign of Henry, and the house as quiet as a church downstairs.

She flapped a hand vaguely at her door. 'He was here. Just now. I saw him. Abbie, I actually *saw* Henry, leaning right over my bed . . . Henry, just like you see in the portraits. You think I'm mad.' She glared at me suddenly. 'You don't believe me, do you?'

'I do. I do believe you.'

'He gave me this.' She held out her hand. The orange might have been made of gold, the way she looked at it.

'Oh my God . . . how could he . . . ? Throw it away. Marina, don't eat it!'

I held up my arms instinctively. Marina had never been a touchy-feely type exactly. But now I just had to get hold of her, somehow grab her wrists. I wanted to shake her. To shake some sense into her.

'Marina, look, get dressed now. You can come home with me, my mum won't mind how long you stay. Stay the night if you want.' I glanced nervously over my shoulder. If Henry was this bold, this active in daylight, what might he do in the long dark hours of the night? It didn't bear thinking about. I tugged at her arm. 'Marina, *hallo*! You can't stay here alone. We'll sort this out, we'll arrange an exorcism. I'll go and see the vicar and ask him for help. He's a bit of a dope but he must know how to do it, you know, the holy water and stuff. We can't do it alone. Marina, are you listening?'

She freed her hand from my grasp and sat smoothing her hair in that vain disdainful gesture I knew so well. Of course she couldn't stay with me. A visit to Smedhurst Road was even more unthinkable than a visit from Henry, it seemed. Didn't I realize by now, she had the family's tea to get, pork tonight, which she'd just got out of the freezer? And anyway, she wasn't a bit scared, just buggy or something.

'You should have seen him, Abbie. He was . . . magnificent. Really fine and noble looking you know . . .'

'No.' I shook my head. 'Marina, I saw him too. Just now, downstairs. Marina he actually *spoke* to me. How can you call him "noble"? He's foul. He's a disgusting dirty old man. He's a bloated old pus-bag, plus . . . plus . . .' I searched for words strong enough to make her see sense once and for all, 'he stinks worse than geriatric dogs' breath. I mean how can you . . .?'

I trailed off as her dark eyes fixed on me. Perhaps Marina was seeing a very different Henry from me.

Henry the troubadour. The Golden Youth 'whose fairness doth outshine the sun', as one brown-nosing courtier would have it. But what did it matter? It was all the same Henry, teasing us, taking his different forms.

'Well look, never mind whether he's noble or not. He could be the hunkiest thing on legs. Fact is, he's not flesh and blood, is he, he's a bloody ghoul. Listen, if we don't do something, he'll be moving in with us permanently. He'll be like dry rot. We'll never get rid of him.'

At last, it seemed I'd convinced her. 'You saw him too?'

I nodded.

Marina was silent for a while. Finally she said, 'All right, if you must. You can organize this exorcism.' She shuddered over the word, as if it was *her* that was to be exorcized, banished to the spirit realms. 'But I don't want this priest of yours sticking his nose in my affairs. I won't have my parents involved. You'll have to make that clear, Abbie, from the start.'

'I will.' I glanced at my watch. 'Look, I'll have to go. I really should catch the last half hour of biology. You know what Mrs Hargreaves is like, she always wants doctors' notes, forensic evidence, proof. These scientists are all alike.'

It was an excuse of course. Anything to get out of that house, to get away from Marina. She looked so small as she stood framed in the doorway, seeing me off. She looked nothing like Aphrodite now, or Anne Boleyn come to that. She was just a small frightened schoolgirl. My best friend.

Chapter Fourteen

'There's some funny business going on with you, my girl. And you might as well tell me what it is, because I shall find out sooner or later.'

My mother glanced up from *Chiropody Monthly*, a riveting little article called 'Toe the Line'. 'You've not been sleeping properly, have you? I heard you last night, pacing about. It's nothing to do with that young man, is it?'

Through clenched teeth, I said, 'No, Mother, it isn't. And how can I pace about in my room when there's, like, an inch of floor space to pace on? Honestly. You must be hearing things. It was probably Mrs Croop, come to think of it, sleepwalking.'

Honestly, it was like living under twenty-four-hour surveillence. Probably my mother had secret video cameras installed in my bedroom. Why couldn't she get herself a life, like other mothers I knew; why couldn't she *neglect* me for heaven's sake? I was the age now to be neglected. I should pension her off, say, 'Hey, Mum, you've done your bit, thanks and all that, but now you can party!' Hah. If only she knew, I thought, slicking shadow-concealer beneath my eyes, the reasons for my not sleeping well.

Nikos was one of them of course. I hadn't seen him for two whole weeks, and now when I tried to summon up his toe-curling gorgeous, sex-god visage, both memory and imagination failed me. If only I might say the same of Henry. Unfortunately, I was seeing far too much of him. Every time I closed my eyes in fact, his bloated form swaggered before me. Henry, who wouldn't let a little thing like *being dead* put him off chasing women. Who was probably about to make Marina his seventh wife, if I didn't do something. Fast.

'Where are you off to now?' my mother called from the living room, as I zipped up my fleece. She didn't come out to inspect. She and Dad were glued to a quiz show by the sound of it. I could hear them, shrieking the answers from their armchairs, as if the contestant might actually hear them and win himself a zillion pounds.

'Just off to see a man about an exorcism, Mother,' I said from the landing.

'You're off what, Abigail . . . Abigail?'

'Just off, Mum. For a walk. Back in an hour.'

And I'd gone.

The Church of St Lawrence was only a couple of streets away. A new, red-brick vicarage with those glary great picture windows stood right next door. On the television I'd noticed that vicars always had starchy housekeepers, so it was a bit disappointing when the Reverend Smiley's wife opened the door to me, jiggling a baby in arms, a bare-bottomed toddler clinging to her skirt.

'Ein bin sick,' the toddler proudly informed me at once.

'Got an appointment, have you?' Its mother looked

as if she could do with being exorcized herself. Hair all over the place and a wild demented look in her eye. 'Well you'd better just knock and go in. Phil's got choir practice in half an hour though, so you'd better make it quick.'

'Oh yes. Thanks. I will.'

The vicar was strumming a guitar as I walked in. My hopes sank at once. He was entirely the wrong sort of priest for what I had in mind. You just could not imagine him casting demons out of frothing-mouthed victims with Latin incantations, and holding the crucifix aloft.

'Sorry . . . Abigail, isn't it?' He squinted at me, as if he was trekking across the desert in search of an oasis, half-blinded by the relentless sun. 'I didn't quite catch . . . did you say . . . *exorcism*?' The word seemed to catch in his throat.

I'd decided to come straight out with it. Everything. The seances, the spirit writing, objects flying around, even Henry's personal appearances. But when I put them all together like that, they did sound a bit much.

'We just wondered,' I said, 'if you had any experience of casting out demons, or anything like that. At all.'

It sounded daft I had to admit, in this bright, centrally heated vicarage, with Mrs Smiley yelling at her kids, and the sound of saucepans clanking in the kitchen.

'Demons?' the vicar pondered. 'Ah . . . Demons . . . hmmmmm . . .' He was fiddling with a bunch of leaflets on his desk. I managed to read them upside down — *The Church and Young People Today — Growing in the Family of God*. Oh dear. I knew he'd much rather I'd come to discuss some nice juicy social problem, boyfriend troubles, going on the pill, drugs . . . anything but demons.

'Exorcisms,' he repeated, as I finished talking; there had never been much call for that sort of thing in his parish he was glad to say. His flock were a pretty down-to-earth lot on the whole.

'So, you won't help us then?' I said, feeling hopeless suddenly. 'But isn't there someone who could? I mean don't you have anyone in your church who specializes in that sort of thing?'

He chuckled nervously. That kind of thing belonged in the old days of superstition and witchcraft. The church didn't go in for 'that kind of thing' nowadays. He looked at me sternly. 'In my experience, it's best not to tamper with such things as Ouija boards and so on. These things are best left . . . uh . . . alone. The Devil finds work for idle hands and all that. Now let's see,' he said, pushing a leaflet into my hand about the Friday evening youth club. 'Now you come along to one of our Friday evenings, Abigail, and you'll forget all about your ghosties and ghoulies hah hah! We get up to all sorts of fun, I even strum a bit for my sins. Why don't you bring your friend along . . . er . . . what was her name again?'

'Marina.'

'Yes, well, strictly speaking of course, she's not in our parish, but we never turn anyone away from God's door. Well that's it,' rubbing his hands together. 'We look forward to seeing you then.'

Useless at casting our demons he might be, but his wife seemed pretty adept at casting out needy parishioners. Before I knew it, she'd bundled me onto the doorstep, the toddler informing me from between its mother's legs, that 'Ein bin sick again.'

I stood there for a while on the step, feeling like an outcast. The Church had let me down. Let *us* down. I would have to think of another way.

'We can have a kind of do-it-yourself exorcism,' I told Marina the following evening, after school. Rather than discuss such matters in her house again, where *he* might hear, we'd crossed the park towards the Garden of Remembrance.

Already Bromfield Park was taking on the shades of autumn. The horse chestnuts were the colour of toffee apples. There was a rustling of squirrels in the canopy, while children rummaged beneath, filling their bags with sticky, unripe conkers. The sky was a beautiful, dusky violet. There was a slight shiver in the air.

'How do you mean, do-it-yourself?' Marina had that sneery dismissive sound to her voice, as if she had more important things on her mind. Although, how could she?

I explained the 'Casting Out' ritual I'd been reading about in the Feng Shui manual. 'All you need is a few herbs and some sand in a bowl, well preferably one of those silvery-lined seashells. Then you light the herbs and flick the smoke about the room with a feather.'

I glanced up at the pigeon flying clumsily overhead. Turkey- or goose-feathers were best apparently. The turkey would be difficult, in this part of North London, but . . . 'If we go down to the lake, we might find a Canada Goose-feather, and—'

'A goose-feather and a bit of smoke to get rid of Henry?' Marina said scornfully. 'You're so naive sometimes, Abbie. You can't believe everything you read in those books.'

I glanced sideways. Marina's head was in the air again. She was wearing a black leather coat over her school uniform, and black knee boots with spiky heels. The heels added at least another six centimetres to her height, so that her dark head was level with my fair one.

Naive, she said! It made me fume. When there I was, only two weeks ago, on the verge of true womanhood, and all thanks to her cousin.

We came to the black wrought-iron gates set into the wall. A notice said that *This Garden will be closing at four thirty from the end of September.*

It was four o'clock now. There was no one else there. Only me and Marina, our long twin shadows looming before us as we walked beneath the pergola. The place had a neglected feel since we'd last been here in midsummer. A few frazzled roses clung to the stone pillars, and there was a smell of moss and stagnant water.

'Well, what do you suggest then?' I said, feeling a bit huffy, when I'd gone to so much effort.

'Nothing.'

'Nothing?'

'Exactly. I haven't seen anything for a few days now. It will all die down naturally. If I lie low for a bit, do as my parents want. I've been thinking about it. It was probably my fault, turning my back on my family, on their way of living; trying to be like you lot.'

I was stunned. What was she trying to tell me? 'Like

us? But, you've never been like us. You've been the perfect daughter.'

Marina gave me a furtive sideways glance. 'No, I haven't been perfect at all. You don't know all of it. Yes, I've done the chores, the cooking, the housekeeping and so on.'

'Oh, is that all?'

We'd arrived at the stone memorial for the dead. From here, a number of circular steps led down to the fish pools and terraces. This time, though, we sat where we were, on a bench in the arcade.

'Listen, Fab, if I tell you something, you must promise me not to tell the others.'

Marina wasn't looking at me. She was staring straight ahead. She had a noble resigned look. The goddess again, I thought, promising at once and flattered to be singled out for a confidence. There was a silence, and then she said, 'My parents want me to marry, now that my GCSEs are over.'

'What? But you can't. What about your A Levels? Marina, you can't get married at your age. It's not fair. What about college? What about your career? OK, you can do both, but not if you're saddled with babies . . .'

'How does anyone know what they want at our age?' Marina said in that chilling brain-washed voice. 'My parents know me better than anyone. They know what's best for me. I didn't think so at first. We had some terrible rows. Now I'm sure that's what caused . . .' She paused. 'All the trouble.'

'I don't believe this. You're not going to? You're not *really* going to get married? I mean, don't you need to be in love first or something?'

I imagined some hideous, remote great-uncle, shipped over from Cyprus. It was like something out of the Dark Ages, and here was Marina, meekly accepting her lot.

'It's not the end of the world,' I heard her say.

'No. Just the end of your life. And who is the lucky guy? I don't imagine your parents are going to let you choose for yourself, I mean, you've only got to sleep with him for the next sixty-odd years and bring up his sproggs.'

I stopped. Out of sight of our bench, from the far shadowy end of the pergola, the iron gates jangled softly. I heard the familiar clunk of the catch. A kind of tremor shivered through the thatch of vines, as if the garden braced itself for intrusion.

Marina was standing up, doing that sort of imperious swivelling thing on her spiky heels, saying she should have known better than to confide in me.

I tried again. 'You don't think getting married is going to get rid of Henry, do you? Henry isn't some kind of punishment for your sins, Marina.'

Marina sighed. 'Listen: the seances, all that, it was just an escape. I realize now. We all have to face it sooner or later.'

'Face what? Marriage you mean?'

'Reality.'

'So, does that mean you're, like, a prisoner for the next few months? Hiding away, waiting for your husband to carry you off? What about the fair? The fair's coming next week. You promised you'd come with me and Lauren.'

'I'll come to the fair,' Marina said coolly. 'Getting

married doesn't stop me enjoying myself, does it? It doesn't stop us being friends. Of course I'll come. Listen, listen, can you hear it? It's that music again.'

I listened. To catch the notes that hardly seemed to be there, you had to listen not just in the usual way, with your ears, but with every sense. The music seemed to be in the very air, like some terrible perfume blowing off the decayed roses, the stagnant pond weed. A sound not meant for everyone. Only for us.

'Notice something else?' I whispered to Marina. 'The birds. The birds have stopped singing.'

Now I didn't claim to be some kind of bird-spotting boffin, identifying the tune of the Great Spotted Warbler. Nothing like that. But the happy twitter of birds is one of those everyday things you take for granted. Only when it stops do you hear the deep and terrible silence it leaves behind. The birds knew. The birds had more sense than Marina and I did. They knew that something foul and old had snuck into their domain on its velvet jewelled slippers, flap flap flap with its flat pus-ridden feet.

Just above us, a crimson rose drifted suddenly down from its stem, its thorns catching on Marina's coat as it fell. She bent to pick it up and looked at me.

'It's him!' She whispered like a love-struck girl, 'Henry's here.'

'Come on.' I yanked at her sleeve. 'Come on, Marina, let's go.'

Marina shook me off. 'Just a minute. Wait.'

Cradling the rose, her eyes searched the entire garden. The music seemed to be getting louder. Now you didn't need every sense to hear it. It was in the air, a tuneless strum-ti-tum, like someone endlessly tuning a guitar before a concert.

'Marina, for God's sake! Well, I'm going if you're not.'

Clumsily I began blundering through the dead leaves, beneath the columned arches towards the gates. Just in time. Glancing back I saw him. Not *my* Henry, but Marina's. As if he'd been waiting for me to leave, emerging nimbly from behind a rose bush, one hand extended. Somehow I'd expected a musical instrument, Henry in Wandering Minstrel guise. But, instead of clutching a harp or lute, perched upon his gloved arm was a great hawk, its head all but covered by a hood. Only the cruelly curved beak could be seen, glinting even from this distance, like a blade.

It struck me suddenly how unfair it was. I mean how come Marina was getting a different version of Henry to me? How come she was visited by the fit young hunk, while I got the bloated old windbag? Still, whichever guise he came in, Henry was essentially a ghoul, a ghost, a spook, a fact that Marina seemed prepared to overlook.

I glanced up into an empty sky. Of course. Hawking was another sport that young Henry supposedly excelled at. No wonder the birds had stopped singing.

'Marina!' I yelled from the gates.

No reply. She just stood there, clutching the rose like an idiot, as Henry, gold hair smooth beneath his cap, leaned over, bent to . . . oh my God . . . Don't say he was kissing her hand. The kiss of death!

'Marina, come on!' my voice shrieked into the silence. 'We've got to get out of here before they lock the gates!' I rattled the catch of the gate, gently at first, then furiously. 'It's locked! Oh my God, Marina, it's bloody locked! Let us out, hey, we're in here!'

I never was any good with gates, doors or turnstiles of any kind. If they were meant to be pushed, I was sure to pull. Now I must have been panicking, for the gates gave suddenly, pitching me through them, even as Marina joined me, breathless, still clutching her rose.

'Did you see him? Did you see Henry?'

Marina was positively glowing. She couldn't wait to tell me. I was going to get the complete run down, like it or not.

'He actually spoke to me, Abbie. "Mistress," he said. "Mistress, I see you are well recovered from the sweating sickness. My heart fills with joy at the . . ."'

I stopped her. 'Look!' Safely through the gates, I clutched at her arm, pointed to the sky. Freed from its hood, the hawk hovered motionless over the garden, then plummeted out of sight.

The sight of the hawk seemed to bring Marina to her senses. She held out her hand, as if it belonged to someone else. In a shocked voice, she said, 'Oh, Abbie, oh my God, he kissed me. His lips actually brushed my hand. I felt them. They were icy cold, ticklish like dead leaves.'

I stared. Poor Marina. Her very first kiss. And from a dead man!

I took hold of her arm, and we ran then. Maybe the last time we would ever run like this together, for Marina was getting married to person unknown. She would be married, respectable, and we could never be friends again.

Chapter Fifteen

'Can you believe it,' I said to the others. 'My parents are away for, like, the *entire* weekend. I could stay out all night, if I wanted to, and no one would ever know.'

A week had passed since Henry's last appearance in the garden. A whole week without any sightings whatsoever, and no suggestion from Marina that we should play the Henry Game. Thank God.

Maybe things were looking up. Now the fair was in town, and it was like someone had waved a magic wand over Northgate and turned it into Glastonbury for the night. I took a deep breath of that lovely wet-grass-and-hot-dog smell peculiar to fairgrounds, as we staggered up the sawdusty aisles; the stall-holder women watching our progress with hard, day-glo eyes.

For this one night at least, we could forget our troubles. Lauren could forget that she was a walking allergic reaction, Marina that she was about to be married off to some mysterious oik, and I could forget I'd been dumped by the hottest hunk this side of Hollywood.

Well I could try.

What's more we could all forget about Henry. I mean he wouldn't come here to the fair, would he?

'Where have your mum and dad gone then?' Lauren passed the bottle of wine, which Marina had filched earlier from her dad's vintage selection. 'I thought you said they never went out.'

'They don't. Usually. This is some sort of national conference. *Chiropody in the Community.* Riveting stuff, eh? What's more, it's in Devon, squillions of miles away, so they have to stay the night in a hotel. Have another glug.' I passed the bottle back to Marina.

'They didn't fix up a baby-sitter then?' Marina laughed, somewhat enviously I reckoned.

'They muttered something about Mrs Croop keeping an ear out. Which is like a major insult to my general intelligence and maturity, don't you think?'

Lauren shook her head as the bottle came her way again. 'I think I might be allergic to red wine,' she said, as some Goths drifted past with their graveyard faces, ghostly under the lights. 'My head feels strange. Everyone looks grotesque, as if they're off another planet or something.'

Marina smiled. 'Don't worry, it's not the wine. I know what you mean. This place reminds me of one of Henry's "Disguising Pageants". They had these amazing spectacles, you know, music, poetry, mock battles. Everyone was masked; no one was quite what they seemed.'

'Let's not get on to Henry, puh . . . lease . . .' I pleaded with her.

Actually Lauren was right. Everyone *did* look grotesque. Even the weather was bizarre: fat blobs of rain that would splosh in your eye then stop just as suddenly, winds whirling your hair into whipped peaks. Clouds blurred the face of the moon, like bruises.

The three of us out together was novelty enough. Lauren, Marina and me, arms linked, Marina stuffing herself with hot dogs like she was just an ordinary girl, out for a good time.

How had she ever persuaded her parents to let her out after dark? Probably she had to make some impossible deal in return, like in a fairy tale, eternally sweeping leaves into the eye of the wind, or collecting water from the bottomless well. I couldn't help thinking of Marina that way, as some strange, ethereal creature who might just have vanished if Lauren and I hadn't wedged her firmly between us.

We came to a halt as Lauren bent double, suddenly. She seemed to be choking, spluttering out bits of hot-dog bun. It sounded serious.

'Where's the First Aid Tent?' I looked around wildly.

'She doesn't need First Aid.' Marina gave her a hefty thwack between the shoulder blades, which amazingly did the trick.

Lauren seemed pathetically grateful for the thump. 'Imagine the total humiliation! Choking to death on a hot dog.'

I handed over the wine and told her to wash it down. 'What set you off anyway? Hot dogs don't have bones in them, do they?'

'It's not that.' Lauren scooped a wing of floppy brown hair behind her ear, and pointed up ahead of us. 'Look up there, the stage.'

A few yards along, to the right of us, was a makeshift stage. Earlier on that evening it had been used by local groups for entertainments: kids tap-dancing, an aerobics group bobbing about, a Tai Chi demonstration.

Now the stage was ashimmer with gauze and voile and organza, the strangely erotic tinkle of silver bells, as the women practised their warm-up.

The loud-speaker trumpeted the shocking announcement: 'We are proud to present the Ladies of the Muswell Hill Belly-Dancing troupe – *THE MUZBELLES!*'

Lauren clutched hold of my wrist, as if to keep her balance. 'My mother. That . . . that *creature* is the woman who gave birth to me! I'll kill her, showing me up like this. I'll kill her.'

I shook Lauren off. 'Don't be pathetic. You should be proud. Look, your mum's right at the front. She's looking amazing! Isn't she, Marina?'

'That's your *mother*?' Marina looked wistful, as if she'd like to be up there too, a ruby glowing in her navel, decked out like a Bedouin bride.

Izzie Alexander must be wearing a wig, swathes of fiery red hair cascading to her hips. The hips were undulating, faster and faster, as if somehow they'd come unhinged from the rest of her. They switched from side to side, a bit like the Pirate Ship at Alton Towers, until you felt almost sea-sick just looking at them. A chorus of whistling and 'Get your kit off, girls!' broke out among the crowd.

'Cretins!' Lauren threw her snootiest glance at the stubble-headed yobs gathered close to the stage. 'That's what she gets for making an exhibition of herself. It's obscene. Listen, you two can watch if you find it so fascinating. I can't. I can feel my sinuses clogging up already.'

Behind Lauren's back, Marina and I exchanged a

meaningful smirk.

'OK, keep your hair on. Tell you what, we'll go and check out those tents over there.' I gestured across the shadowy sweep of grass, where several marquees were clustered beneath the trees.

Marina rolled her eyes in dismay. 'You can't be serious. Not the WI jam stall, and all that country craft stuff?'

I shook my head. 'I think it's where the psychics and mystics hang out.'

'Fortune-tellers you mean?' Lauren said doubtfully. 'Aren't they a bit, you know, tacky in these places?'

I shrugged. 'You stay and watch the Muzbelles if you prefer. It's up to you.'

'Not much of a choice, is it?' Lauren grumbled. She trundled reluctantly behind Marina and me, as we crossed the field towards the tents.

Maybe this wasn't such a great idea. In the past few minutes a wind had come up. An unnatural mad sort of wind. The kind that seems conjured out of nowhere by some old hag, hurling scraps of litter and dead leaves and horrible gritty stuff into our eyes. It was uncanny. Almost as if the wind was blowing us backwards, back to the fair.

It wasn't so bad for me and Lauren. We were both wearing our baggiest jeans and those shrunken sweaters that look like they've been hand-knitted by a myopic granny. Marina, though, was nearly whisked away in her swishy skirt and silk shawl from Cyprus. Her hair tossed about like a rough dark sea.

'I just hope this so-called fortune-teller's worth it,' Marina said, as we finally reached the marquees.

'Oh yeah, I think she is. Hey, you two, I think we've struck gold.'

I was already reading the notice board outside the end tent. Wavery gold letters announced:

IRIS BLOOM – CLAIRVOYANT £5.00 for full reading
What does the future hold for you?
Frightened? Confused? Or merely curious?
Why not allow Iris to set you on the right path?

Why not? It was the stuff beneath this blurb that really got me though. Newspaper cuttings of famous murder cases which Iris had helped solve.

'Look at this stuff. Impressive or what! She's the real thing all right.'

'Hmmm . . .' Marina peered over my shoulder, sneering. 'Iris Bloom, though. What kind of a name is that for a clairvoyant?'

'Names aren't everything,' I said. 'Why shouldn't she be Iris Bloom? I mean, just because she sounds like some sort of dried flower arranger. Don't you see, that makes her all the more convincing. If she was Gypsy . . . I don't know, Gypsy Magenta or something, she'd probably be a total fake, wouldn't she?'

Personally, if I was ever a mega-famous palmist to the stars, which I intended to be one day, I should call myself Madame Fabiola. But I decided not to share that inspired idea with the others right now.

'What d'you think, Lauren?'

'She sounds totally naff, if you want my opinion,' Lauren disloyally asserted. 'Anyway, haven't we had

208

enough messages from the Other Side? I mean, what's the point?'

'It's not the same thing at all,' I snapped at her. How could she be so dense? Iris Bloom was hardly going to order her to burn her granny's heirlooms for a start, was she? Also, she might have a real message for me, about Nikos. All I ever got out of Henry was the same old tedious line . . . *Master Nicolas is a rogue* . . . Well. Tell me something new.

'You'll go in as well?' I turned to Marina.

'All right then.' Marina acted as if she was doing me a big favour. 'If you're sure she's so marvellous.'

Lauren wasn't so keen. 'You two go on. I might take a wander back. Only Andy said he might meet up with me later, and I don't want him to see my mother got up like some disgusting old slapper. That would just be the end of everything.'

'Oh come on. I thought this was meant to be kind of a girls' night out?' I was a bit annoyed about Andrew Warrender sticking his geeky nose in. 'Sure you won't come? Moral support?'

The truth was, I felt a bit nervous. I'd never met a real psychic before. At least, not that I knew of. But Lauren was already lumbering away, arms folded and stooped against the wind. She called over her shoulder, 'I'll meet you both at the dodgems. In about twenty minutes, right?'

'Go on then.' Marina was prodding me through the flaps of the marquee. 'You go first.' She said this as if it was a generous offer. I bent my head, and immediately smelled that under-canvas smell of stamped-down grass and stale air.

Iris Bloom was blowing her nose as I entered, and popping a fruit lozenge into her mouth.

'Hallo, dear. You'll have to excuse me, I've got a sore throat. Talking all day I expect. What's your name, dear?'

'Abbie.'

'Abbie, short for Abigail the Unwanted. Sit down then, dear. Make yourself at home.'

Abigail the Unwanted? Obviously my mother had got that one wrong! At once I was disappointed. The woman must be a phoney after all. She looked like a clone of my mum's friend Vi who worked in the wool shop. What with the glasses, and the puff of blueish-grey hair, she could easily have been a chiropodist like my mother. Anything but a fortune-teller.

She didn't match up either with the dream-catchers dangling from the roof, the vulgar kind with dyed pink feathers, and one of those naff indoor water features, a concrete-cast nymph, eternally emptying her urn over a mound of pebbles.

I would have left right then, pretended I didn't have enough money or something. I would have, if at that moment Iris Bloom hadn't whisked a purple silk cloth from the object on the table, and revealed, in all its glory, the crystal ball.

I'd never seen a real crystal ball before. It seemed to me the most beautiful thing, as if Iris Bloom had captured the moon itself and was dusting it gently with the silk cloth. The more I stared the more spectacular it was. Colours flickered on the surface, blue and purple and green lights, shadows like the Sea of Tranquillity. Mesmerized by its beauty, I handed over my crumpled fiver and sat down.

'Well then, dear,' curiously, Iris Bloom's voice brought me back to the real world, 'what have you come to see me for? Is it some sort of problem you think I might help you with?'

Her eyes were a mild blue behind the glasses. She sounded just like a school counsellor, as if she was about to whip out a leaflet on contraceptive advice.

'Perhaps, if you could just tell me whatever comes up?' I suggested half-heartedly.

'Whatever you want, dear. What comes up, eh?' She had the wrong sort of hands, I noticed, the fingernails short and pearly. Not psychic hands at all. I could do a better job myself. Where, I wondered, could you get hold of crystal balls, and would she be offended if I asked her?

And yet, as she cupped the silvery orb in both hands, tenderly, as if it was a baby's head, I held my breath.

It was uncanny how much she knew about me. That I had no brothers and sisters for instance. That I'd had an operation two years ago, 'Somewhere in the region of your tummy, dear.'

'I had my appendix out.'

'Ah, that would be it. And your mother, is she a religious person at all, dear?'

I tried not to snigger. 'Not really. I mean she goes to church sometimes, but I wouldn't say she's religious.'

Iris Bloom looked puzzled. She could see my mother down on her knees a lot, she said. The light dawned on me suddenly. 'Oh, she's a chiropodist, she looks after people's feet. That's why.'

'That would explain it. Now . . . let's see what the future holds in store for you, shall we?'

Ah. Now we were getting down to business. Who

wanted to hear about my parents and the boring old past anyway?

Iris Bloom must be concentrating. Still lightly cupping the marvellous globe, she closed her eyes. My heart beat fast as I watched her face, wrinkly blue eyelids, wonky red lipstick smelling of fruit drops.

When she opened her eyes again they looked straight into mine. It was unnerving, the way her glasses flashed like the crystal ball. I could see my reflection in them, my wind-torn mop of blonde hair.

There was a funny look in her eyes too. Sort of accusing. As if I knew what she was about to say. Perhaps . . . she recognized a kindred spirit? She would pat my hand and tell me that I too had the 'Sight'.

But then she said, 'I think, my dear, that you've been a bit of a silly girl.'

'Sorry?'

'Two silly girls I see. You have a friend. Small, dark, pretty?'

'Well yes . . . but . . .' This was a bit rich. Here was I, a paying client, and she was onto Marina already.

'This girl, your friend, she is in some danger.'

'I don't understand.'

'I see your friend, and I see a man too, dark like her with the same eyes. He lives not far from here, from this place. He is looking for you.' Her lips tightened as she peered from the crystal ball to my face.

Looking for me? A deep joy took hold of me, as if the world tilted suddenly towards the sun, flowers bloomed, and angels sang to heavenly trumpets.

'And . . . will he find me?' I wished she'd just get on with it, tell me what she saw.

Her hands made passes over the globe like clouds. 'You want to know if you'll get married, have babies,' she said rather wearily.

I shook my head. Of course I didn't. A girl like me, with no ambition beyond a husband and kids? That was rubbish. Nonsense.

'Well, I can tell you, dear, that this man is no good for you, and it would be better for you if you never saw him again. Also . . . there is someone else . . .' Her eyes strained as if to see a long way off. Something was happening to the ball, a darkening, swift and sudden, like a shadow passing over the moon. I thought I smelled something too, something that wasn't just the stuffy, grassy scent of under-canvas. Something foul and old.

'Another man. Excuse me.' She sipped at a glass of water, as if the strain of reading my future was too much, and she needed cooling down.

Another man, she said. Well naturally. There were sure to be other men. I imagined a kind of identity parade of assorted sex-gods, lined up in my future waiting to be picked out. But for now Nikos was all that mattered. Nikos looking for me! I was impressed. There were a million more questions I wanted to ask Iris Bloom but she was already shrugging off her cardigan and asking me to send my friend in.

'My friend?'

'The little dark-haired girl. She's waiting outside, isn't she? Well send her in then, dear, and don't forget what I told you.'

Outside, quite a queue had formed behind Marina. I stuck up my thumb. 'She's amazing. And she knows all about you.'

213

Marina gave me her Mother of Cyprus look, as if it was only natural that her famed beauty and general gorgeousness would spread throughout the world like some new religion.

It was only as she ducked beneath the canvas that I recalled those other words: Your friend, she is in danger.

Knowing Marina she'd probably make sure she got her money's worth, and be in there for ages. I wandered off to look round the other tents. It was the usual stuff, a girl with dreadlocks painting kids' faces, an Indian head massager, and a woman who could read the pupils of your eyes.

Somehow my wandering in a happy daze, thinking of Nikos, led me back across the grass to the stage again. There was no sign of Lauren. No sign of the Muzbelles either.

The man at the shooting gallery opposite, yelled at me to 'Come on, darling, give it a go, eh! Knock Anne Boleyn's head orf. Only a pound. Win a cuddly toy.'

What did he say? I thought at first I was hearing things. Then peering through the heads of the punters aiming their rifles, I saw her. A mechanical figure gliding squeakily back and forth. Someone had gone to a lot of trouble to make her convincing. She had the long dark hair, and that pearly head-dress, the same saucy come-and-get-me-look she wore in her portraits. That look she must have given Henry when they first began courting. Until, that is, someone scored a bull's-eye. Then the head pinged off, dangling horribly.

'Come on, love, three shots a pound. See if you can knock her block orf.'

But someone got there before me, a father carrying his

214

toddler on his back. The child triumphantly waving a plastic bag containing a goldfish.

Hurrying back to the tents, I had the feeling suddenly that this Anne Boleyn was no accident but part of some weird conspiracy. Wasn't it usually fat ladies, ducks, cartoon characters? Was there no getting away from Henry? From the Henry Game?

'Did a girl come out just now?' I asked the couple at the front of the queue for Iris Bloom. 'A girl with long dark hair?'

'Went off towards the gates, love.' The young man gestured away from the fair, to the tree-lined avenue at the edge of the park.

'Are you sure?'

'She came out in a hurry,' the girl said cheerfully. 'Colin reckoned she must've had bad news.'

'Oh God!'

I ran round the back of the tent and looked across the park. I could just pick her out, Marina, a swirl of purple stumbling against the tides of people drifting through the gates. I didn't think I'd ever seen her running like that before.

'Marina! Hey, wait a minute!' The ground felt hard beneath my feet as I pounded over the grass. She couldn't hear me, of course, above the fairground noise. Only when we both reached the main gate did she turn and frown.

'What?'

'What d'you mean, "what?"? I've been shouting my head off. Where are you going?' I was panting, leaning my hands on my knees. 'Did she say something? Iris Bloom? Did she say something to scare you?'

'My parents have come home early, that's all.' Marina shook back her hair with a flash of her old pride.

'She saw your parents in the crystal?'

'Yes.'

'But you said they'd allowed you to come. Lauren is waiting back there for us. And the shooting gallery, did you see it, with Anne Boleyn? It's totally weird. And we haven't been on any of the rides yet.'

I might as well have saved my breath. As I watched her anxious running-walk out through the gates, across the pedestrian crossing, I was furious. So she hadn't got the OK from her parents after all? But she'd come anyway. And now her dad was at home and raving about his Hermia, the pig! Why else would she run like that, as if for her life, for her very honour?

It was only as I crossed the grass again to find Lauren that I remembered what Iris Bloom had said about seeing 'another man'. Not a tall dark handsome stranger. It couldn't have been, for her to gulp her water like that.

And then, telling me to send my friend in quickly – Your friend, she is in danger.

It could mean only one thing. Marina had been shown something, something a hundred times worse than her enraged parents in the crystal ball. I could only imagine what this might be. Henry perhaps? She had seen Henry there, Henry fixing her with his suspicious, unforgiving eyes.

MISTRESS I CHARGE YOU TO FORGET THESE STAR-GAZERS AND CHARLATANS, AND SPEED YOU BACK TO COURT WITHOUT DELAY.

Chapter Sixteen

My first thought now was to find Lauren. Meet at the dodgems, she'd said, but where exactly were they? I seemed to have lost all sense of direction. What's more, it was raining, those fat heavy drops that soak you through to the skin in minutes. The rain released a fragrance from the earth I'd almost forgotten, a musky sweetness, as all around me people ran for cover, jackets pulled hastily over their heads.

I wasn't going to meet up with Lauren again tonight. Somehow I knew this, as if I'd seen it in the crystal ball, plain as daylight. Fate was nudging me in another direction altogether.

Passing the shooting gallery, I had that feeling you get when you're going down with the flu. An ominous shivery feeling, as if something dark and inescapable waits for you in the shadows.

'Knock Anne Boleyn's block orf. Three goes for a pound!'

I looked away, and in doing so came upon the hot dog stall. Too late. Someone was laughing, a deep mischievous cackle I knew only too well.

Nikos had his back turned towards me. His short leather jacket made him look chunkier than I remembered. The girl with him I recognized at once. It was that incredibly elegant blonde from Stefan's bar, the one whose stool I'd dropped *Poltergeists* under. I watched as she stumbled suddenly in those ludicrous spaghetti-strap sandals, Nikos catching hold of her arm.

'Careful, sweetheart. Nearly lost you then.'

Pity she hadn't broken her ankle!

Please don't notice me, I prayed silently as I drew level with Nikos and the blonde. Surely I could feel their eyes on my back? I imagined the blonde nudging him: 'Haven't I seen that girl before somewhere?'

Nikos would shrug and hurry her away. 'Her, oh yeah, she came into Stefan's place once. Brought her Bible with her.' He would tap a finger to his head. 'Bit of a screwball, know what I mean?'

Perhaps I'd take a detour. Away from the path, it was surprisingly dark. Weaving my way among the caravans and trailers wasn't easy. Not that it mattered. All I could think of was the blonde and Nikos.

'He's looking for you,' Iris Bloom had said. Well that was tosh for a start. Iris Bloom was a fraud. I might have known with a name like that.

Emerging at last from the trailers I found I'd worked my way round to the far side of the fair. It was livelier here. Girls shrieked from the Big Wheel, motor-bikes whined on the Wall of Death, while loud-speakers blared tinny old Tamla Motown tunes from the Dark Ages . . .

What becomes of the bro . . . ken hearted? Who had lur . . . ve that's now departed?

I rubbed the tears from my eyes where the lights dazzled them. My head was so full of Nikos and the blonde, I hardly noticed myself drifting towards the crowd. They were gathered at the Wall of Death, lads

bristling with studs and chains, and the hip-hop fanatics, vaguely sinister as they stood hunched in their hoodies.

Not that I had the slightest interest in motorbikes. Why anyone would rocket round a mini bullring like a demented blow-fly until they broke their necks was beyond me. Also, the stench of scorched rubber and oil fumes made me feel sick. Or was it the thought of Nikos and leopard-print sandals? Together.

'Who's the fat geezer?' one of the hoodies yelled in front of me. 'Jesus, look at the guy. Look at that lump of lard. Ya . . . hooo! See that guy move!'

Standing on tip-toe to see over the bristly heads, I made out two stunt-cyclists. They were no more than dark blurs in their leather jackets emblazoned with unreadable logos they moved so fast, just missing each other by some miracle.

One of them – a massive Hell's Angel type, ram horns spiralling either side of his helmet – was surely defying gravity? My head swivelled as he spun round the very rim of the wall, the bike like a child's toy beneath him, striking sparks from the steel surface.

The crowd gasped.

'He's gone over the frigging top!' someone shrieked. The audience broke up, surging forward and taking me with them.

The biker had pulled the most amazing stunt. He'd actually cleared the wall and could now be spotted weaving his way through the caravans back towards the tents of the psychics and mystics.

Well. So what? Some fat maniac just risked his neck for some dodgy applause. What did I care?

Breaking free of the crowd, I retraced my steps across

the field. I'd decided. There was no point now in looking for Lauren. By now she'd be all snuggled up to Andrew the Geek. Might as well sneak on back to lonely old Smedhurst Road. Maybe I could join Mrs Croop in a cup of cocoa? I wiped another tear from my eye. What a waste. What a total waste of my mother's chiropody conference.

By now I was halfway across the field. No one about. Not a soul. Just the slow puttering of a solitary motor-bike behind me. I turned, blinking in the beam of the headlight, then stood aside to let the bike past. But the bike didn't pass. It circled slowly, the beam of light like the eye of a wolf, waiting for the kill.

Oh for God's sake, what now? Not the biker. The fat biker had spotted me in the crowd by some miracle and somehow taken a fancy to me. Perfect end to a perfect evening.

I shouted above the whine of the engine . . . 'Look, why don't you just sod off, fatty? Whoever you are.'

Really I'd just had enough for one evening. Whichever way I moved, the bike hemmed me in, closer and closer, until I found myself backed up against a tree. The bark was rough beneath my hands; rain plopped from the canopy of leaves.

Silence. The biker switched off the engine. He just sat there now, astride the machine, some moron in a terrible mask, trying to scare me. But why? My fingers closed over my mobile in my jeans pocket. I held it up to show him. 'I could call nine, nine, nine. Now. This minute. You want me to call the police?'

It was then I heard it. Laughter. He was laughing at me! But worse than that. Oh God. No. Please no. My heart leaped into my throat like it would choke me. I knew that laugh . . . wheezy . . . gasping . . . a dirty old man laugh, like stale air squeezed from a pair of bellows.

And the mask! Suddenly I recognized it, the satanic curl of horns, the iron teeth, the hawk nose, the same mask in that illustration from *The Pleasure of Kings*. This was the famous Jousting Mask, given to Henry by some emperor or other.

As for the biker's jacket, a spear of light from the fair slanted diagonally, illuminating the words: *DECLARE JE NOS*. Above the inscription was what looked like a heart engulfed in flames.

'*Declare Je Nos*', meant 'Declare I dare not'. I only knew this because Marina had scribbled the words in some of her early spirit writings. We'd both looked it up afterwards. Apparently, what Henry 'dared not declare' was his passion for Anne Boleyn. There had been some fantastic jousting tournament and the motto had been embroidered on Henry's surcoat and the trappings of his horse.

This was no ordinary biker. *This was Henry.*

'Well, Mistress,' Henry roared. He removed the mask with a triumphant flourish, as if expecting applause. 'What think you of my disguising, eh? I had you fooled. Admit it. You were quite taken in by my merry jest methinks.'

My fingers closed tighter on my mobile. What use was the stupid thing to me now? Even if I did call 999, what service should I ask for? All three together couldn't do a damn thing about Henry.

'Well what say you?' Henry urged impatiently. Without the mask he was like one of those pigs you see at rare breed farms, mean-eyed and tusky beneath the gold bristles.

'Not *you*.' It was all I could think of to say. 'It was you all the time, on the Wall of Death.'

Henry let out a guffaw of laughter, as if his court jester, the famous Will Somers, had cracked a stream of rib-tickling one-liners.

'Is that how you call it? The Wall of Death? 'Tis a merry sport. The beast that roars,' he slapped the flank of the bike, 'it has the strength of ten fine horses. Would that I had such a beast for the hunt.'

'It's a motorbike,' I said miserably. 'And you look ridiculous on it.'

Henry let this one pass. Obviously he didn't recognize the word 'ridiculous'. Actually I didn't feel half as brave as I made out. Something peculiar was going on with my heart. It felt like a fish I'd once seen, writhing hopelessly on the fishmonger's slab.

'And what tricks this marvel can play.' Henry went on extolling the bike. 'Did you not hear the crowd, Mistress? Did you not hear them roar their approval?'

I shook my head. Suddenly I could find no words. All I could do was plead silently in my head, *Please just go away*.

'See how I still command my realm?' Henry was boasting. 'The people know their King.' The light in his eye was menacing suddenly. 'What say you, Mistress? Thy tongue is idle. I like a wench who can prattle saucily.'

'For a start I'm not your wench. Why can't you . . . ?'

But really I was running out of words. I could hear the tears trembling in my voice. This was worse than that time in Marina's house. Who could help me out here in the darkness, swallowed up by the glare, the dazzle of the fairground? I might scream my head off and no one would come, my cries drowned by the squeals of mock-terror from the Big Wheel.

'Come, Mistress,' Henry crooned in that wheedling voice, as if I was being unreasonable. As if I was some silly girlie having a row about nothing with her boyfriend. 'Come come, you must not be afeared of your King, eh eh? Lord of all Christendom I may be, but flesh and blood like you . . .'

This was even worse. Henry crooning, wheedling, trying to reason with me.

'No! That's what you're not. You're not flesh and blood!'

As if to prove me wrong, he began easing his bulk from the 'beast that roars', shedding the jacket as he did so, transforming himself into the old Henry, with fur-tipped cape, the jewelled cap, the gleam of metal at his side.

'Get back!' Remembering my crucifix suddenly, I tugged it from under my sweater, and held it aloft, the way I'd seen priests do in horror films.

But Henry was no Dracula. The crucifix posed no threat to the Lord of all Christendom. Quite the reverse.

'A pious wench I see.' Henry's vile squeezebox laugh was in my head now. Taking a further step towards me, head cocked, fat jewelled hands held up in a false gesture of surrender, he made me think of a farmer approaching a chicken, whispering 'easy does it', before wringing the poor thing's neck. 'Piety in a woman is a goodly thing,' Henry murmured.

223

Another horrible thought now shoved the others to one side. Was Henry trying to seduce me? Was he aiming to carry me off in triumph to his bed of worms and bones? I swallowed hard.

'Please,' I sobbed, pathetic now, and helpless with fear. 'Please leave me alone.'

'Come come, sweetheart, if the guising displeases you I am sorry for the jest. Come, dear heart, come let thy King comfort you.'

Comfort? Henry was trying to be gentle. I closed my eyes tight. I prayed for the turbulent spirits to leave me be.

Please, I'm sorry I've been rude to my mum. I should have gone to work in Victor Values. I should never have done what I did with Nikos . . . Sorry sorry sorry.

This whole thing had gone far enough.

I ran then. Blindly. Running until my throat hurt, the blood in my ears like waves pounding. Towards the lights, the noise, the crowds, that was my first instinct. Yet how could you run from a ghost? Henry didn't need his bike to catch up with me. He could get me any time. Anywhere. If he made up his mind, nothing would stop him.

Oh God . . . oh please God . . . I heard myself crying, as if it was someone else . . . and then, wham! He'd got me. Henry had got me! I'd slammed right into him. A man, bulky, strong, a man holding my arms.

I opened my mouth and felt my lungs fill with air. And then I screamed. I screamed and screamed and screamed. Did anyone hear? My screams were lost, absorbed by the gull–like cries of all those minute figures on the Big Wheel, spinning slowly round and round.

Someone was shaking me by the elbows. 'Abbie . . . Abbie . . . S'all right, it's me, it's me, Nick.'

I opened my eyes. The eyes I found myself staring into weren't mean and piggy at all, but brown, a deep velvety chocolate.

'Nikos?'

'Yeah, Nikos.' He looked relieved. Relieved that I'd stopped screaming I supposed. 'What the hell's going on. I thought I saw you with some old greaser.'

Nikos, not Henry. Nikos's voice. I was crying, I realized. My face buried, not in gold, not in rancid foul-smelling ermine, but the creaky leather of Nikos's jacket.

'It's all right, all right. Where is he? You want me to go after him?'

'No . . . no . . .' I drew back my head. 'It's nothing really. No one.'

He looked doubtful, 'Sounds like it. You screaming your head off like that, sounded like you'd found a dead body, seen a bloody ghost or something.'

'Hah . . .' Was I laughing or crying? Both, it seemed like. It was true, you could laugh and cry at the same time. My nose would be going red. Vanity suddenly over-came terror. I must get a hold of myself. I must not behave like a gibbering wreck.

He was holding me to him. 'Why didn't you stop when I yelled at you? Didn't you see us? Back at the hot dogs? We were waiting for Stefan, and Sara said she thought she recognized you from that day in the bar. I called out but you'd disappeared between the vans, like you were in a hurry to go somewhere . . . Here . . .' He drew back from me. 'Blow your nose.'

225

The handkerchief he gave me was brilliant white, freshly laundered. When I handed it back, he took hold of my chin, dabbing my eyes, as if I was five years old.

I tried to focus on Nikos's face through my tears. Nikos my saviour. That tender look of concern making him even more irresistibly gorgeous than I'd remembered.

'Stefan and Sara?' I said finally.

'Yeah. Remember Stefan? How could you forget him, slobbering all over your hand, right?'

'Him and Sara . . . they're like, together?'

'They were when I last saw them on the Tunnel of Love. Listen, are your mates around somewhere? Cos if they aren't I'll drive you home. You shouldn't be wandering around like this you know.'

In the warmth of the car my hair dripped flat against my skull. I didn't care. I felt so relaxed suddenly, I could almost have fallen asleep. Here was Nikos beside me at last, and yet I could think of nothing whatever to say.

Nikos was doing all the talking luckily. 'See, you should've given me a call. Come to the fair with me, had a good time. You young girls should be careful you know, wandering about these places alone. Some of those fairground types are heavy characters, know what I mean? Take advantage an' that.'

I stared out the window. Nikos was lecturing me! He sounded almost like somebody's dad.

'What you need is a proper boyfriend. Someone to look after you, right?' He said this as if he was trying to

226

think of a suitable candidate. 'You think I'm a bastard, don't you?' he added unexpectedly.

'No . . . I . .'

'I don't blame you or nothing, for thinking that. The thing is, see, Abbie, I'm honest that's all. I don't play games. I'm not gonna promise a girl all that happy-ever-after shit, just to get what I want.'

Already we were turning into Smedhurst Road. My heart sank at the sight of it, so soon. I felt so warm, so comfortable. I would have been happy just to stay like this, with Nikos driving me round the country for an eternity.

It was only as we pulled up outside the flat that I remembered the chiropody conference! I glanced nervously up at the front-room window. For the first time ever in my entire life, I was coming home to an empty flat. No telly, no cocoa, no cross-questioning about where I'd been. No parents. Only the dark empty rooms, where I'd be alone, all night, with thoughts of him . . . Henry.

I glanced at Nikos. 'I er . . . I don't suppose you'd like to come in for a cup of coffee, would you?'

Nikos looked kind of eager and uncertain all at once. 'Meet your mum and dad you mean? Well I . . . maybe another time, eh?'

'Actually, my parents are away for the weekend. They've gone to a conference.'

'A conference?' A look passed over Nikos's face then, as if he'd just won at the races.

He patted my knee. 'Yeah, all right then. A cup of coffee. You've persuaded me.'

Well what else could I do? Rummaging in my bag

for my front door key the thought came to me that, in a bizarre sort of way, Henry had driven us apart, and now he was bringing us back together again. Me and Nikos. Nick and Abigail. It sounded right. As if it was meant to be.

Chapter Seventeen

Funny how Nikos looked a bit out of place in our flat in Smedhurst Road. It was as if someone had stuck some swanky leather-upholstered designer chair in amongst the shabby old stuff we'd had for years. And our living room was smaller surely? It seemed to have shrunk to doll's-house size, what with Nikos prowling up and down like a caged tiger.

'You're sure about your mum and dad, then?' He sounded edgy.

'Of course. They won't be back till tomorrow night. D'you want to sit down?'

There were only two armchairs in the living room, those tapestry effect fireside chairs you get in old folks' homes, each with a strange arrangement of green ruffled cushions for my parents' individual back problems. No wonder he shook his head.

'I'm all right for the minute, sweetheart. Just have a bit of a stretch an' that.'

That word 'sweetheart' gave me a jolt. Hadn't Henry called me that earlier? *Sweet Heart . . . Dear Heart.*

'Bit of a stretch,' Nikos said. The way he was pacing, and rubbing his hands together, and flexing his shoulders, he looked like someone just stumbling off a long-haul flight to Australia.

Oh dear. Perhaps I'd made a mistake bringing him

back here. *Big Mistake*. The kind of Big Mistake that triggers cosmic blushes for years afterwards, that makes you cringe decades later when you're married to someone called Gordon and have three kids and a perm.

'So . . . this is *IT* then . . .' The flat, I supposed he meant, the way he kept glancing around, pulling at the cuffs of his jacket. He looked as if he was in a hurry to be off somewhere. But where? And now that I'd got him here, what the hell was I going to do with him?

'It's a bit small.' I found myself apologizing for the flat, something I did with all my friends. Also I was trying to shuffle a tatty copy of *Chiropody World* under a cushion without him noticing. 'It's a bit of a mess actually. But I didn't expect to bring anyone back here.'

Whoops. That sounded pathetic. Like I didn't have any friends to invite or something. But Nikos said it was fine. 'It's cosy enough for the two of us, yeah? It's not like we're throwing a party.'

Cosy, he said. *The two of us*. That was better. The very words gave me a contented sort of glow. Maybe this really *was* Love. Real True Love that would drive Henry into the furthest shadows, into the darkest recess of hell, never to bother me again. Henry didn't even seem real now that I had Nikos here with me. Maybe I never really saw him at all? It was just some nasty chemical in that wine, giving me hallucinations.

The gas fire made that popping sound as I set the match to it. An open log-fire would have been better of course. We could have stretched out in front of it, talking into the small hours, our faces bathed in the rosy glow from the flames. We might even have toasted crumpets on it, if we were hungry.

'I'll make us some coffee then,' I said.

Nikos cleared his throat, and said no thanks, he wasn't that thirsty.

'Something else then?'

I prayed he wouldn't ask for something we didn't have. Which was pretty inevitable really, when there was only the sherry left over from last Christmas and enough Ovaltine to put you to sleep for a thousand years.

'Something to eat then?' I blurted desperately, as he shook his head again. 'I think we've got some muffins somewhere.'

'Muffins yeah?' He gave me that slow smile that made my stomach flip. 'Aren't muffins the same thing as crumpets then?'

'No,' I said, ignoring the crumpet reference. 'No I think they're quite different actually. Muffins are, like, muffiny, and crumpets are more . . . sort of . . . like, toasty . . .'

That was as far as I got on the 'muffin' definition.

'Bit like you then,' Nikos murmured pulling me close. 'You're sort of *toasty*.'

I couldn't pretend it wasn't nice, what he was doing to my ear, that tingly thing which was kind of his speciality. But still this wasn't going the way I'd hoped. We still hadn't talked. Suddenly I wanted to tell him *everything* about myself.

As gracefully as I could, I wriggled free from his clutches. 'Nikos, you know that day you turned up at Marina's and Lauren was screaming, and I said it was a spider?'

Nikos stood smoothing his hair. He looked confused. Clearly he'd forgotten all about that day. 'Yeah . . . ?' uncertainly.

'Well I didn't tell you the truth.'

He grinned. 'Oooh, what's this? Confession time or something?'

'Sort of. The thing is, you see, we were having a Ouija board session, you know, calling up the spirits.'

The grin faded. 'That right?'

'Well, I know this is, like, hard to believe, but we did get a spirit – actually we got a lot more than we bargained for. You'll never guess who turned up.'

Nikos took a deep wondering breath, a bit sarcastic, like he was indulging some kid in a silly party game. Well he *was* an Aries of course, and Arians are major sceptics, so I should make allowances. Then again, it was a typical Cancerian sort of thing that made me want to cling to his manly chest, and blubber on about my 450-year-old stalker.

What I really wanted was a fairy-tale ending. Nikos would take me in his arms, and tell me he had this brother, who just happened to be a priest and a world famous exorcist with years of experience. *Don't bother your pretty little head about it,* he'd say, *that Henry guy, he's history.*

Instead of which, he said, 'Let me see now . . . who turned up . . . Elvis Presley? John Lennon? No? I give up.' He held out his palms in a gesture of defeat.

I took a deep breath. Dare I say the demon's name aloud? In my own home? 'Actually,' I looked directly into Nikos's warm brown eyes, 'actually it was Henry the Eighth.'

I'd expected he might be a bit impressed at least. But all he said was, 'Oh yeah? Who's he when he's at home then?'

'Henry? Well he's . . . he's . . .' I was astonished. How could anyone not know who the most famous King of England was?

But my attempt at a history lesson didn't stand a chance. Nikos grabbed me suddenly, knocking me off-balance and toppling us both into the armchair. Not the most comfortable place for two people to topple into; it had a bony, rigid, disapproving feel, as if one of my parents was still sitting in it, doing the crossword in the evening paper. Just the thought of my parents put me right off. I tried to lever my arms back, but in pushing at Nikos's weight, I only propelled the chair back from under us, until we were both sprawling, half on the floor.

Determined to explain myself still, I blurted, 'Me and Marina, we believe in life after death. Do you believe in life after death, Nikos?'

'I believe in life *before* death, darling. And do me a favour, let's stop talking about your friend Marina, shall we?'

'Nikos . . . this isn't . . . I mean, it's not the best place . . .'

This flat, I meant of course, my childhood home. The idea of Mrs Croop, head cocked towards the ceiling when she heard the juddering wrench of the armchair, followed by the thump of two bodies on the living-room floor.

Nikos misunderstood me. 'OK, where's the bedroom then, sweetheart? You going to lead me to your chamber, or d'you want me to carry you?'

'No, no, we can't go to my bedroom.' Somehow I'd wriggled half-upright, the bony chair-frame digging into my spine.

233

For a start it wouldn't do to have him see my room, unhappily still without lava lamp, and smelling of TCP and spot-concealer. Also my duvet cover was in the wash and my mother had put on this really babyish one with teddy bears on it.

It just wasn't the kind of bed for losing your virginity on, even if you wanted to. Not that I did. Want to, I mean. Not tonight anyway. It's hard to feel sexy when you've been practically assaulted by a ghost.

'Nikos, what I saw at the fair just now, when I was screaming. It wasn't, like, an ordinary biker, it was . . . well it was . . .'

Nikos let out an exasperated kind of sigh, as if I'd tried his patience beyond endurance. That Roman conqueror look had stolen over his face suddenly, cold, resolute.

'Listen, do me a favour, love, can we stop this pissing about? You didn't bring me back here for tea and muffins, did you?' Then seeing my stricken face, he turned it into a joke. 'What's wrong with your bedroom then? Hiding someone in there, are you?'

'Course not.' I felt myself blush. 'I mean, Mrs Croop, her room is right underneath see, and she'd hear . . . everything, and she'd probably ring the police or . . . or . . .' I broke off, startled. The telephone *was* ringing. I was psychic after all! It must be her, Mrs Croop. *Are you all right, lovey? Thought I heard a thump just now.*

'Leave it.' Nikos held my face between his hands, as if it was a bun he was about to take a massive great bite out of. 'Probably some berk selling double glazing.'

'At this time of night?'

'Prats work all hours, don't they?'

I wriggled out from underneath him. 'I'd better

answer it. It might be my parents.'

More than likely it *was* them, checking up on me. If I didn't answer they'd probably call all three emergency services at once, just to make sure.

Close behind me, I heard Nikos sigh again. His arms fastened so tight about my waist it felt like I was wearing one of those Victorian whalebone corsets. The kind that used to make women faint away onto sofas, and have to be revived with smelling salts.

His breath tickled my ear. 'Just get rid of the old folks, eh? Tell them you couldn't be better.'

'Hallo?' I tried for my usual bored telephone manner, expecting my mother's voice to come hurtling down the line at me: *Are you all right, dear? You sound a bit funny to me.*

But it wasn't my mother. It was Marina.

'Abbie, Abbie, is that you?'

'Marina? What's up?'

'Abbie, you've got to help me!' Marina's voice at the other end had a horrible controlled sound, as if she was forcing herself to stay calm, not to panic.

'Marina, what's wrong? What's the matter?'

Nikos let go of me at once. 'What the hell is this? What does Marina want?'

'I'm ringing from the box outside the park,' Marina said. 'I can't go back. I won't go back in the house.' She paused, and this time there was a kind of hiccuping sob in her voice that chilled me. 'It's happening again, Abbie, he's been in my house, in my room . . . My family are all out, I'm on my own. There are doors slamming all over the house, and I'm so cold . . . so cold . . .'

'He's been in your room?' I repeated stupidly. 'You mean Henry . . . ?'

'You said you'd help, you promised you'd help if I needed you!'

'Yes, I . . .' But that was as far as I got. The ringing tone buzzed in my ear like tinnitus. Dead.

'All right, what's going on?' Nikos stood looking at me, his arms folded. Suddenly he was all stern and self-righteous. He had that 'game is up' look teachers get when they catch you out in something.

'It was Marina,' I said stupidly.

'Yeah yeah, I gathered that. What's wrong with my cousin is what I want to know? And who the smeg is Henry?'

'I told you about Henry. I told you just now!'

I wanted to cry suddenly. How could he turn just like that? How could he be pleading and nuzzling me one minute and so cold the next? Like I meant nothing to him. Now when he grabbed hold of my shoulders, it was only to shake me. 'You never said anything about this Henry. You never told me Marina had a boyfriend.'

'Not a boyfriend.' The shaking seemed to jerk my voice out of me, halfway between a laugh and a sob. 'Henry . . . he's not a person, not real. He's a spirit, an earthbound spirit. Henry's a ghost!'

'Listen, love, don't piss me about, OK? I know you girls protect each other, you tell each other things. You know about Henry. He's screwing my cousin, right?'

He let go of me so abruptly, I fell back against the dresser. The terrrible chinking of Mum's collection of Portmeirion teacups brought a rush of tears to my eyes.

'Where are you going?'

He was tugging on his jacket. 'Just tell me where she is!'

'I promised to help her.'

Funny how quickly tears dry up in a real crisis. Marina might be his cousin, but she was also my friend, and NO WAY was I going to be left out of this.

He was out in the hall already, tapping his car keys on the banister rail. 'Tell me where this bastard Henry is, and I'll punch his flaming lights out!'

'No. I won't take you. I won't tell you where she is, unless you take me with you.'

'Right, if that's the way you want it.' He grabbed my arm, thumping downstairs in a manner guaranteed to bring Mrs Croop scuttling from her web. *Everything all right, lovey?*

But Nikos was too fast for her. We were out of the house and into the car in seconds, Nikos driving like a maniac through two red lights, over pedestrian crossings, taking the corners so wide we almost hit a traffic island.

I clung to my seat. 'Slow down. Nikos, slow down, please. I keep telling you, Henry's not a real bloke or anything. He's only a spirit.'

'You keep telling me lies. Frigging ghost stories. You think I believe that crap? You think I'm a complete dick brain or something?'

'She's in the telephone box,' I shouted, 'outside the park.'

We screeched to a halt outside the booth. The thought came to me that had I plunged through the windscreen at that moment, Nikos would probably have driven right over me. Marina ... Marina ... his thoughts were all for Marina.

Just for an instant I almost hated Marina for coming between us. That is until I saw her, sort of crumpled in

237

the telephone box, her arms crossed over her chest, staring at nothing, like a stone saint. When Nikos leaped out and bundled her into the back of the car, she didn't even flinch. It was almost as if she'd expected Nikos and me to arrive together, to rescue her.

Chapter Eighteen

'This guy Henry, he crazy or something? He did this?'
Nikos whistled softly when he saw the state of the
house. He muttered something in Greek to Marina.
When she didn't answer he turned to me.

I nodded. 'Yes, Henry did it. But not the way you
think.'

This time it would take more than a quick whizz of
the Dyson, a few flicks of the duster to put things
straight. The house was gutted, curtains ripped from the
windows, stuffing pulled from the cushions. The relatives
squinting short-sightedly through the smashed glass of
the photo frames. Across the mirror, which miraculously
had stayed put on the wall, was a familiar scrawl in
crimson lipstick. Nikos read the words aloud: MISTRESS
ABIGAIL IS A WHORE.

Nikos looked at Marina and me, from one to the
other, as if finally he understood: 'So that's it, eh? You
two, you're both in this together. You're both at it with
this Henry bastard. Yeah, yeah, it all makes sense now, I
should've known.'

He turned to Marina with a pleading note in his
voice. 'And I thought you were a good girl, Marina.
Know what, I'm sadly disappointed in you. This Henry
bloke, what else did he do then apart from wreck the
place? He didn't touch you, did he? Marina, tell me he

didn't touch you!'

But Marina wasn't telling anyone anything. I couldn't take my eyes off her, the way she stood rigid in Nikos's arms. He was murmuring urgently into her ear, the way he'd done to me, only what . . . an hour ago?

Well, he was her cousin of course. It was a family thing. Or was it? As I stood shivering and miserable, feeling like one of Henry's rejected wives, the light slowly dawned. Of course. Was I really that thick? Why hadn't I seen it before? Why else would he be shaking her like that, crooning in her ear one minute, nagging at her the next? Nikos and Marina. Marina and Nikos.

I see your friend, Iris Bloom had said, *I see her with a dark man*. Nikos was the wonderful husband lined up for Marina. So that was it. He thought he'd have a pop at her friend first, before tying the knot. What a two-timing, miserable hypocrite!

'I want to know!' he was yelling at Marina now. 'I want to know, 'cos if he laid a finger on you, I'll have his . . .'

What he was going to have we'd never know, because at that moment, Marina seemed to come to life. She shook him off with a kind of imperious flutter, like a queen brushing away the court fool. Then she tossed back her hair in one magnificent gesture and uttered the immortal lines that Wyatt had written for Anne Boleyn: '*Noli me tangere, for Caesar's I am*.'

Well. This threw Nikos a bit. He dropped his hands to his sides in a kind of despair. He turned furiously on me. 'What's she on about? She on drugs or something? Look at her!' waving his hand at Marina. 'The girl's out of it, high as a kite. He's given her something, that Henry's

240

given her something. What is it then? Coke, Ecstasy? You'd better tell me, darling, 'cos I'm calling her mum and dad in a minute, and then I'm calling the police.'

'You do that, you call them. They can't do anything. Why won't you listen to me? Why are you so *thick*? Henry is a ghost, and this . . .' I indicated the room, 'this is the work of a poltergeist. You know what that means, poltergeist? Marina's possessed. She's been so repressed by her family, it's no bloody wonder!'

If I hadn't been so worried for Marina, I might have lobbed some of the broken china at him. Instead I went to my friend and took hold of her hand; that hand which had promised so much, the psychic fingers, the terrific Mount of Venus. Now it just felt like an ordinary girl's hand, small and icy with sweat.

'Marina.' I stared into her eyes. 'It's me, Abbie. You're OK now. It's all going to stop, I promise. You're not Anne. You're not her. You're Marina, Marina Paulos.'

'Someone at the door,' Nikos said suddenly, as the doorbell rang. 'Now who could that be? Oh I know, maybe it's that Henry the Eighth fella. Great. Now we can all have a party.'

'Don't say that!' I yelled at him. 'It's not funny. Stay there, Marina, I'll get it.'

Marina made no move to answer the door in any case. She hardly even blinked when Lauren burst in, hair all over the place and red-rimmed eyes like she'd been crying for a week.

'So who's this?' Nikos snapped, exasperated, as if the sight of Lauren was just too much to take.

'It's a friend of ours, if you don't mind,' I snapped back. 'Sorry, Lauren, but we're having a bit of a crisis here. I'll explain later. What happened to you?'

'To me? What happened to you two, you mean?' Then, noticing Marina's trance-like gaze, the state of the room, 'Marina, what's wrong with . . . oh my God, not *him* again?'

'Yup,' I nodded. 'Henry must think it's a monastery or something.'

'So she knows Henry too?' Nikos stood there nodding. 'Sheesh, the guy must be quite a stud. How many of you girls are there?'

'Ignore him,' I said to Lauren. 'It's just Marina's cousin. I won't bother to introduce you, seeing as he's such a total prat. Anyway, where did you get to? I thought you were with Andrew?'

This set her off. Lauren could really blubber when she got going. I had to dash off and bring a toilet roll from Marina's bathroom to mop up her tears.

'Don't talk to me about him,' Lauren snorted into a mile of lavender tissue. 'Everything was all right, until he saw my mum.'

'Your mum? Oh dear. You mean in her belly-dancing costume?'

Lauren nodded. 'It was just so embarrassing. I mean there she was, practically falling out of her bra, and planting a whopping great kiss on Andy's cheek. She was, like, all over him. You should have seen his face. Like this!' Lauren did an impression of a gob-smacked fish. 'His mouth just hanging open, like he'd never seen a belly button before in his life. Well not with a jewel in it anyway.'

I passed her another load of toilet roll, as a fresh outbreak of howling broke forth.

'So I said,' Lauren continued, 'I said, if he was so fascinated why didn't he join the Muzbelles, and then I said I was going to look for you, and he said that he'd seen you with some Hell's Angel sort from the Wall of Death. And then . . . and then . . . I was running and running in the darkness, and I bumped into Henry.'

'Oh no, not Henry.'

'Yes. Really. Henry.'

'Argh, that's it!' Nikos was practically tearing his hair out. 'That's bloody it! You girls, I give up, I wash my hands of you. You're all crazy, you know that?' Tapping his head. 'You've all got screws loose. You need putting away, the lot of you. Locking up. If I was your dad, right—'

'Which you're not.'

'If I was your dad, I'd lock you all up and throw away the key.'

Nikos began storming round the room, just like Henry must have done earlier, except he was trying to put things straight again, hoisting the chairs upright, saying something about how he couldn't let his aunt and uncle see the place like this.

'Abbie, you make Marina some black coffee, get her sobered up, for Christ's sake. Her parents will have a fit if they see her like this. And on second thoughts, we're not having the police involved, we're not having shame brought on our family, right?'

I turned. Nikos was standing in the middle of the room, hands on hips, legs planted apart, wagging his finger at me. There was something about this lordly, arrogant posture that reminded me of someone else. Henry.

243

Henry when he ordered the executions at the Tower, Henry ignoring the weepings and wailings and pleadings of those women he had happily tumbled in that great bed with the fringe of Florence gold. Henry stalking out of the birthing chamber in disgust when Anne Boleyn brought forth yet another feeble girl child. He wasn't a man to give up either. Henry was coming back. Now. I could feel him.

Ignoring Nikos totally, I turned to Marina and Lauren. 'Get ready, you two. Henry's coming back and he's jealous as hell.'

'Jealous? Why should he be jealous?' Lauren said.

Leaving my own tragically doomed and going nowhere relationship out of it, I told her instead about Marina and Nikos. 'It turns out they're actually, like, *promised* to each other. And just to make Henry even more green, there's you and that Andrew . . .'

'But there *is* no me and Andrew,' Lauren protested. Then, panicking, 'We haven't got a pentagram. We should have drawn a pentagram!' Lauren wailed, pinching her nose against the familiar stench. I almost gagged myself. It was like the Big Cat House at the zoo, a vile mixture of fur and animal dung and putrid festering pus. Henry was coming. Not the gallant young hunk who had so captivated Marina, not *that* Henry. This would be Henry at his worst. Furious, bitter, betrayed, half out of his mind with pain and old age.

Nikos was flapping a hand at the air. 'What's that bloody stink? Smells like a ferret's armpit.'

'Close,' I said. 'It's Henry. He's coming back.'

I was beginning to feel sorry for Nikos. He had no idea. He had no idea what was about to happen.

'Hold on tight,' I murmured to the others. We were huddled together by now, Marina still with that terrible blank look in her eye, as if she'd gone beyond fear. As if nothing Henry did could frighten her any more.

'Your crucifix . . . try your crucifix,' Lauren hissed at me.

'No good. Tried it already. He likes a pious wench. He told me so himself.'

'What then? There must be something . . .'

Yeah, there had to be something.

'Trouble with Henry is, he never did scare easy. Reckoned himself a hero, except for his, like, total paranoia about diseases and stuff. He was a real wuss when it came to death.'

'Well that's a big help,' Lauren said, 'seeing as how he's dead already. So what does that leave us with?'

'Well . . . well . . . we could try laughing at him I suppose . . '

'Laughing.' Lauren looked at me as if I'd finally lost the plot.

I couldn't blame her for being sceptical. Laugh at Henry? When we felt like we might all just die of sheer terror? Yet the whole Henry thing of the past few months now blazed in my mind like a series of flash cards. Here was the very first seance when I'd cracked up over the words 'Sweet Ladies'. Hadn't the glass stopped moving long before the letters were scattered by Lauren's sneezing? Then there was the time Henry sang for us in his tuneless screech, and Lauren got a terminal dose of giggles. It had taken all Marina's powers of flattery to bring him back. And what about the time he'd farted, heaving himself from the recliner?

245

I'd practically split my sides at that. By the time I'd come to my senses he'd gone. Laughing at the King was a treasonable offence according to Henry, but he hadn't stuck around long enough to do much about it. Also hadn't there been something too, in the poltergeist book, about spirits not having a sense of humour?

'It could work,' I said to Lauren. 'Anne Boleyn laughed at him. She used to laugh at his crap poems.'

'Yeah, and look what happened to her.'

'I know it sounds mad, but trust me on this, Lauren. If we can just wound his pride, maybe we can wound him as well. Like, fatally. Think . . . think of something hilarious.'

'Something hilarious?' Lauren said sarcastically, listing her recent misfortunes. 'You want me to think of a joke, when my love life's in ruins, my gran's priceless clock is a heap of ashes, my mother is a Jezebel . . .'

Nikos wagged his finger directly at us. 'You lot need a head doctor. I've had enough of this game. I'm ringing the police. Now.'

Nikos was taking control. With a lordly air he sat on the table, beneath the chandelier, very slowly drawing his mobile from his top pocket, fingers hovering over the buttons.

'Bunch of raving weirdo druggies, all of you,' Nikos was mumbling to himself. 'I tell you what, whoever this Henry bloke really is, he has my sympathy, putting up with you lot. I mean the bloke must be desperate . . .' Nikos stopped, his fingers poised mid-air, his mouth open . . .

For there Henry was. A blur of silks and velvets and bloated flesh, as if he'd just crept up on Nikos, charging

246

out of the unknowable darkness of the other side, whirling his silver sword above his head, roaring his battle cry: 'You dare to sully the honour of my maids! I'll have your cods for the crows. The devil take you, Sir!'

And the devil of course, did take him.

Afterwards, it seemed to me that everything happened in slow motion. The whirling sword, Henry roaring, and Nikos . . . well, Nikos cringing is the only word to describe it. The look of absolute horror, of disbelief, on his face, was a sight to behold. What came next I seemed to know already, as if I'd seen it before.

The slight shattering tinkle of something giving way, coming loose, that split second when I *might* have called out, warned him to move . . .

But I didn't. I just closed my eyes as the great jellyfish chandelier, caught in the whirl of Henry's sword, came crashing down on Nikos's handsome woolly ram's head. It was all quite graceful really, the way he crumpled to the carpet, crowned by a million tinkling fragments of glass.

'Oh my God! Is he dead? He's dead, isn't he, Abbie? Shouldn't we ring for an ambulance?' Lauren stood hopelessly, practically chewing the end off her thumb.

There were lots of things we *should* have done. But administering the Kiss of Life to Nikos was only likely to enrage Henry further.

Now that he'd tasted blood again, Henry was almost his old tyrannical self. He was swivelling triumphantly round in Mr Paulos's leather recliner-chair, roaring something about 'goodly thrones', and how we were 'well rid of that foul churl, Nicolas'.

I suppose we might all have run screaming from the house at that point. But we didn't. For one thing, I was sick of running. I was even more sick of Henry having things all his own way. Funny, because Cancerians usually cower away in their shells when the going gets rough. But Henry had just pushed me too far this time, and I went for him, pincers out.

'Suppose that makes you feel big, does it, attacking a defenceless man? Hardly a fair fight, is it? But then that's just the sort of thing you'd expect from a wuss in tights and a cod-piece.'

'Wuss, you call me? I like not the sound of this "wuss". What's this, something amuses you, Mistress?' Henry wanted to know, as Lauren sniggered fearfully behind me.

'Yes, *you* do. She's laughing at you . . . hahahahha-hah . . .'

Oh dear. Fortune-teller to the stars I might be one day, but I'd never make an actress. That was about the most unconvincing attempt at hilarity ever. Still at least the THING seemed disconcerted. Just a little.

Lauren seized her chance: 'You look hysterical in that skirt-thing, doesn't he, Fab?'

'Hysterical,' I agreed.

'In face you look like a total geek, that's my opinion,' Lauren bravely asserted.

'Greek!' Henry raged. 'I will hear no more about the Greek. Understand me, Mistress. The Greek, Nicolas, is no more!'

Which set us both off. Strange, because unlike me,

Lauren wasn't the giggly sort, whereas I had been known to wet my knickers over practically nothing. So maybe it really was a kind of nervous hysteria that had us both gasping for breath and doing a sort of cross-legged dance across the room.

'Fie, fie, Mistress, this ribaldry doth not become a maid methinks . . .'

Henry's voice was like the hiss of air whistling from a punctured balloon. As for Henry himself, he seemed to waver, the way the picture does on the TV when weather conditions affect the signal. We were getting a poor reception suddenly. Was Henry still there, or wasn't he?

I managed to speak at last, spluttering between the hiccups of mirth. 'I think we've got him.'

Then I noticed Marina. Even as Henry faded, Marina seemed to revive. She crept towards the body on the floor.

'Mind the glass,' Lauren fussed protectively. 'Mind you don't cut yourself.'

But already Marina was crouching over Nikos. Tentatively she laid a hand on his cheek. Her hair swished forwards over his face, like a bolt of dark silk. My heart contracted. What would she do now? Throw herself, wailing and keening, on his prone body perhaps? The princely cousin, the marvellous husband-to-be, so carefully chosen by her parents.

But all she did was turn and gaze at Lauren and me and with a look of wonder in her eyes. 'That's Nikos,' she told us. She spoke in her normal self-assured every-day voice, just like the old Marina. 'That's my cousin, Nikos Andreas. I was going to be married to him next year. I was going to be Mrs Marina Andreas. That's where my parents are tonight, talking weddings with my aunty Rosa. They were meant to be fixing the date, making it official. And now look . . hah ha . . . hah.'

Marina's astonished laughter sobered Lauren and me up in an instant. It was so unexpected. I mean what kind of girl would laugh to see her fiancé crowned by a chandelier? Presumably she'd had some feelings for him? He was her cousin after all.

'Out cold,' Marina howled with mirth. 'Some bride-groom he'll make, won't he? They'll have to carry him down the aisle.'

Obviously there was something about Marina's laughter Henry didn't care for. Or, maybe he thought she was tittering at *him*? I suppose it was the final straw, his 'Dark Eyed Dove', his 'Lily', cackling like a common harlot.

In a voice that seemed hardly Henry's at all, but faint with old age, he trotted out all his favourite phrases, the old threats, the warnings we'd heard a million times before during our Ouija board sessions.

'Accursed whores,' Henry protested feebly, as if with his dying breath. 'No better than the Night Crowcrowcrow . . . Remember, Mistress . . . no head . . . is too fairfairfair . . . Remember, Mistress . . . no head . . . Roguerogue . . . chopchop . . . burnburnburn . . . Tick-tock . . . Green Grows the Holly O, oh, Know you the punishment for Treeeeea . . . son?'

The word treason died away, fading like the whine of a mosquito. I had just one last vision of him, chest thrown out, hands on hips, outraged at the indignity of it all, before he vanished, taking the stench with him, leaving only the faint scent of oranges on the air.

Funny how exhausted I felt suddenly, all floppy like a rag-doll. My throat was sore. My stomach muscles ached from laughing. It was all I could do to offer Marina a length of toilet roll to dry her tears, as her laughter gave way to dry gulping sobs of disbelief.

'It's OK, Marina, he's gone. Those were his dying words, didn't you hear? Our laughter has killed him. It's like he's just died for a second time, and he's never coming back.'

Chapter Nineteen

He's never coming back.

It was, let's see . . . three weeks ago, that I said that. And so far, so good. Marina, Lauren and me, we're all getting back to normal, whatever 'normal' is. I used to think 'normal' meant safe and boring. Well, so what? After what we've been through recently, *safe and boring* is fine by me; safe and boring is just what we need right now.

In fact, I reckon we all got off lightly, considering. Although, of all of us, it was Marina who came closest to losing her mind, if not her head. Poor Marina. I decided not to tell her about me and Nikos in the end, mainly because there was nothing to tell, thanks to a *certain person*.

Not that it matters much anyway, because the wedding is most definitely OFF. When Marina's parents walked in, at the very moment we'd vanquished thingy, you could say they went totally mega-ballistic. Just couldn't get it out of their heads that we'd had some kind of wild party, that a bunch of hooligans had come over from the fair and trashed the place. What's more, they blamed Nikos for allowing it to happen! Irresponsible, they said, and no way for a future son-in-law to behave, even if he was seriously injured in the process. As for us girls, we were surely on some kind of drugs the way we were screaming and laughing and crying all at once.

You have to feel sorry for parents really. They're all the same. The way they always get everything totally, absolutely wrong.

Still, the outcome for Marina isn't so bad. I mean she seemed almost normal when I last saw her, just a few days before her convalescent holiday in Cyprus (doctor's orders, what with her nerves being so frayed and that). She didn't mention Him, not once. Neither did I. He's become like, a TABOO subject. A non-person. Like he never existed. The theory being that if we don't even think about him, he can't come back.

Anyway, I've given up all that stuff now; no more Ouija boards, no more poring over the stars, or scrutinizing my palm, or gazing into crystal balls. Nowadays, when the girls at school stick their hands under my nose and shrill at me, 'Hey, Fab, will I be famous? Tell me, Fab, per . . . please!' I tell them to put it away for God's sake, and how should I bloody know?

Lauren and I have got better things to think about. Next summer we're going abroad. Izzie and her belly-dancing mates are planning a package tour of Turkey, home of the art of the Pelvic Swivel.

'See if we can pick up a few tips,' Izzie says. And, 'Why don't you and Abbie come along, darling? Help you to chill out a bit?'

That's because Lauren hasn't been sleeping well since the . . . well, you know. First, she got this mega-outbreak of eczema, like, all over her body, and her herbal therapist at the allergy-clinic said it was because of some guilty secret she had, causing all the toxins to build up in her body. So then she blurts out the whole business about the clock to Izzie. Which is OK as it turns out, because Izzie says life's too short to worry about an old clock and if Lauren's nice to Harv-wit, who is moving in on a permanent basis, then her gran need never know, need she?

It turns out too, that Harv-wit is an ace cook, and drives me and Lauren anywhere we want to go at the drop of a hat, so things could be a lot worse, as I tell Lauren.

I go to the hospital, just once, to see Nikos. It's a bit of a shock to see his beautiful head all wrapped in bandages, with two black eyes and a broken nose (and God knows what else is broken).

That blonde, Sara, is there, who's supposed to be Stefan's girlfriend. A likely story, the way she's feeding him grapes! Even peeling them first, and calling him 'poor lamb' and all that stuff. It makes me feel sick to my stomach to see Nikos lying there, lapping it up, nurses fluttering around his bed like demented butterflies.

'I brought you grapes too,' I say. 'Green ones.'

'Thanks, sweetheart,' Nikos says, then adds, 'What're you doing tonight then?'

The blonde glares at me, and says I shouldn't take any notice, the poor mite is still suffering from concussion and not thinking straight.

'He keeps talking about some King Henry, poor darling. Completely away with the fairies.' She looks me up and down. 'Probably better if you don't tire him out, you know, too many visitors . . .'

But she needn't worry, at the mention of that name, I'm already out of there. 'I've grown out of the likes of Nikos,' I feel like saying to the blonde, very, you know, experienced woman-of-the-world-ish. 'And you, my dear, are quite welcome to him.'

Funny how I feel kind of free after that visit, as if I'm just practically levitating all the way home. Because Nikos is in the past, and suddenly I have, as my mother is always so fond of saying, got my whole future before me.

It's typical, of course, that just when you're feeling like everything could go right for you at last something has to spoil it. I mean here I am, congratulating myself that I've come through the whole thing unscathed, no eczema-outbreaks like Lauren, no practically losing my marbles like Marina, nothing.

Then the very day after my visit to Nikos, what happens? I go down with this raging fever is what happens.

'Must be the flu,' is my mother's diagnosis. 'That'll teach you to go prancing about in the rain half-naked. It's bed for you, my girl.'

'Mother,' I tell her, 'if you mean the fair, that was three weeks ago, and an inch of bare belly-button is not half-naked.'

It's delayed reaction probably. I'm thinking this as I toss and turn under the teddy-bear duvet, teeth chattering one minute, hot flushes the next. Because there *is* no flu going round that I know of. Maybe I've picked up some disgusting lurgy in that hospital? Or maybe just seeing Nikos again has done this to me? Something I need to get out of my system, like those toxins Lauren goes on about as if they were 'turbulent spirits'.

Luckily, the mysterious plague doesn't last much

longer than a couple of days. In fact, I'm just thinking about getting dressed, when my mother comes thudding along the passage. She drops a package onto the bed. 'I think your friend Lauren must've left these for you. Pity I was out. Mrs Croop heard a noise and when she went outside, she found them in the porch. What a sweet girl she is, thinking of you like that.'

'Yeah,' I say, 'sweet.'

Thing is, I know this gift has got nothing whatsoever to do with Lauren. I don't even need to look inside the bag. I know what's in there already. The scent of citrus wafts up to me. Oranges. Five of them. Huge. Perfect. Freshly plucked from a Spanish orchard, and prettily nestled in gold-edged tissue.

'I think there's a card,' my mother says, squinting nosily, 'but I haven't got my glasses.'

'No,' I say. 'No, there's no card.'

I get to it before she does, conceal it tight in my hand. When she's gone I'll rip it into millions of incy shreds, and then I'll probably set a match to them. And after that I'll take the ashes and bury them in a deep pit some-where, or I'll take the train to Southend and hurl them out to sea, just to make sure.

But before I do any of that, I can't resist a peep.

The card is gold-embossed, with this picture of a heart engulfed in flames, and beneath it the words: TO MISTRESS ABIGAIL — DECLARE JE NOS.